Acclaim for *Guardian of the Dawn*

"I had no idea the terror wing of the Catholic church penetrated as far as the sub-continent; yet Zimler testifies to thousands of Jews, Muslims and Hindus who perished in the *autos-da-fé* . . . Zimler paints a portrait of a cosmopolitan but paranoid colony suffering under a regime so corrupt that 'they'd arrest Christ if he dared show his face in this wretched city'."

Guardian

"*Guardian of the Dawn* is an exciting adventure story of a victim of injustice seeking revenge. But Zimler's seductive charm also draws readers into undue confidence in his narrator . . . Revenge may be justified, but its sweet taste corrupts the soul and obscures the mind. Zimler shows great novelistic skill in confronting readers with this corruption, as Tiago, the noble young man we identify with, turns into Iago, the murderous outsider of *Othello*."

Independent

"The strength of *Guardian of the Dawn* lies in its rich historical setting and in Richard Zimler's creation of an idiomatic language that reflects the religious and cultural diversity of place and period . . . remarkable."

Times Literary Supplement

"[A] meaty historical epic . . . an involving study of evil, alive with local colour and well-researched detail."

Daily Mail

Hunting Midnight

"I defy anyone to put this book down. It's a wonderful novel: a big, bold-hearted love story that will sweep you up and take you, un-complaining, on a journey full of heartbreak and light."

Nicholas Shakespeare, author of
Bruce Chatwin and *The Dancer Upstairs*

"Enthralling . . . *Hunting Midnight* is a shamelessly sprawling histor-ical novel, spanning continents, Napoleonic wars, a secret Jewish family, Kalahari magic, and slavery in South Carolina."

Sydney Morning Herald

"Zimler is always an exhilaratingly free writer, free of ordinary taboos . . . *Hunting [Midnight]* . . . [his] powers."

Magazine

"This is an epic melodrama, spanning three continents and more than twenty-five years, building up to a genuinely moving climax."
Literary Review

"Zimler covers the distance from innocence to self-knowledge with deep insight, told in a richly poetic style that makes reading this tale a truly literary experience."
Hadassah Magazine

"An historically rich exploration of important ethical issues and an exciting read as well."
Peter Singer, bestselling author of *Animal Liberation* and *One World: The Ethics of Globalization*

"The unforgettable cast of *Hunting Midnight* will break and mend your heart."
Elizabeth Rosner, 2002 Ribalow Jewish fiction prize-winning author of *The Speed of Light*

"A wonderful novel that spans generations and crosses continents, told with unforgettable narration."
Esther Benbassa, author of *The Jews of France* and *Sephardic Jewry*

The Last Kabbalist of Lisbon

"Zimler [is] a present-day scholar and writer of remarkable erudition and compelling imagination, an American Umberto Eco."
Francis King, *Spectator*

"Drenched in atmosphere and period detail."
Wall Street Journal

"A riveting literary murder mystery, his novel is also a harrowing picture of the persecution of 16th-century Jews and, in passing, an atmospheric introduction to the hermetic Jewish tradition of the Kabbalah."
Independent on Sunday

"A fascinating novel with spellbinding subject matter."
Elle

Richard Zimler was born in Roslyn Heights, New York. After gaining degrees in Comparative Religion from Duke University and Journalism from Stanford University, he worked as a journalist in San Francisco for nearly a decade. In 1990, he moved to Porto, Portugal, where he has taught journalism for the last fourteen years, both at the College of Journalism and the University of Porto.

He is the author of five novels including *Unholy Ghosts* and *The Angelic Darkness*. *The Last Kabbalist of Lisbon*, the first in his series of independent historical novels about the Portuguese-Jewish Zarco family, was named 1998 Book of the Year by three British critics and became a bestseller in eleven countries. The second in the series, *Hunting Midnight*, and third, *Guardian of the Dawn*, have also been international bestsellers.

Zimler has won many prizes for his writing, and has lectured on Sephardic Jewish culture and Portuguese history all over the world. He reviews books for the *San Francisco Chronicle* and *Os Meus Livros* (Lisbon). When not writing, he enjoys gardening at his weekend house in the north of Portugal.

For more about how the book came to be written, with background to some of the themes and issues it explores, see the interview with Richard Zimler on p. 245.

The Search *for* Sana

RICHARD ZIMLER

CONSTABLE • LONDON

Constable & Robinson Ltd
3 The Lanchesters
162 Fulham Palace Road
London W6 9ER
www.constablerobinson.com

First published by Constable,
an imprint of Constable & Robinson Ltd 2005

Cover photo: Ferdinando Scianno/Magnum Photos
Cover design by Ken Leeder

A copy of the British Library Cataloguing in
Publication Data is available from the British Library

ISBN 1–84529–078–X

Printed and bound in the EU

1 3 5 7 9 10 8 6 4 2

Acknowledgments

I am very grateful to all those who read an early draft of this book and who gave me their insightful comments: Alexandre Quintanilha, Ruth G. Zimler, Michael E., Judith Ravenscroft and Timothy Hyman. Many thanks, as well, to everyone at Constable & Robinson, particularly Nick, Gary, Andy and my wonderful editor Becky Hardie.

Preface

I met Sana on my third day in Perth, on the afternoon of February 9, 2000. I'd flown there to take part in the Perth Writers' Festival and to do a promotional tour of Australia and New Zealand for my new novel, *The Angelic Darkness*. She and I talked at any length only once, and in hindsight I guess that part of the reason this casual encounter was to start me on a three-year investigation of her life was that I'd been so fragile and excited at the time.

I'd been so vulnerable because I'd had a presentiment of death while riding the London Tube to Heathrow Airport before my flight to Perth. With an ache opening in my gut, I felt as if I were treading water in a night-time ocean, a hopeless distance from the lights on shore. Leagues of cold brown water beneath me were pulling me down. In my drowning panic, I turned to talk to one of my neighbors. But the profile of the elderly man next to me looked as grim as the winter branches rushing by the windows.

Even more than begin a conversation, however, I wanted to shed my skin.

This moment of panic changed my life. For about two years afterward, I felt as if I were enclosed inside parentheses, not quite living the life meant for me.

That night, aboard my plane, I pressed my nose to the window and surveyed the stars in the vain hope of finding some sign of an eternal life awaiting me. Time zones passed. And through one of these gates I must have lost some of my resistance to chance. A constellation not in any of the star charts formed for just a moment and led me first to Sana and then Helena. Though perhaps Sana had plans that made our meeting less than a mysterious coincidence.

I have suffered two periods of deep depression in my life, the first when I was twelve and the last when I was nineteen, and by the time I arrived in Perth I was very worried that I was about to have a third strike. As a result, I found it impossible to fall asleep for more than one or two hours a night. So I was also sleep-deprived when I spoke to Sana.

Exhaustion, mixed with the feeling that I was carrying my death in my pocket, made me look to her for reassurance; I longed to see permanence in her and to feel it reflected onto me – and *into* me.

Given this hope I placed in her, I saw what she did as a personal betrayal for a time. This was silly, of course, since we were not even acquaintances – and selfish, as well, given the circumstances. But a quivering mind that finds it is about to fly into a flame rarely reaches for appropriate choices.

In the weeks following my departure from Australia, I frequently fantasized that I might have been the one to change our futures. I guess I've always wished I had magical powers – like her, as it turns out.

Chapter One

My plane from London touched down inside the summer dawn in Australia on February 7, 2000. On my arrival at the Rydges Hotel in downtown Perth, I was told that my room was not yet ready. From the front desk I put in a call to Alex back in Portugal, where we live, and told him all was well. I lied and said my trip had been uneventful. But we'd been together twenty-one years by then; on hearing the catch in my voice, he told me not to get depressed, that he'd join me nine days later on in my book tour, 3,000 miles east, in Sydney.

The restaurant was just off the lobby, and while waiting for my room to be prepared I went to sit outside at one of the sidewalk tables. The street led off toward a dusty horizon in both directions. Passing cars were already shimmering with the frantic energy of the summer sun. I ordered a Coke and gulped it down, then had a cup of tea with milk.

Men in white shirts and black sunglasses, pale and thin, their noses painted with white cream as part of the ongoing Australian battle against skin cancer, began striding down the sidewalk. They carried briefcases and wore bush-hats, like Crocodile Dundees who'd accepted jobs as accountants after the film royalties had stopped coming in.

The Rydges Hotel was a concrete and glass megalith, but the neighborhood around was old-fashioned; across the street were a second-hand bookshop, a mom-and-pop grocery, and an appliance store. Further away, a juice bar advertised wheat grass, clumps of which sat on a counter facing the street like neat wedges of putting green. I tried some later that morning. It was blended down to a greenish broth and served in a tiny white dental-style paper cup. Terrible. The young man with a metal ball spiked through his tongue who handed it to me told me it had high levels of anti-oxidants. During our conversation I told him I'd just arrived from Portugal, and he said that wheat grass was just the thing for jet-lag – "like eating twenty carrots."

To which I replied I'd never eat twenty carrots.

"And now you don't have to, mate!" he beamed.

Such is the irrepressible nature of Australian enthusiasm.

Perth looked to me that morning like it had been modeled on a Hollywood set of a Victorian outpost town. I would not have been surprised to see horse-drawn carriages and maybe a shootout. White sperm-like shapes darted across my vision whenever I gazed up into the blue-blue sky; thoughts trailed through my brain like opalescent smoke.

I was mired in a brightly polished and arid jet-lag for my entire week in Perth, as though a desert were inhabiting me. Temperatures baked us to 104°F. I roamed around squinting like a mole. At times, all the joy of the sun made me as giddy as a twelve-year-old emerging from the nine-month prison of school into summer vacation. I wore shorts except in my hotel room. There, the windows didn't open and it was nearly always too cool. It was like living in my own climate-controlled space capsule.

When I wasn't at the Writers' Festival, I rummaged in bookshops, visited the Art Gallery of Western Australia, and bumbled through Asian markets in search of mangos and custard apples. I studied the geography of dots on the gallery's Aboriginal paintings to see where I might be. But I didn't seem to be anywhere except outside my real life.

At the Festival, when not listening to one of the writers, I bantered with the waiters at the café, all of whom were blond, handsome, gay, and obviously waiting to be discovered by Gianni Versace or his southern hemisphere equivalent. I practiced my Australian accent by saying *razor blade* the way I'd heard one of them pronounce it: *rizeur blied*.

I made good friends while my sanity lasted. Most of them were other writers: Dermot Healy and his wife Helen, Rodney Hall, Timothy O'Grady, and Nicholas Shakespeare and his wife, Gillian.

I particularly remember Dermot's wine-scented breath gusting hot in my ear while he sang one of my favorite Marianne Faithfull songs: "Love is a Teasing." Though it was two in the morning and he could barely keep his Rasputin-blue eyes open, the gravel in his voice still held the tune.

At breakfast on my third day in Perth, while making quick work of bran flakes and mango slices, a slender woman with prickly black hair sat down at a nearby table. She swiped at the air as though to seize tiny birds darting across the room. Then she closed her fists, which began to pulse with the small imaginary lives beating inside. After peering in at these winged creatures through cracks in her fingers, she opened her hands palms up – like a magician presenting a treasure to her audience – and released them. A slender man in a white T-shirt, with a blue, green, and yellow tattoo of a tropical fish on his bicep, came up to her just then, picked up one of the fairy birds from the edge of a nearby table, and sat it on her head. He kissed her cheek and walked off without a word. The woman leaned her neck down under the weight of the bird. I could feel its little feet bunching up her hair as she winced.

Taking her invisible companion in her hand and putting it on her shoulder, she turned her attention to the buffet table. Her profile surprised me in its sternness – her eyes were sharp, her lips pressed together as though to censor her thoughts. Her skin was a dark, pleasant olive, and tendons arched tautly in her slender neck. Deep lines fanned out from her eyes and her eyebrows lifted up and away like butterfly wings. There was a small scar just below her hairline. I thought that she was probably an actress here for the Arts Festival. I imagined she might be Iranian, or even from India or Pakistan.

Then she turned to the bird on her shoulder. "Well, don't just sit there, tell me what you want!" She spoke in the impatient but affectionate tone people usually reserve for their children.

After she'd gotten some yogurt and fruit from the buffet table, she noticed me staring and feigned a clown-like stumble, nearly tossing me her bowl. We laughed.

"Pretty good," I said.

"Thank you, kind sir," she replied, making a little bow.

She gazed around the room as though watching her bird flapping around. She made little kissing noises and held out her hand. The creature alighted on her index finger, which lowered just a bit, and she placed it back on her shoulder.

I didn't catch her gaze again while she was eating her breakfast. I suspected she was always in danger of performing and needed to be strict with herself.

When I got up from my table, she gave me a girlish wave.

"See you later," I said.

"Hope so," she replied. Taking the bird from her shoulder she tossed it up in the air in my direction. I held out my index finger and let it land, then eased it onto my head. I sniffed at my hand and shook it free of the droppings I imagined it had left behind. She grinned at that. I hoped I'd have a chance to talk to her during my stay.

I saw her again in the late afternoon, when I returned from the Writers' Festival. She was seated at the bar, sipping something amber-colored, probably Drambuie, since I later learned it was her favorite drink. She was wearing a fluffy pink sweater with a high black collar. She looked very regal. When I waved, she waved back, but with her hand opening slowly, then snapping closed, like the snout of a wolf. Her solemn brown eyes followed me as I crossed to the elevator. I thought she might want something from me. A delicate blue California hibiscus blossom was now tucked behind her ear. With her arms crossed, she leaned back as though to listen to the flower's whispers about me.

6

I put my hands into a position of prayer, as though to say: *I hope what you are whispering to each other is friendly.*

She nodded that it was. I was about to walk over to her, but she suddenly looked away and didn't turn back. I reasoned that she didn't want to be disturbed.

The next day, while I was seated alone at breakfast, she walked over to me carrying a copy of the British edition of *The Last Kabbalist of Lisbon.*

"I was afraid to approach you before," she said. A foreign accent added a rise to the ends of her words. "Despite the impression I tend to give people, I'm shy."

There was no photograph of me printed in the edition she carried, so I asked how she knew I was the author. "I read the Brazilian edition when it first came out. You're right there on the flap. And you're also in the Festival brochure."

When I asked about her excellent command of English, she told me she'd lived in New York City for two years.

"Do you still live there?"

"No, I left three years ago and moved to São Paulo." She circled her hand around her neck and made gagging noises. "The Americans nearly lynched me."

To my further questions, she said that no, she wasn't Brazilian. She'd been born in Israel. It was at that moment that I made the wrong assumption that she was Jewish.

She said she was here with the Paulista Dance and Mime Troupe and that they were performing *Lysistrata.* This was her second time in Australia. The group's production of *Waiting for Godot* had been a hit at the Adelaide Festival two years earlier. They mixed mime and dance to tell their stories.

She surprised me then by asking if she could hold my hand. I can still feel the taut strength in her fingers.

"It's so odd to meet you," she said, giving my hand a squeeze. "I mean, I looked at the brochure they sent us, and so I knew you'd be here, at the Festival. But I didn't know we'd be staying at the same hotel." Tears glistened in her eyes. "Or that I'd run into you." She dropped my hand and wiped her

7

eyes. "Your book put some things in order for me . . . no, that's not right . . . it helped me slow some things down so I could see them properly and know what to do. Even the things in it that I didn't like, its flaws, they didn't seem to matter so much at the end. Your novel is like a life well lived." She wanted to say more but had lost her voice. She stepped her index and middle fingers through the air between us – till I could see a horse prancing. Then she stopped and pointed toward my eyes. She touched her fingertips to my closed eyelids. I felt the pressure as though it came from inside me.

I didn't know what she meant by that gesture. I still don't. I was too stunned to speak. Maybe it was a kind of sign language. I had the feeling she was getting to know me through her sense of touch.

Before I could say anything, she laughed in a burst and covered her face with her hands like a little girl caught at a secret game. "You must think me silly, and that maybe I'm upset – with all these tears. But I'm not. I'm very happy. I'm just particularly sensitive right now."

"You're not at all silly. I'm glad you told me. It's always good to hear that what you write has a positive effect on someone. I'm very grateful."

"Listen, would you autograph my book? Or is that a bad thing to ask?"

I took it from her. "Of course I will. Who should I sign it to?"

"Make it to Helena."

"Just that – no last name?"

"Helena is enough."

I dated my inscription and wrote: "For Helena, Thank you for telling me of the effect of my book on your life!" In parentheses, I added, "Going on strike for peace remains a worthy cause."

When she saw my message, she gasped.

"What is it?" I asked.

"Just the oddness of everything in the world."

I was referring to *Lysistrata* with my parenthetical statement, of course. In that play, the women of Athens refuse to have sex with their men until they end the war with Sparta.

We talked some more about Perth, then she reached into her canvas bag and handed me two soaps with pink and white swirls, scented with rose, that she'd bought at the art gallery. "I wanted to give you something for writing your book."

She started crying again when I gave her my thanks.

I'm not usually so bold, but I stood up and hugged her. In her trembling, I felt her vulnerability – and also an extraordinary power pressing into me. She was so thin that I could feel the contours of her ribcage. Just holding her reassured me about the solidity and rightness of my life for a moment. I was grateful.

Also, for the first time I thought it might be wonderful to write a play or movie – something in which she could act.

"Do you ever perform in anything with words?" I asked.

"I have, but not in a few years."

"This is a crazy idea, but if I were to write something for you . . . I mean, write a play or film, would you consider looking at it?"

She brushed my arm. "Of course. But you must not write anything only for me. It would be too . . . too limiting. Write something beautiful and good, that's all that's really important."

She kissed my cheek and without any explanation rushed off for the elevator. She raised her hand high above her head and waved goodbye without turning back, as though she were afraid to look at me one last time. As she walked, she pulled invisible stones from her pockets and tossed them to the side. She raised up to her tiptoes, lighter with each step, and leaped into the elevator, arms unfurling out, as though to fly.

What would have happened if I'd run after her and insisted on talking more?

I never spoke to her again, though I saw her once more. Martin, one of the Perth Festival organizers, was sitting outside with me the following evening, around six. It was an evening of baking heat. I was eating some delicious corn chowder. Martin was smoking and nibbling mouse-like at my bread.

We heard glass shattering from above us. Shards sprayed down and I threw up my hands to keep from being hit in the face. Martin ducked and yelled something.

I jumped up at about the same time Helena hit the ground. She made a dry thud, like a door closing. A thin line of blood sluiced from one of her nostrils. Her eyes remained open but were seeing nothing in this world.

Chapter Two

We heard the rumors that Helena had left a note for her fellow dancers, but the police would not tell us what it said. I asked the people at the Writers' Festival to try to find out, but all they could learn was that no one suspected it was anything but a suicide. An article in the *West Australian* newspaper soon confirmed that:

> A spokesman for the Perth Police said yesterday that the death of Sana Yasawi, artistic director of the Paulista Dance and Mime Troupe of São Paulo, Brazil, has been registered as a suicide. Yasawi, 53, jumped from the seventh floor of her room in the Rydges Hotel, having broken the window first with a desk chair.

I noticed, of course, that she was not called Helena in the article. I reasoned that Sana must have been her stage name. I flattered myself that she had trusted me enough to give me her real name.

Undoubtedly on purpose, Helena – or Sana – had waited till after the last performance of *Lysistrata* to kill herself. The Paulista Troupe left the hotel the next morning for the airport, while I was eating breakfast. Most of them wore sunglasses, and they filed out into a white van, whispering among themselves, clutching their bags as if they contained stolen goods. I wanted to run to them. I wanted to ask if she had received some terrible phone call the previous day – news of an illness spreading through her body, her mother's death – but I didn't want to invade their private grief.

*

11

After the ambulance had taken Helena away, and after I had vomited my corn chowder, I called Alex. While the phone rang, I started sobbing. He wasn't at home or at his office. I shivered while watching the city out my hotel-room window. Light and death – they seemed made of the same cruel element.

I froze that night, unable to control my body temperature. In the morning, I took a warm shower and let the water touch fingers to my closed eyes – just as Helena had done, it occurred to me later that day. I pulled on the thick black sweater I'd brought with me just in case we hit unseasonably cold weather and went down to the lobby; mortality was pulsing inside me and I didn't want to be alone. I sat with Nicholas and Gillian Shakespeare. A knot in my chest was making me think I might have a heart attack. They ordered me an Irish coffee – to loosen up my congestion, they said. After I'd become wobbly and weepy, a boyish police detective with golden blond hair identified himself to us and asked me to sit with him in the lobby. I told him about Sana catching her invisible birds, listening to the whispers of a hibiscus blossom behind her ear, jumping into the elevator. I said she'd liked a novel of mine. It had helped her slow some things down so she could think more clearly.

"More clearly about killing herself?" he asked.

"I don't know."

"Did she look troubled?"

"No."

"Did she say anything that might have made you suspect her intentions?"

My neck seemed to turn around a rusty winch as I shook my head. "No, as a matter of fact, she said she was happy."

When I reached Alex that evening and told him what had frightened me the most, he replied, "People don't commit suicide because they like a novel."

"So you think it's impossible?"

"Of course."

The next morning, I walked over to the art gallery again. I

didn't know why I'd gone back there until I saw the soaps Helena had bought me in the giftshop.

Two of my novels were stocked on the shelves. Maybe she'd noticed them and bought her copy of *The Last Kabbalist of Lisbon* here.

I asked the woman at the cash register if she remembered Helena. I described her and said she might have been walking with an invisible bird on her shoulder. *Slender, with short hair, tall, young-looking, though she was in her fifties . . .*

The woman shook her head. I asked a guard too, but he didn't remember her either. I went to the bathroom and locked myself in a stall. It smelled sweet and acrid at the same time. Holding my head in my hands, I wanted to imitate the women in *Lysistrata* and go on strike – to make a stand against the unfairness of life right here and stay inside till I understood why this had happened.

That evening, I flew to Melbourne and stayed at an old brick house owned by Michael Rakusin, the head of the company that distributed my books in Australia. It was in a quiet residential section of a trendy but shabby neighborhood, where kids in baggy shorts and ripped T-shirts roamed around as though looking for windows to break and walls to deface with graffiti. I was alone, which was a mistake. I slept with a light on in the living room. I imagined that there were murderers waiting to break in and that I'd never get back to Portugal and see Alex again or finish my latest novel. I considered calling a taxi to take me to a hotel downtown, but I stayed put out of embarrassment.

Once, I awoke to find myself making gulping screams. I didn't recall what I'd been dreaming, but I felt as if I'd been bathing in ice-water; my inner thermostat was still badly broken and would remain so for the next several days. With my teeth chattering, I piled on the blankets and shivered to sleep.

*

Over the course of my three days of interviews and readings in Melbourne, I lost so much ground to insomnia that I began to believe that collapsing on live radio and being rushed to a hospital would be by far my most promising option, both in terms of health and publicity.

I took my Qantas flight to Sydney on the night of the 16th. Alex had arrived just before me, from London, and when I saw him waiting by my baggage carousel I ran for him. We hugged and laughed like kids. Then, at the hotel, I wept again. I tried not to think of death – of having to say goodbye to him one day – but even in his arms I could not shake the feeling of treading water in a barren ocean. I told him everything Helena had said to me, as though sharing the story would take some of its power away. But it was too soon for that.

The Last Kabbalist of Lisbon now seemed so entwined with Helena's death that I thought I must have written a fore-shadowing of it in its pages. Something there mirrored the thoughts and emotions that prompted her to take one last leap. And yet, neither Alex nor I could come up with any connection that seemed reasonable – not in Australia, not on my tour in New Zealand, and not back in Portugal.

After arriving back in Porto in early March, I immediately descended into the landscape of my new novel, *Hunting Midnight*, shuttling between the nineteenth century of the book and my own life. One of the central characters – Midnight – is a healer from southern Africa who is sold into slavery. Near the end of the novel, he describes his arduous life on a rice planta-tion in South Carolina as being "buried one stone at a time." As I wrote those words, I remembered Helena taking the stones from her pockets. But Midnight was not like her. He had survived, even after having to carry the weight of those rocks around with him for nearly two decades.

Why had Helena given up? By tossing stones from her pockets, was she telling me that she'd thrown off the burden of the world and it no longer had a hold on her, that she was

14

free? Maybe she was claiming her right to be unhappy and to take the nearest exit out.

I began an e-mail correspondence with one of the members of the Paulista Dance and Mime Troupe, Mário Ungaretti, after getting his address from the people at the Arts Festival in Perth. He'd been good friends with Helena – or Sana, as he called her, since that was the name she'd always used with him and the other members of the group. He had even taken in her Shetland sheepdog, Margot, after Sana's death. She had made him promise to do that before leaving for Australia. When he'd asked her why, she spoke about getting bitten by a poisonous snake in the outback. They'd ended up laughing about her paranoia. Mário dismissed the possibility that she had already been contemplating suicide. He thought it was more likely that she'd been assailed by some sudden loss of balance. He told me that she'd been a very sensitive and spontaneous person.

In one of his e-mails, he wrote, "People don't realize that we're hanging on by a thread. All it takes is something to cut it and then . . . we fall."

He didn't know what – or who – might have severed Sana's hold on life. He said she had not left a suicide note.

Mário was the man I'd seen in Perth with the fish tattoo on his arm. He told me that Sana was sometimes moody and apprehensive, and that she had had a fiery temper, but that he had never known her to be depressed.

The only unusual thing, he told me, was that she almost never spoke about her past or her family. Only once had he heard a reference to her father, whom he believed to be living somewhere in Italy. She had told Mário she had been born there, but never told him where. Her mother was dead. At least, that was the impression he had gotten, since she spoke of her always in the past tense. As far as he knew, she'd always used the name Sana, though he supposed she might have taken it as a stage name years earlier – before moving to Brazil.

He also told me that she had not had any health problems that he'd been aware of. At my request, he confirmed her fitness with the mime troupe's administrative manager. Mário also managed to speak with her personal doctor, who said that all her latest blood tests had been completely normal.

He put me in touch with other friends from Brazil. They all concurred that she had been a moody person and could switch from rage to giggles in a matter of seconds, and that she'd been born in Italy. I wondered, of course, why she had told me Israel.

Ana Morais, another member of the troupe, wrote to me in June of that year to say that she'd once spoken to Sana about *The Last Kabbalist of Lisbon*. Sana, she said, had been taken with the character of Farid, a Muslim young man who is a deaf-mute. He and the narrator, who are intimate friends, speak in a sign language that they developed as little children. Sana had told Ana that what she found so amazing was that a good part of the narrative is a translation of the conversations they have in sign language. In effect, we are all reading a translation, no matter what language we read the book in.

I could see, of course, how this aspect of the novel might be of particular importance to a woman whose art was based on hand and body movements, but I couldn't believe that that was all there was.

In February 2001, a year after my trip to Perth, my British publisher launched a new paperback edition of *The Last Kabbalist of Lisbon*. It sold well at one of the English book-stores in Paris – W. H. Smith – and I was invited by the manager to give a talk there. I gave my slide-show about being a secret Jew in Portugal in the sixteenth century. My publisher came, along with his assistant and production manager. We ate a gigantic dinner together at Le Soufflé, just off the rue de Rivoli.

Also at the event was a retired American who asked if I would give a talk for an organization he belonged to, the Paris Jewish Connection. He was friendly in a fatherly way, which I found endearing, and I accepted his invitation. We picked a date about a month away, at the end of March, because I had to return to Paris then to meet with a French photographer for whom I was organizing an exhibition in Porto that fall, to coincide with a writers' festival I was organizing.

My talk was held at a large, elegant apartment near the Arc de Triomphe. I recall giant Chinese vases and Persian rugs, and French waiters carrying hors d'oeuvres on silver trays. The slide projector sat on top of a baby grand piano. Though most of the guests were dressed casually, I kept feeling as though Joan Collins and the rest of the *Dynasty* cast might just wander in at any moment.

I spoke for about forty-five minutes. Then, after the buffet dinner, I mingled with the guests. One of them was a woman with puffy eyes and a pale, gaunt face. She looked ill and embittered, as if she'd seen way too much, and her frazzled gray hair made it seem as though a fire had recently ravaged her emotions. She wore a loose-knit red woolen sweater and a long black skirt that gave me the impression she was overweight. She chewed her bottom lip when she was silent.

I assumed from her accent that she was French, though she carried a British copy of *The Last Kabbalist*. We talked mainly about Sephardic song, since that was the subject of her Ph.D. thesis at the University of Paris. She had a substantial English vocabulary, having devoured all of Jane Austen and most of Charles Dickens. She also told me she'd scoured the collections of various British libraries to find materials that might be helpful for her doctoral research. She spoke very carefully – as though she was in grave danger of being misunderstood. Occasionally her eyes would glaze over, however, and I thought she might be on some sort of medication, maybe tranquilizers.

Before leaving her, I said, "If you want I can sign your copy of my novel."

"Thank you, but you signed it already," she replied.

We were sitting opposite each other on two large armchairs. Leaning forward, she opened her book to the inscription I'd written on the title page:

For Helena, Thank you for telling me of the effect of my book on your life! (Going on strike for peace remains a worthy cause.)

A sense of impending death gripped me; I was here and in Perth at the very same moment.

"Is something wrong?" she asked.

"Would you mind telling me where you bought that copy?" I thought that it must have been sold by whoever had inherited Sana's possessions and somehow had ended up at a second-hand bookstore in Paris.

"A good friend mailed it to me from Australia. You . . . you must have met her there. She wrote to me that there was a writers' festival taking place and that you were there – that she saw you. You remember her?"

"Of course, I do! So Helena sent you her copy?"

She pulled her head back and gave me a puzzled look. "No, Sana mailed it to me."

"So she *was* Sana . . .? I mean, if that was her real name, then . . . then who is Helena?"

"Me. I'm Helena. She sent the book to me. She thought I would like it." She tilted her head. "Sorry, I don't understand. Sana did not even tell you her name?"

"No. She said to sign it to Helena. I just assumed that that was her."

"Hah! That is perfect Sana!" she howled. "She loves confusions and being a big mystery – and making believe she is me. She has done this since we were kids. She makes phone calls to strangers and says it is me. She orders refrigerators from stores and says it is me." Helena's voice was animated for the first time, and her green eyes were sparkling with delight in her friend's mischief. She laughed to herself. "Once," she told me breathlessly, "Sana called up the Israeli Defense Force to join and gave them my name! I nearly killed her when we were kids – many times."

"And she really was Sana? It wasn't just a stage name?"

"No, it was always her name, since birth."

"So she always intended the book for you?"

"I think she must have."

"Did she say . . . Did she say anything more about meeting me?"

"Just that she liked your face."

"Did she tell you why the book was important to her?"

"No, she only said I would like it."

"I've wanted to find out more about her ever since meeting her."

Helena bit her bottom lip, as though considering how to respond. She took my shoulder. "You know . . . you know she is dead."

"I saw. I was there when she hit the ground. I was right there."

"Oh, my God . . ."

When I asked Helena if she'd tell me what she knew of Sana's life, she said she didn't feel comfortable speaking about her with so many people around – and that it would take many hours.

"Are you certain you want to know?" she asked me, with a kind of menace in her voice, as though it might not be advisable. She moved to the edge of her chair as she spoke, not wanting anyone to overhear.

"Helena, I've thought of Sana every day for a year. Doesn't that tell you something?"

We made a date to meet the next evening for dinner at the Bonaparte Café, in the St-Germain-des-Prés neighborhood. I would have preferred to get together with her in the morning, to give us more time to talk, but she said she never went out before dark.

Chapter Three

That night, I dreamed I was sitting at the bottom of a well, though it looked more like a sorcerer's tower buried upside down in the ground. Crows began dropping out of the sky on top of me, flapping around like fish out of water, their wings breaking with an awful cracking sound. Upon waking, I could hardly get my breath. Wiping the sweat from my face and neck, I shuffled off to pee and remembered it all while staring at myself in the mirror. I recalled, too, that several of the birds had human faces. One of them was that of my older brother who had died eleven years earlier, after a long illness. Another was that of a man whose wife had been killed in an anti-Jewish attack in Paris in 1982 and whom I'd interviewed for United Press International.

This was the dream that had first assailed me in Melbourne.

I scribbled some notes about the upside-down tower and the crows before falling back to sleep, which is how I remembered the images so clearly the next morning. I thought then that the falling birds were a pretty obvious reference to Sana's manner of death – and to how I'd seen her miming when we'd first met. And maybe that's all they really represented. Except that I have had the dream on many subsequent occasions and it always reminds me of those old newsreels – filmed at the Nazi death camps – of goat-ribbed Jewish bodies tossed like skeletons into pits, their arms and legs flailing. So to me, the dream has come to signify that we each can envision a suffering worse than death. In fact, that was precisely what I wanted to learn from Helena – what it was that Sana regarded as worse than killing herself.

*

The next evening, as Helena and I spoke into my tape recorder resting between us on a table at the Café Bonaparte, I didn't have the slightest suspicion that she was holding back much of what she knew. Of course, if I had been in her position, discussing intimate matters with a stranger, I'd have probably done the same.

Helena was wearing a frayed corduroy coat – dark blue, with black pockets – that looked as if it had been picked from a rack at a Salvation Army center. She'd put on pretty pearl earrings as though for the contrast, but they were only visible when she swept her ravaged hair back behind her ears, a nervous gesture she made with some frequency. In the dim lighting her eyes seemed haunted.

I asked her first if Sana had been ill or had received some terrible news.

"Not that I know of. But I was not in contact with her for a few years."

"So you don't know if she'd been depressed?"

She took a deep breath. "I don't know how to reply. I don't believe so, but she may not have wanted to reveal her feelings. She could be secretive. And even if I said to you now that she was depressed, would that mean so very much? If you are really interested, you will have to hear all about her . . . about what made her who she was. Life takes time to go wrong . . . to go really wrong. I'm beginning to see that now." She flashed an embarrassed smile. "I'm sorry if I sound difficult or . . . or morbid – that's not my intention. What I mean to say is that I think it takes years to jump, even if it takes just an instant."

Helena looked out the window at a group of scruffy young people standing in front of the St-Germain-des-Prés Church. "Look at those beautiful kids. Two or three must be very lonely. Who knows, one may even be thinking about killing herself. But it's a secret." She looked back at me and touched her finger to her forehead, then her heart. "It's in here, hiding deep inside, and no one ever knows. Maybe she will kill herself in twenty years, or even thirty, because of something that happens today, something that starts her traveling on a road toward a window on the other side of the world. But how can we know that?"

"Helena, I want to hear all about Sana. But I need to know if you at least *think* you know why she might have committed suicide?"

She shrugged herself free of her bulky coat. Despite what I'd thought earlier, she was dangerously slender. The tendons in her neck arched like spokes into her collarbone. The coat and bulky sweaters were camouflage.

She put her cigarettes and a plastic lighter down on the table. "Look, Sana is new to you but she is old to me. I can't pretend she is someone with easy answers. I might want to, but I can't." She closed her eyes to gain some composure and I could see how struggle had aged her face – particularly in the furrows by her mouth, which gave her the hinged jaw of a marionette. Opening her eyes, she said in a whisper, "Would you want your life reduced to a single answer?"

"No, of course not."

"I probably knew Sana better than anyone. Maybe one of the things I know made her kill herself – maybe two or three of the things. You will have to decide that. But only after you know who she was. So I'll only talk to you if you really want to know about her, where she comes from, who her parents are . . ."

"Look, I liked her – I liked her *a lot*. And I can't get her out of my head. I think of –"

"If you want to get her out of your head," she interrupted coldly, taking a cigarette from her pack, "then maybe we should not be talking." She spoke as if to accuse me of betrayal.

I felt cornered, and a bit angry, but she was already looking down, ashamed of her words perhaps, or simply too emotional to continue speaking. Her movements to light her cigarette were hesitant. I was beginning to think she demanded the truth as her only way of surviving.

I said, "It's just that I'd prefer not to always see the last image I have of her – of her fallen on the pavement. I wish I could go back to when we met and talk to her some more."

She looked up, surprised. "So you feel that way, too?"

"Yes."

She gave me a touched expression. "I'll tell you something, I think we all wish we could have prevented her from making that jump. That is her last revenge." She leaned back and gazed away. From her unblinking stare, I was sure she was seeing her old friend. I imagined them standing together on a Parisian street piled high with winter leaves. Helena's face grew stony, her eyes blank. Ash curled at the end of her cigarette, then fell to the table.

To explain my need to find out more about Sana, I began to repeat what she'd told me in Perth about *The Last Kabbalist of Lisbon*.

Helena wrapped her arms around her chest and leaned forward to listen. Though gratified by her attention, I was frightened by her urgent eyes, as if she were looking for too much inside me. When I'd finished, she said in a resentful voice, "It's terrible being connected to a person who kills herself. Like we also have a foot inside the grave, no?"

"And like she's taken a book of mine down there with her."

"But she hasn't," Helena smiled reassuringly. "She sent it to me instead. I have it. You understand?"

"I think so. Helena, did you come to my talk last night because Sana sent you my book?"

"I came because Sana was right – I liked it when I read it. Though I must say I didn't so much like the story. I am not fond of mysteries. And the rhythm of the narration seemed wrong in some chapters. But I liked your characters. They are good people – good people who did not deserve to die."

"How long did you know Sana?"

"Since we were kids."

"Did you meet at school?"

She shook her head and drew in deeply on her cigarette. "No, no, long before that. We were born nearly together. We lived two houses apart for many years."

"So your parents knew each other. Were they friends?"

"More than friends." She looked off again to gather her thoughts. On the tape there was a pause of just less than a minute, but it didn't record the hard tension in her face as she gazed out the window. "Look, I'm going to have to start with our mothers," she said, snapping her head back to gaze at me. Her eyes were deep green, but rimmed with black, and her stare was very unnerving. "There's just no other way," she continued. Believing she might be speaking aggressively again, and aware, I think, of the effect her penetrating look had on me, she apologized and said, "I would like to tell you quicker, I wish I could, believe me. But it wouldn't be fair to her – to Sana. And I will not add to the unfairness of all that has happened to her. That is something no one can make me do."

Her hands were trembling. Watching her finish her cigarette, as if slowly drugging herself was her only solace, I only then realized the obvious: Sana's death had changed everything about Helena's life – and was threatening to sever her last hold on it.

As I ate a salad with melted brie, Helena began by talking to me about their mothers, Rosa and Zeinab. I didn't need to ask her questions; her story peeked outside hesitantly at first, then began to race for nearly three hours. She downed a cappuccino in a few gulps, then had several glasses of white wine. She smoked half a pack of Marlboro Lights as well, licking her lips to keep them moist and occasionally staring out the window to reflect. Her voice was heavy with emotion, and gritty from all the smoking. Sometimes, as she spoke, she would smile shyly, as though unwilling to give in to the humor in what she was saying. When she did laugh, it was in a glorious burst. I wanted to ask her to pin back her hair so I could see how she'd look without that tangle, but didn't dare. Twice I offered to buy her dinner, but she said she'd only eat later – she'd only gotten up at one in the afternoon and usually ate supper at eleven. I had the feeling that she wouldn't allow herself food before freeing herself of what had been kept silent. She said she was in the habit of staying up to see the dawn, then taking a pill and sleeping straight past midday. She only came out after sundown. I didn't yet ask why. Perhaps she thought I was going to criticize or chastise her, however, because she rushed to add, "Don't tell me, please – I know all my habits are wrong. But I've always felt most comfortable when people disapprove of me. It is a relief that everyone thinks of me as beyond help. If you are nice, you will do the same."

24

As she told me about her past with Sana, Helena would occasionally look at me as though surprised by something in my eyes. After a few seconds she'd turn away from our shared gaze, or I would, because the intimacy was too much. Sana linked us, and neither she nor I were sure that was such a good thing.

Chapter Four

S ana and Helena had both been born in September 1946, in Israel, in a dusty alley at the fringe of Wadi al-Nisnas, a rickety old neighborhood of small houses and shops huddling together in the morning shade of Mount Carmel. That made Rosa and Zeinab sisters by circumstance, and pretty soon the young mothers were changing diapers for each other, borrowing olive oil and flour, and gossiping about the neighbors. On hot nights, they sometimes even slept outside in Rosa's back garden. Helena remembered hearing them talking in lowered voices as she fell asleep. She'd never felt so protected – as if those intimate conversations were building an awning over her life. Early on the two young mothers also forged a winking complicity against the international conspiracy of men, led in their cases by their husbands, Samuel and Mahmoud.

Both women were short and dark, but in those strategic places where Zeinab's pilfering of date cakes and halvah rounded her out into rosewater-scented fullness, Rosa remained as compact as a secret. Zeinab always told her if she ate like a woman and not like a waif then her Polish husband – who, being from a cold climate, needed more visual inspiration than a Middle Eastern man – would never crawl limp into their bed ever again. And it would cure his atomic-bomb snoring, too. In reply, Rosa told Zeinab she was far too nosy and that a more attentive Polish Jew in her bed would only ride her into the ground. She had no intention of being flattened like a Passover *matzo* at this point in her life. As for Samuel's snoring, she found it comforting, because it meant that after surviving *back there* – which was her codeword for Nazis, Auschwitz, starvation, pneumonia, memories of her lost family, and many other

26

perils and sadnesses much harder to name – she and her husband were both still breathing at the very least.

Rosa was made of hissing steam – a tiny dust devil with the darting, all-seeing eyes of a *djinn*. It was rumored by neighbors she was telepathic and could move objects with her gaze. A snap of her fingers was enough to send dogs and cats scurrying.

Zeinab was a fertile valley of irrepressible waters. She liked to tell stories without endings, to sing lullabies and dance, to make children laugh. Neighbors swore that she could have been a movie star, just like Faten Hamama, the Egyptian actress who was the heart-throb of many a man in Wadi al-Nisnas. They told her she ought to take a boat to Hollywood and dance for Jimmy Stewart and Rock Hudson. She'd start with small roles – Italian sex kittens, Gypsies . . .

"Hah!" Helena laughed. "All those horrible Hollywood films Sana and I saw with Mom and Zeinab . . . When we were older, we used to go every week, sometimes twice. For them, for us, Hollywood always seemed so far away and so . . . so exotic. It couldn't be the same for you, an American. But for us, it was like watching a distant planet. My God, how we loved those films!"

Helena told me that her mother once tried to dye her hair blonde with a package ordered from America after seeing a Doris Day movie in which the actress seemed to be made of polished plastic – apparently considered a desirable look in some areas of Israel in the 1950s. Something went badly wrong. After the toxic-smelling meringue was hosed out of Rosa's hair on to the tiles of the back garden, her curls shimmered pink as cotton candy. She and Zeinab skipped around like madwomen, howling with glee, till they collapsed in giddy tears. Rosa looked like a neon sign, a Dr. Seuss character, a child's drawing of a lollipop . . . Zeinab said she had to keep proof of this mis-adventure and snipped a lock from behind Rosa's ear, tying it with a red ribbon. It was Helena who would inherit this tiny bouquet a little over a decade later.

Now, at our café, Helena made a game of peering around to see if anyone was eavesdropping. "I'll show the pink hair to you someday," she whispered, "though Mom would kill me!" She thrust a make-believe knife into her chest and pulled it out with a comic groan.

Back then Haifa was an old ramshackle city snoozing in the sun around the base of Mount Carmel. Each year, like a child growing, it sent dusty suburbs a few hundred yards further north toward Lebanon and south toward Tel Aviv. No one there believed that the rest of the world could even find the city on the map. But that was just fine.

Helena told me that Haifa had been a predominantly Palestinian city before the fighting that followed the Arab rejection of the United Nations plan to partition the territory – previously administered by Great Britain – into two states. It fell to Israeli forces on April 23, 1948. The Arab militias and most of the civilian population fled, including Sana, her parents, and grandparents. Thousands funneled toward the port to board English ships bound for Acre, which had been part of the British Mandate and which was – at the time of the creation of the state of Israel – originally supposed to become part of an Arab state. The frantic crowds twisted out of control. Scores were crushed to death, including Sana's maternal grandmother.

In the shaky peace which followed Israel's final victory in 1949, thousands of Palestinians snuck back from newly independent Arab states, particularly Lebanon, to Haifa, patching the broken windows of their old homes with plastic, sweeping out the mouse droppings and ants, and tossing the moldy lemons from their gardens into the street. Most returned without the permission of the nascent Jewish government.

Sana's family had lived inside their squat two-bedroom house for as long as anyone could remember. It was locally famous for its tin chimney pipe dating back to the nineteenth century. Sana's great-grandfather Gadallah had, in fact, been called Tin Pipe, since he was the one who had put it up.

Helena heard the stories about Tin Pipe from Zeinab, who used to sit the girls down for tea and cakes and jabber away as though she were giving them gifts they'd need to pass on to their children. Helena always called Sana's mother Tia Zeinab, meaning *Aunt* Zeinab in Ladino, the traditional language of Sephardic Jews like Rosa (and similar to medieval Spanish or Portuguese).

"You know, your face changes when you speak of Tia Zeinab," I told her. "Your eyes – they open wide, and your lips . . . they twist with humor."

"Tia Zeinab was all the comic parts of life," Helena explained. "But she was more than that. How can I explain? She was music. And she was light. Do you love these things? Yes. But it's more than that – it is everything. She was the person . . . the person who could always make us smile – me and Sana, I mean. She made everyone in our neighborhood smile."

Sana's parents lived in those days with her father's younger brother, Abu-ai-Rayhan, and wife Karaz. Abu-ai-Rayhan was the only one in the family who had refused to abandon Haifa during the Israeli siege, convinced that powerful Egypt – his family's homeland for several generations – would come to the aid of the Palestinians. He had remained locked inside their house for four days and nights during the Israeli bombardments, living on bread and oranges. So when the barrage was over, he was ready to wait in line for residence papers for the family. He succeeded in getting them for himself and his wife, but was denied authorization for Sana, Zeinab, and Mahmoud. Although Abu-ai-Rayhan had had the foresight to bring their photographs with him, the official in charge told him that at least one member of their family had to appear in person to ask for residency. Nevertheless, Sana and her parents scraped their way back from Lebanon as soon as they could, sneaking into Israel because they hadn't secured legal authorization.

Helena's family lived two doors down, in the House of Blue Hydrangeas, as it was called, because of the bushes Rosa had planted out front on first arriving. She had lived in Salonika, Greece, until she was seventeen, and her lawyer father had created a resplendent garden there. She was the only one of her family of four to survive the deportation of that city's 45,000 Jews to the death camps. Most members of this community – including Rosa's parents – were Sephardic Jews who could trace their families' origins back to late-medieval Spain or Portugal, though all of them had been Greek citizens.

Rosa's own younger sister had been taken from her arms and led off to be gassed. Irene's last words to Rosa had been, "Try to keep me in your memory!" She spoke as though her voice were clinging on to a fraying rope.

"At first, my mother couldn't understand why Irene said this particular thing," Helena told me. "After all, how can a girl forget her younger sister? Mom thought about that all the time, and when she was a few years older, she understood that Irene was really saying, 'As long as you remember me, I will be alive in some small way.'"

But making a living being – a *golem* – out of memory proved beyond Rosa's reach; each year added to the separation between them, despite all her prayers to the contrary. Irene would always remain a little girl turned to smoke in Auschwitz, and Rosa would grow up to become a mother in Haifa.

Helena's father had avoided the camps by taking a steamer from Danzig to England in 1932, studying botany at the University of London. Upon receiving his doctorate in 1937, with a thesis on the history and structure of the bitter orange tree, he hopped on a boat for Palestine, eager to create a green paradise out of the desert sands. He labored sun-up to dusk on a farm near the Dead Sea for five years, experimenting with hybrid varieties of citrus fruit, trying to find specimens that took to the scalding climate. Then, in 1942, he moved to a scabby little house near the port in Haifa, having been recruited, it was said, as a spy for the British. Fluent in both English and German, and conversant in French and Arabic, he made several trips to Damascus, Beirut, and Amman in their service. Whenever Helena asked him about this time he would cup his hand behind his ear, give a sweet laugh, and say his work had merely been *eavesdropping*.

Helena said her father was a wonderful man – tiny and strong, with the gentlest hands of anyone she'd ever met and eyebrows like hairy caterpillars. He had taught her the art of caressing pollen from the stamen of a flower with a delicate ermine brush and placing that wondrous powder onto the pistil of another bloom to make a cross. He had let her make hybrid grapefruits and lemons. He liked to read French newspapers and smoke his pipe. Helena would sit on the floor between his legs and squeeze his feet together around her.

After the war, Samuel opened a small florist shop. In the window he kept an eight-by-ten-inch photo of Marlene Dietrich in *The Blue Angel*. He idolized the actress for defecting from Germany. One day, a doe-eyed young woman stopped by to admire the photo. She was wearing a red hat with a long white feather. Samuel ran out to her and asked if he could be of some help. He learned her name was Rosa. They were married three weeks later and purchased the House of Blue Hydrangeas from a Palestinian family off to a new life in Beirut. Several years later, Samuel secured a professorship at the University of Haifa and closed his florist shop. Rosa took in ironing and sewing. Reading was her favorite pastime, and she would often sit all morning with her face in a book – novels ordered from Madrid and Paris. She devoured everything she could find by Erich Maria Remarque, Thomas Mann, Kafka, Dostoevsky . . . She liked a good story – preferably one with some really strange and cruel happenings. She hated happy endings. "If at least half the people don't keel over or get sick, or just plain vanish into nothing, why should I believe it?" she used to tell Helena.

Sometimes, when Samuel wasn't home, Rosa would show Helena the tattooed number on her forearm and let her touch it. The young mother would tell her daughter it was a sign that God would prevent the Nazis from turning her to ash, because it ended with the numerals 1 and 8. In Hebrew, a language in which the letters are also numbers, the verb "to live" (*chai*) adds up to 18.

These stories of the camps scared Helena, but also comforted her, because Rosa would always end them by saying, "My path may have been crooked, but every turn led me to you and your father. So whatever else you do in life, Helena, for God's sake keep walking."

Rosa and Samuel spoke mostly French at home, since it was the one language they shared. As the years passed, however, they switched to Hebrew, especially with Helena, whom they wanted to be fluent in the language of their adopted homeland. They were also conversant in the local Arabic dialect, having lived among Palestinians for years.

Sana's father, Mahmoud, was an olive-skinned, sad-eyed

man, a bank clerk who had been apprenticed in his father's office in Cairo. To make extra money, he kept the books for several local businesses. He was often already gone when Sana woke and back only after sundown. Helena told me with a dark look that he was the kind of man you respected but did not feel comfortable with. Why he and his brother had moved from Cairo to Gaza and then to Haifa no one knew for certain, but it was believed that an argument had split their family in half. Mahmoud was exceedingly polite, yet he liked silence too much to be of much good to Zeinab and Sana. Maybe in consequence, they always tried to get him to demonstrate his affection in other ways. Mahmoud's brother, Abu-ai-Rayhan, was more buoyant, and sometimes sang with his niece or danced her around the house. Helena said he was a nice man when they were alone with him, but mostly kept to himself around other adults. He wasn't comfortable with people outside the family – not even with Samuel and Rosa. Maybe because they were Jews.

As though to mark the end of her stories about the past, Helena took a last sip of wine and said, "My dad's family name is Verga. He told me it's Portuguese."

"It's a very common name in Portugal," I replied.

"And what does it mean?"

"Wand or switch . . . or even stick."

"Hah!" She cut the air like Zorro with her imaginary *verga*. "So maybe it is my destiny to save Sana . . . to save her with my sorcery. Though all my incantations do not help so much in the end, do they?"

"You can't hold yourself responsible. It isn't –"

"Don't bother to say more, I'm okay," she said, waving away my attempt at encouragement – sensing, most likely, that too much of it was for myself. "Your novel has a character named Verga, remember? That was another reason Sana sent it to me – though she didn't say so in her note."

Solomon Ibn Verga was one of the few real persons in my book. He'd been renowned for his treatise on Jewish history called the "*Shebet Yehuda*" – "The Scepter of Judah."

"Do you still have the note she sent you?" I asked.

"You, sir, are in luck." Winking, she lifted out a folded sheet of cream-colored paper from her coat pocket and opened it on the table between us. She smiled, happy to be helping me.

It was in Hebrew, and the script was very neat. When I pointed that out, Helena replied, "Yes, Sana has very proper handwriting. *Pas comme moi* – not like me. She was a good calligrapher in Arabic, too. She could do anything, that girl. In fact, I believe she could do too much."

"What do you mean 'too much'?"

"Talented people have so many problems. They are too . . . too visible."

"They stand out."

"Yes. And they draw jealousy to them."

"Were you jealous of her?"

She smiled as if I'd caught her out. "Of course, but only when I was not with her. In her presence, our force . . . what we'd create together, it . . ." Looking for the word in English, she rubbed her hand across an imaginary board in the air between us.

"Was erased," I suggested.

"Yes, my jealousy was erased by what we made together."

Helena let me hold the note for a while, then translated it for me:

My dear Helena. I send you love from Down Under. I had this book signed by the author – I hope you like it. I think you will. I met him here. I think he has a nice face. Think fondly of me. I love you like the moon smiling over Wadi al-Nisnas. As for the flower – no papers!

I didn't understand that last reference. Helena explained that Sana had sent a pressed hibiscus flower in the envelope.

"And what does 'no papers' mean?"

"In the first years after the War of Independence, Israeli soldiers would arrest Arabs without residence permits – like Sana and her parents. They took these people across the border to Lebanon. So the women would stand at the top of the steps at the end of our alley to shout when the soldiers were coming. So when our Arab neighbors heard their screams, they would run away and disappear."

"The soldiers came at any time?"

"Night, day . . ." She flapped her hand in disgust. "They came when they wanted. Zeinab refused to . . . to risk causing trouble for her brother-in-law and his wife by hiding at home, so she would grab Sana and rush off. Mahmoud would go with them if he was at home. Sana always insisted on taking her cat, too."

"A cat! What was his name?"

"Plum. He was light gray and very sweet. The only cat in Palestine who loved to eat carrots! He was famous! Once, we couldn't have been more than five or six, I asked Sana why she didn't just leave Plum with me, and she replied, 'No papers.' It became our favorite joke – because we knew the idea of residence permits for cats was *meshugeh* – just like it was for Sana's family, who had lived in their house for centuries. Yet the craziness wasn't ours – it belonged to the soldiers. So whenever our parents wanted us to do something that seemed to make no sense, like wearing a pullover on a hot evening or making our bed, we would look at each other and say, 'No papers!' Later, we would say it to mean anything that didn't make much sense – even good things."

"So sending the dried flower to you . . . It meant that it was a mad idea but that she still wanted you to have it."

"You should be careful, my friend, thinking like Sana can be dangerous."

She squeezed my hand, glad that I was beginning to understand, then thought better of our connection and pulled away from me. She ordered another white wine. I thought she might want to stop talking about Sana for a while, but she said she was regaining her energy.

After I had put another cassette in my tape recorder, she took a big breath and said, "Unfortunately, Tia Zeinab's arthritis in her knee began to be very painful. She couldn't run at all. Mom told her she must hide in our home. Soldiers didn't search the Jewish houses very often, of course. But Tia Zeinab didn't want to risk causing trouble for us. She refused. Then . . . this must be in 1952 or '53, a nice young man from our neighborhood was beaten by the soldiers and taken to Lebanon. He was ordered

34

not to return to Haifa. We never saw him again. *Puff* – he disappeared for ever! But his jacket was returned to his parents and it was stained with blood. Everyone in our neighborhood saw that jacket. It went from house to house. Soon after that, soldiers shot their guns into an old bakery near our house. No one was killed, but two women and a boy were injured. From then on, Mom would not allow Zeinab, Mahmoud, and Sana to go away when the soldiers came. They had to stay in our house. So Dad took one of his saws and cut a . . . a . . ." Helena failed to find the word she wanted and traced a circle in the air with her hand.

"A hole."

"Yes. A hole at the back of my parents' wardrobe. He and Mahmoud, they carry it across the house and put it in front of the little room where we keep old things. Whenever Sana crawls in there to hide, I join her. Plum comes, too." Helena pulled her hair back, taking years off her face. Her eyes opened wide – they were dark with deep joy. "We are seven years old when we first hide like this and the secrecy of it all . . . the secrecy makes us hold our breath till we just explode laughing."

Helena turned away and reached a hand to her brow. After a few seconds, she leaned down. She began having difficulty drawing in air and her face was very red.

"Helena, are you okay?"

She held out her hand to have me wait a few seconds. I took it and gave it a quick squeeze.

"Can I do something?" I asked. "Is it asthma?"

"I need a break after all," she said in a frail voice. She wiped tears from her eyes, then stood up and excused herself. "I'll be right back."

I assumed she wanted to steady her nerves in the bathroom. But through the window I soon spotted her outside, shivering, rubbing her shoulders for warmth. I waved at her and gestured that I would join her if she wanted. She smiled and shook her head, then held her hands over her eyes and peeked out, as if she were a girl needing to hide – making a game out of her fear. I realized I liked her a great deal.

We stared at each other until she tilted her head in apology and looked away. Out on a city street she seemed much more fragile – a girl in a wilderness. I almost went out to her, but I didn't want to embarrass her. A few minutes later, she came back inside.

"Are you okay?" I touched her arm. It was icy.

"A wave of dizziness, it just falls over me – and heat, too. I was so hot. I needed the cold." She patted her belly. "It's a new age for me. *Gil ha-blut* we say in Hebrew – the age of physical decline. Anyway, Prince Charming need no longer worry about making a baby with me." She took a gulp of wine and wiped some beaded sweat from her cheeks with her napkin. "My goodness, what a drama these changes can make."

"Is there a Prince Charming?" I asked.

She made a grunting noise. "I had one years ago and he's not charming at all. Now, I just want a man who can cook. And who leaves before it is time for bed."

"You're sure you won't eat something?"

She shook her head. "There's no food allowed in our hiding place. It is a rule Mom makes after Sana and I once leave chicken bones there. An army of ants comes." She holds her nose, which makes me laugh. "It smells so bad you would not believe it. Mom is *very* angry."

"You're not there now. Have some bread, at least."

She nodded purposefully. "No, we're there – you and me, right now." She pointed to the ceiling. "Up at the top is a single window that Dad covers with a red towel. It lets in a gloomy light. But Sana and I love it. It makes us feel like we're made of colored shadows – and maybe made of dreams, too. Over there . . ." She pointed across the café at the wall by the staircase leading down to the bathrooms. "There's the nail where we hang our coats. You see it?"

"Yes, I can see it. Does Zeinab hide with you here?"

"Hah! Would Faten Hamama crawl through a hole in a wardrobe? Would Elizabeth Taylor?"

"If they had to."

"Well, Zeinab told us she will never join us. She was too afraid of the dark. And she believed it would be better to let the soldiers arrest her if they found her. She probably saw a heroic

36

scene like that in an Italian film . . . a film made by Rossellini. She believed they'd stop searching for Sana once they had captured her. The girl would be raised by Mahmoud and her sister-in-law till she could find a way to return to Haifa. But in case she never returned, she made Mom promise that Sana will go to university – even if Mahmoud does not like it. And that she will be well married, too. I remember that Mom joked that she might just find Sana a nice Jewish boy. Tia Zeinab told her, 'As long as he is handsome and kind and can make a good future for my daughter, he can even be British!'"

"She wouldn't have minded Sana marrying a Jew?"

"Of course not, this was not Israel, this was Wadi al-Nisnas – our neighborhood had its own rules. Or maybe had no rules at all. So Zeinab started hiding in my parents' bedroom whenever the soldiers came, listening in fear to all those aggressive Hebrew voices. She was so very frightened. Mahmoud, if he was home, he sat on the edge of my parents' bed, waiting. Sometimes he'd smoke, too, though that was a risk." She cupped her hands together. "He used a shell ashtray that I would fetch for him. By now, you see, he refused to hide, to make concessions to danger. It was not honorable. Mom always said she'd kill any soldier who tried to arrest him and Zeinab. We could all see that she meant it, too. Mom had eyes . . . they were like black pearls – pearls of survival. No one else I've ever met had them. She would always say you had to live a long time with death close by to have them. She told me once, 'Those soldiers have a very big surprise coming if they think I outlived everything *back there* to see more of my family disappear. Just let them try me!' She said that to me while waving her gun, too."

"She had a gun?"

"Yes, of course. And it was a good one. A Russian soldier who liberated Auschwitz took it from a German and gave it to Mom for her walk across a thousand miles to Greece. He showed her how to shoot it, too. But she never made it home. Just before she began her trip, a man from Salonika who knew her parents told her that they both *went up the chimney*." Helena twisted her hands and raised them in the air, then shut her fists. "So instead, Mom went to Genoa. She walked most of the way. She found a ship there to take her to Cyprus. Then she found another ship to take her to Israel."

"And she really threatened the soldiers?"

"Yes, but wait . . . there's more. By this time, she succeeded in making herself a blonde." Helena grinned; she was enjoying this part of her story and finding her rhythm. "So the soldiers all thought the tiny woman from Greece with the Doris Day hair and black eyebrows had no sense in her brain – that she had left her mind in the barbed wire in Europe. They thought she'd never shoot her gun, too. One time, a young officer came to our door. He had a Yiddish accent and he dared to step into our house without Mom's permission. That was a big mistake. Mom fetched her gun and fired up in the air. The bullet broke a roof tile and scared the chickens in the garden. They started screaming and running around. The soldier told her she was crazy. So she told him, 'So crazy that next time I'll aim for your head, *feshteinzee?*' "

Helena's voice was full of pride. "Mom was great when she was angry. She had this idea then, we all did, that all Israelis were fighting on the same side. So she didn't believe that the soldier would act against her wishes – not now, after she'd shown him she was serious. But the officer grabbed her wrist – grabbed it hard. And he took the gun from her. He told her to calm down in his Yiddish accent – another big mistake. Because now he sounded to Mom just like an SS man. He reminded her so very much of everything *back there*. She became very cold. And all her sense, her reason, it just vanished. She was a ghost of herself. She thought maybe her marriage to Dad and my birth had all been a dream."

Helena's voice lowered, as if she were giving me secret information. "People who believe they may be ghosts are freed from normal constraints," she told me. "Like maybe Sana is – before she makes her jump."

"Why would Sana think of herself as a ghost?"

"Maybe because she has already decided she is as good as dead, no? I think maybe it is like that for her. Though I'll never know. So while the soldier was walking down the corridor to my parents' bedroom, Mom ran to her kitchen for a knife. She stabbed it in his thigh as he opened the door. Zeinab later told me his scream was so loud that it must have broken windows as far away as Tel Aviv."

"Your mom must have got in lots of trouble."

"Not really. At the hearing, she told the judge that the soldier with the thigh wound was damn lucky. She told him that next time she'd take the big knife she used to chop walnuts for the Passover *haroset* and cut out his *kishkas* – his guts. Mom learned all her Yiddish from Dad, you understand. She says to everyone in the courtroom that she already died in the camps many times, so there is nothing more that an Israeli court can do to her that frightens her – nothing! I guess that being a survivor of the death camps saved her, because she is not sent to prison. The judge simply tells her that she must never cause trouble again. And that *was* the last time we ever had trouble, since everybody in Haifa knew by then about the little Greek woman from the camps, with the Doris Day hair and the terrible temper, who lived in the House of Blue Hydrangeas."

Helena made believe she was closing a book, then put it at the corner of our table. "My mom can nearly always make a happy ending."

I saw Sana's miming in the way Helena created imaginary objects with her hands. I was beginning to think of them as sisters. "Is your mom still alive?"

"No, she died ten years ago."

Helena then said something odd: "I once met a man with a web between his thumb and index finger. You could see the veins in the light."

This was to become a common ploy of hers – to divert my attention with a non sequitur whenever she felt tears coming.

When I asked her what that meant, she said, "I am just thinking out loud – about uniqueness." Then she added, "A girl, an angry girl, might never smile – she might prefer to rip her mouth apart rather than smile."

When I asked which girl, she said, "Sana told me that once, and it terrified me."

"What was she so angry about?"

"I don't know. We were in our hiding place when she said it.

She didn't say what she meant. She rarely talked about what was happening inside her. She invented things instead. You had to find clues about her from the stories she told."

Helena rubbed her neck, as though the memories of their times together had left her bruised. She told me then that the first time she had read C. S. Lewis's *The Lion, the Witch and the Wardrobe*, she was convinced that the author must have gone into hiding at some time in his life, because she and Sana used to make up long stories like his when they passed through their wardrobe into the storage room. In truth, they loved being there – the controlled danger, the purposeful quiet, the gleeful knowing that their mothers would protect them. They were happy to be desperados. As all children should be, they were the number one box-office stars of their own lives.

Sana, who had inherited her mother's imagination, would invent stories about desert caravans, sea voyages, scaly monsters . . . Helena remembered she was particularly afraid of a cyclops by the name of Queen Bee who would chase them all the way to Egypt – to the pyramids, down the Nile . . .

"Queen Bee has captured me! Get her away from me! She's stinging me! She's flying me to Cairo."

"I'm coming."

No sooner would Helena tug the monster away with a grunt, then the cyclops would be back, trying to carry Sana away.

"Wait, I've got magic powder," Helena would say, and she'd sprinkle it over the monster. "She's gone."

Later, when their powder stopped working, Helena had to work up incantations in Hebrew and Arabic, and shoot magic arrows. Once, Sana was stung by Queen Bee right in her head, and Helena had to bring her back to life with magic water and a kiss from Plum.

The two girls would sit across from each other and act out their stories until a knock from Rosa or Zeinab would warn them that the soldiers were nearby.

"Not a peep!" their mothers would say.

At these times they conversed with their hands and developed their own sign language. They changed themselves into animals too – mostly butterflies and birds. But never bees.

"Sana loved birds and butterflies – and airplanes, too," Helena told me. "But she hated bees and wasps."

Occasionally, Sana would make believe she was a bird sitting on Helena's shoulder. She'd flex her wings and primp her feathers.

She also liked to give Helena problems in multiplication and long division to solve.

"You cannot believe the length of those numbers she gives me to multiply," Helena said. "And I do it – I make the calculations!" she added, astonished by her past self.

As they got older, Sana also discovered word games. One of them they used to call "Linkages."

I didn't understand Helena's explanation of this game at all, so she took out a scrap of paper from her pocket and wrote the following:

Love Lone Lane Sane Sana

She explained that the idea was to link the first word with the last by changing only one letter at a time. In this case, it took four steps to get from "Love" to "Sana."

"Sana once signed a letter to me like that," Helena told me. "She could invent linkages in any language – Hebrew, Arabic, French, Ladino . . . Her brain never stopped making things. If only she could have rested from herself." Helena rubbed her eyes. "It's no good to think about her. I hate her for giving up – giving up on . . ." Her voice faded.

"On what?"

"On everything. On herself most of all. But I'll be selfish, too – I hate her for giving up on me."

Later, when I got back to Portugal, I told Alex about "Linkages," and he remembered having read of something similar in one of my father's old math books. My dad had loved mathematical puzzles. I soon hunted it down. It was entitled *Martin Gardner's New Mathematical Diversions from* Scientific American, and was published in 1966.

In the book, Gardner mentions a game just like Sana's called Doublets. It was invented by Lewis Carroll over Christmas of 1877, for two girls who, he said, "had nothing to do." That seemed an impossible coincidence. When I spoke to Helena on the phone about it, she confirmed to me that a kind math teacher of theirs named Professor Constantine had taken a special interest in Sana after learning how she and Helena hid together during the raids. He must have studied Carroll's writings and taught her the game.

When I asked Helena how I might find Professor Constantine, she said, "That's a dead end, Sherlock. By now, he'd be a hundred and twenty years of age."

I didn't know anything about Lewis Carroll or Professor Constantine while sitting with Helena at the Café Bonaparte, of course, and so I didn't ask any more about mathematical games. Instead, I asked if Sana had had any brothers or sisters.

"None," she replied.

That was a lie, but it would take me many months to find out.

I asked about other friends I might contact. She said she didn't know about Sana's life in Brazil. They'd lost contact. A husband or a boyfriend? No, she knew nothing – though that didn't mean there wasn't one; Sana had been secretive about her personal life.

I sensed that something bad had happened between Helena and Sana but didn't ask about it. Helena downed the last of her wine. "Then one afternoon Zeinab disappeared," she told me. Stubbing out her cigarette, she called for the waiter and took out her money. "Come on," she said, "I'll tell you more as we walk, but I must go home. I'm expecting a call from Israel."

Chapter Five

In 1982, on graduating from journalism school, I was lucky enough to win a grant from the Correspondent's Fund for an apprenticeship at a United Press International office overseas. My first choice was Rome, but I got a call one day at my parents' house on Long Island to say I was being sent to Paris.

It was there that I had my first real experience with anti-Semitism – and of how Israel, a country I'd never visited, could influence how people felt about me.

Our office was on the rue des Italiens, a few blocks from the Paris Opera. I stayed in a broken-down apartment near Notre Dame that belonged to a scientist friend of Alex's. I could touch the sagging ceiling on my tiptoes. There was no shower and no hot water. Through a series of rubber-man contortions I was able to wash myself in the pencil-thin stream of cold water that came out of the rusty faucet. I slept on an ancient mattress squashed into a metal frame. The only insurmountable inconvenience was the police station next door – motorcycle cops rumbled in at all hours. Stirring from sleep I'd shuffle to one of the platter-sized windows, my blanket around my shoulders, and stare through the diffuse gray light at Notre Dame. I imagined I had awakened into an earlier century. I was in heaven.

On my first day of work, I slunk into the office like a pimply adolescent passing through the unmarked doorway of a brothel, fully expecting to suffer abject humiliation at the hands of experts. The acting bureau chief was pointed out to me by the receptionist. He was stocky and dull-faced, maybe sixty, with wisps of dark brown hair glued down by sweat to his forehead. The tail of his white shirt was sticking out and a heavy paunch rolled over his belt. He had the giant knobby hands of a Van Gogh farmer.

I later learned he was Polish and that he had lived in France since the early 1960s. He had been promised the job of head of the United Press bureau in Warsaw as soon as the Communists were toppled from power. When I met him, he was still waiting for that blue moon to rise over Eastern Europe. I'll call him Pierre, since he may not yet be dead.

Pierre was watching a large TV mounted high on the back wall, in front of a group of burly men. I presumed they were our reporters, but they turned out to be our two French photographers, Stéphan and Giles, and journalists from other news agencies sharing our telex machines. A French station was airing a report about the Israeli military razing a Palestinian village. Pierre flapped his hand and cursed the soldiers as though wishing to spit in their faces. When the report was over I introduced myself, and he snapped in French, "I only hope you're not another Jew."

I felt my head shrinking turtle-like into my shoulders. If life were a Martin Scorsese movie, I would have had the snide calm to gaze around and reply, "You talkin' to me?" Instead, hoping to ease the tension squeezing in my gut, I smiled weakly and said, "For better or for worse I am indeed Jewish."

"Hmmmnnn," said he, looking me up and down. An insect about to be squashed might feel as encouraged as I did at that moment.

I worked for Pierre, the Polish anti-Semite, all of July, August, and September of 1982. He and the reporters rolled their eyes at the very idea of abandoning the bureau and doing any pen-in-hand-style reporting, so I was sent out to cover ministerial press conferences, burst water mains, golf tournaments, movie premieres and, most exciting of all, the World Pong Championships (pong being the Model T of the computer games industry). There were also a great many anti-Zionist demonstrations in those days, since it was a cause around which French academics and intellectuals could comfortably sip their Scotch. At a rally in the Place de la Concorde, I learned the going chant, which had some nice rhymes and referenced the then Prime Minister of Israel, Menachem Begin:

A bas Begin, A bas Reagan,
Vive les combattents Libanais Palesteniens . . .

Down with Begin, Down with Reagan
Long live the Lebanese and Palestinian fighting men . . .

All that was missing at these fist-in-the-air demonstrations were a few real-live Palestinians of course, and maybe Vanessa Redgrave looking chicly defiant in her camouflage jeans and tank top. But the Palestinians exiled in Paris were busy working for a living, and La Redgrave was evidently stuck in rehearsals in London.

If I am making light of these protests, it's certainly not that I disagreed with much of what the demonstrators wanted to change about Israeli policy. One didn't need special powers to know by 1982 that the Jewish settlements in what ought to have been sovereign Palestinian territory would become the major impediment to peace over the next few decades. Rather, it was because my intuition told me that at least a few of these champions of fraternity and liberty had also painted the graffiti that I'd seen around the city equating the Israelis with Nazis, and many of them would not have lost a moment of sleep if all of Israel had been bombed into the sea – except for maybe the oldest parts of Jerusalem, since French intellectuals appreciate the value of a good archeological site when they see one.

To my skeptical eyes, their gatherings seemed like adolescent excuses for shrieking clichés and primping testosterone-coated feathers, though maybe it is in the nature of such protests to appear less well meaning and heartfelt than they are. Also, it is possible that my easy dismissal of them was provoked by embarrassment, in the sense that I myself was doing nothing to oppose ongoing injustices in the Middle East.

What I remember most from these rallies was the profound disappointment in the Jews that I sensed in the French Leftists. Their voices were so hoarse with outrage that anyone looking on would have guessed that each of them had been personally betrayed by Zionism. I couldn't understand why they might have felt that way – and why it was they always demonstrated against Israel rather than against far more horrific regimes in countries like China and South Africa – until fifteen years later, when I read Jorge Semprun's memoir, *Literature or Life*. Then I understood how, for many European intellectuals, the Jews had come to represent the exploited and victimized everywhere. Supporting them had become the outward sign of one's firm pledge to fight against evil in all its guises. On page 36 of the English edition, Semprun notes that he created a Jewish friend in one of his novels for precisely this reason. He writes, "The Jew – even passive, even resigned – was the intolerable embodiment of the oppressed." When I read that, I understood what I hadn't all those years before, while watching that anti-Zionist rally in the Place de la Concorde: that the Israelis, in rejecting the role of passive victim – that most tolerant of traditional Christian representations – had also rejected the terms of friendship with the European Left. If Semprun was right, then they'd broken a tacit pact that said, *like me for being brutalized*.

In fact, by crushing their Arab enemies in successive wars and brutalizing their Palestinian neighbors, they had burned this pact for ever and scattered its ashes over the Occupied Territories. As a result, European intellectuals could no longer evidence their commitment to fighting injustice everywhere simply by supporting the Jews. All those well-meaning professors and politicians had to start over. Even worse, they'd been forced to switch allegiances to the Palestinians, a people with whom they had little shared culture and almost no shared history (and who usually spoke French with thick Arabic accents!). No wonder their voices were hoarse with rage.

I spent hours perfecting my articles about the anti-Zionist rallies. Nothing of what I wrote was of interest to readers back in America, however, and not a single story I filed with our editors in New York ever made it into print. Instead, given the nature of American journalism, the story I had major success with was the following, which hit the front page of the *San Francisco Chronicle* and several other newspapers that July:

'Pooper Scooters' May Save Paris

As every Parisian walking down the Champs-Elysées knows, there is trouble underfoot in Paris. Dog excrement litters the streets. But Parisians, ever creative, have decided to battle the problem in a new way. Mechanical "pooper scoopers" attached to the back of slow-moving scooters will take to the streets in full force by September 1.

Working away at the back of the scooter is a brush and hydraulic lift that deposits dog droppings neatly in a bag. City officials anticipate that a force of 45 scooters will be needed to clean the streets. The city has contracted a private company to man the scooters, which will carry out their mission at a speed of about 3 m.p.h.

My busiest day at U.P.I. that summer began when news came in over the Agence France-Presse wire that Princess Grace of Monaco had been injured in a car accident while driving through the steep canyons above Monaco. No one had yet been informed that she was actually dead. Speculations about whether an underage Princess Stephanie had been at the wheel were making the editors in New York grow fangs. Unable to find their way back to the land of composure, they demanded updates every half-hour from our bureau, praying to Pulitzer, the god of newspaper scoops, that teenage Stephanie had indeed been driving, and that Grace was – at the very least – seriously injured, since the story would then take on criminal and tragic dimensions: *Underage Stephanie Takes Wheel Before Crash and Maims Princess Mom: Monaco Holding its Breath as Former Hollywood Star Lies in Coma.*

I was all by my panicked little self in the office at the time because the only other journalist on duty, Pierre the Polish anti-Semite, was drowning his despair at being unable to move back to Jew-free Warsaw in the cheap Chablis of a Transylvanian-dark pub around the corner, as he did every afternoon.

The editors in New York shouted expletives each time I repeated over the phone that he must have been taking an extra long lunch or had maybe stumbled on to an earth-shaking event in the street – a gigantic anti-Zionist demonstration, perhaps. I distinctly recall one referring to him as "That fucker!"

I was not displeased. I volunteered to find him and inform him that he was in great demand.

The editors instructed me not to leave the office to locate "that fucker," however. So I manned the phones and filed the first stories by myself, adding quotes from various sources in Monaco to the French-language copy chattering constantly over the wire from Agence France-Presse. I even managed to track down the man who claimed to have found Princess Grace unconscious after the accident, though he proved satanically resistant to all attempts to elicit a moving or dramatic quote over the phone. "Yup, I found her," was about all he could come up with. It sounded as though he talked while chomping his gums, like a French Gomer Pyle. Talking to him, I imagined that the hill people of Monaco had been inbreeding for a bit too long.

My worst day was August 10, 1982. The day before, two assassins from Abu Nidal's terrorist group, the Fatah Revolutionary Council, had tossed grenades and fired machine guns at customers eating in Jo Goldenberg's, a well-known deli-style restaurant on the rue de Rosiers, the main street in the Jewish quarter of Paris, the Marais. I was off duty when it happened and didn't read the newspaper that day, but the next morning I was sent first thing to the Hotel Dieu, the centuries-old hospital next to Notre Dame and my apartment, to interview an American who'd been hurt in the attack. (Dead or injured French persons were of far less interest to newspaper editors in America, of course.) Six people had been murdered and twenty-two wounded. One of the victims had been the American man's wife. For some reason, I cannot find the article I wrote about our encounter, which was published in several newspapers, most prominently in the *St. Louis Post-Dispatch*, since he and his wife were from there. I remember the name of their daughter though – Clara. She was three. She didn't yet know her mother was dead because her father, in shock, couldn't think how to tell her.

He and his wife were academics and had been spending their summer vacation doing research at the libraries in Paris.

Clara's father was shuffling across his hospital room when I arrived. He was thin and pale, and there was a cavernous hollowness in his cheeks that I have, ever since, associated with death. In fact, I sometimes see his face in the repeating dream I have had since Sana's suicide.

I explained who I was and said I would leave if I was intruding, but he had been desperately hoping for a chance to speak to someone fluent in English. I sat with him all morning, mostly listening to his glassy-eyed account of the attack and what had happened since. He and his wife had tried to crawl together to the back of the restaurant, but she had not made it. He thought he had covered her with his body, was sure she'd been protected. He couldn't understand how she could have been killed. Or why. It made no sense. If either of them had to die, he should have been the one.

After the first hour, I stopped taking notes. What he was telling me of their lives together was too personal. This wasn't news – at least not as I defined it; this was a marriage blown to fragments.

While I was sitting with him on his bed, one of the Rothschilds – I believe it was Baron Philippe – stopped by to offer condolences on behalf of the Jewish community of France. He was elegantly dressed and had a stooped walk. We shook hands. He did not look surprised by the violence. I would imagine he was wondering if the Golden Age of anti-Semitism was about to come around again – and gain a Middle Eastern polish this time.

I left Clara's father with Baron Philippe for a time to visit one of the other victims of the attack, just down the corridor. She was an elderly Frenchwoman with closely cropped hair and large brown eyes. We talked for a time and she was glad to have company. Her legs and arms were so pocked and perforated with shrapnel wounds that she looked worm-eaten. In a hesitant voice, she asked if she looked as frightening as she felt; they'd taken the mirror out of her room and she could not trust her son and daughter to tell her the truth. I replied that she looked fine – that none of the wounds looked deep enough to cause scars.

She didn't believe me. "Let's put it this way," she said in French, covering some of the crusted holes on her chest with her hand, "if I were dropped in a swimming pool, would I sink right to the bottom?" Her mixture of bravery and humor made me burst into tears as soon as I reached the hallway.

When I got back to the bureau, the reporter who covered fashion began shrieking at me. I'll call her Marlene, because she too may still be alive. She was a barren, yellow-eyed bitch whose hennaed hair seemed to have been cut around the rim of a soup bowl and who, despite having lived in Paris for forty years, insisted on speaking with a gum-chewing American accent that was meant to arouse hatred in all our French employees, whom she despised for not being Americans.

"Why the hell didn't you tape-record your conversation with that guy whose wife was killed?" she demanded. She explained to me that U.P.I. had a radio service and that we could have cut up the interview into bite-sized morsels for eager listeners all over the world. I could even get Clara on tape. It would be a major scoop.

If Clara doesn't yet speak so well, you can just get her crying. Marlene didn't use those words, but she implied it. I told her I didn't consider a recording of the girl or her father appropriate.

"Appropriate!" she sneered. "Give me a fucking break!" Crashing her small recorder into my hand, she told me to get my ass back to the hospital.

When I explained what my orders were to the grieving American, he said in a terrified voice that he really hoped I wouldn't record what he had to say.

For bringing a blank tape back to our office I was railed at by both Marlene and Pierre the Polish anti-Semite later that afternoon. He screamed at me in both English and French, since one language couldn't contain his anger. God only knows how he cursed me in Polish inside his head. I was just thankful that he didn't spit on me.

So it was that I learned that I didn't really want to be a journalist, though for the next eight years I would make believe

I did. The irony was, of course, that here I was back in Paris with Helena, nearly twenty years later, trying my hand at it for the first time in ages.

On our way out of the Café Bonaparte, Helena made a detour to the bathroom. While waiting for her on the street I was thinking of my work at United Press. The motherless girl, Clara, would be in her mid-twenties by now. I wondered if she still lived in St. Louis and if she had come back to Paris many times over the last two decades. Did she squat down outside Jo Goldenberg's and look for slivers of broken glass bearing her mother's name? Perhaps she went into the restaurant and forced herself to eat the corner of a sandwich, hoping to feel the sickness in her gut that ought to accompany memories of a parent's violent death. And her father, was it possible he ever thought of me, that awkward young man who'd risked taking his hand while he talked of his murdered wife? How curious it was that we'd never seen each other again.

Maybe he'll read this and know I haven't forgotten him.

I wondered too whether he and his daughter were occasionally awakened at night by nightmares – by crows falling on them as they sat on their haunches at the bottom of a well. Or maybe they imagined themselves as hollow-eyed Jewish stick-figures being tossed into the common grave of a death camp. Maybe that nightmare united us as well.

As for Pierre the Polish anti-Semite, if I were to recognize him as that bald old man now standing with his arms crossed by the entrance to the Deux Magots café, would I tell him what I had thought of him, and if so, what would have been the point of berating a fat old drunkard? A man capable of hating Jews after all they'd suffered in the death camps of his own homeland – of despising people who'd been made into fertilizer for the cabbage fields of the thousand-year Reich – was hardly going to lose any sleep over my opinion. And I wouldn't even want to change him. No, let him die with the dead hating him back.

*

Clouds had wafted in from the northwest, from Normandy. I zipped my coat and balled my hands in my pockets. Helena came out bundled in her big coat, holding black-and-white photographs in her hand. She said she'd nearly forgotten she'd brought them for me.

One of these four photos came to be the most important to me. The girl on the left is slender, all elbows and skinny ankles in her white blouse and dark skirt, and despite her glare of pent-up rage there is an undeniable comic sweetness to her, since she is acting at being angry and not doing a very good job. Her long hair is parted in the middle, and she is holding the two scraggly ends with her fists, about to give a yank and a hellish shriek. The tendons in her neck are straining, as though she's doing a miniature imitation of the Incredible Hulk. She is performing for the camera, which must mean she is already, at age nine, thinking of future glory. She most definitely plans to laugh over the finished product with the other girl in the photograph – and maybe the little boy in it as well. In her eyes there are golden seeds of mischief.

That, at least, was my first interpretation, standing with Helena outside the café, but there is another possibility; given what I was to find out later, Sana might also be experimenting with the rage she would like to express more openly. It is permitted during that fraction of a second caught for ever by a camera, when everyone assumes she is acting. At other times, it will be punished.

When Helena pointed to their feet, I saw that Sana was wearing two right shoes, and the girl beside her, Helena, two left ones. "It was just an idea Sana had," Helena told me now, shrugging. "Not everything we did has a meaning, you know."

As I look at the photograph now, on my desk in Porto, I find it easy to summon up Sana's face in Perth, for what was irrepressible about her, the daring, gentle, off-center oddness that made her reach for the bird on her shoulder and speak to the hibiscus flower behind her hair, was already there. Maybe Zeinab recognized the creative fire in her the day she came crying into the world. I like to think so. I like to think that she had a mother who looked deep into the eyes of the wondrous child she had. From what Helena tells me, I think she did.

Maybe we should be glad that Zeinab did not outlive her daughter; I have been told by two mothers who have seen their adult children die that there is nothing worse. Yet if Zeinab had lived, then perhaps Sana would not have chosen to dive out of our world.

In the same image, Helena's mouth is a slit of forced silence, as though she has taken a vow not to show emotion – not to laugh most likely. She is holding her breath, and her eyes are looking up and off, as though they might just fly out of her head, since if she were to glance for even a moment at the camera or the person taking the photograph she would lose control – and maybe even pee in her pants out of glee. Her hair is auburn, I would guess, and it falls to her shoulders. On her hip she carries a little boy who stares at the camera with his mouth open, as though he is looking at a miracle.

What strikes me the most about Helena is that she is a strong girl – certainly more powerful than Sana. Yet there is something about their position – with Sana leaning toward the camera and Helena tilting away, almost wishing to run – that makes it clear that Sana is their tactician, their commander-in-chief.

"We were such troublemakers," said Helena in a tone of awe as we stared at her black-and-white past. "I can see why our parents were always giggling when we were together. You know, my father always called us the two demons back then. But he said it in French, of course – *les deux démonettes*!"

She allowed herself a quick laugh. Then she angled her head down sheepishly.

"What is it?" I asked.

"Bad thoughts come when I'm most happy. I can't prevent it. Let's get going." She surprised me by hooking her arm in mine, and we set off.

"Who's the boy in the photo?" I asked.

"My brother."

"How much younger is he than you?"

"Almost six years."

"Where is he now?"

"Oh, he's still in Israel – in Tel Aviv."

Helena stopped abruptly and asked to see the photographs again. I spread them before her, in the light of a streetlamp, as if doing a card trick. She picked the one we'd been looking at and leaned down toward it eagerly, much like Sana had toward the camera. For a moment I could see them together as adults, switching positions and personalities. I realized the obvious: growing up together, they must have taken on many of the same habits and gestures.

Helena shook her head as though to free herself of the memory of that day. "Sana, she threatened to hit me on the head if I spoiled the scene." Looking up toward heaven, she added, "Sometimes I think she is still here and that she still might."

"Ducks fly in a V-formation because there's less wind resistance – it makes it easier for them to fly."

We were nearing Helena's home when she said this.

"Excuse me?" I replied.

She flapped invisible wings. "Sana told me that once. But the first duck still has difficult work – flying ahead of the others. You see?"

Did she mean that Sana took the lead when they were children and made it easier for Helena to fly, that she sacrificed herself for her friend's benefit? Or was Helena referring to the suicide?

When I asked her to explain, she replied in a challenging tone, "I don't know – you're the writer. I'm waiting for you to tell me."

A year later, Helena would explain this sudden confrontation. We were talking on the phone at the time, and I was taping the conversation.

"You can't know how worried I was at that moment that you would write the story all wrong," she said. "Or that you would tell it in so many pieces that people will read a distorted impression of Sana and of the past that we made together. I spoke so long at the café, and I suddenly saw that you still didn't understand the most important things. It was not that I cared what you might say about me, because I was still there to defend myself. But Sana . . . I was worried that you would make her into a person different from the way she was. Then I realized that you would make mistakes. It is inevitable. You cannot prevent it. By writing down some of what happened and by leaving out some other things, you are going to tell only a part of the story. Maybe the things you will decide to exclude, or that cannot be expressed . . . maybe they are the most important things. So standing with you there on the street I felt that I had already said too much. You were not inside the photograph and you could never be there. You could stare at it but you could not jump inside. That's what I wanted to make clear to you. And that is what I wanted you to say in what you would write."

"I don't understand. What precisely do you want me to say?"

"That what you are writing is only a small part of the story – even if you get all the facts and feelings just perfect."

This was during a period when Helena was calling me once a week to add little things about Sana and their shared past, and I promised her I'd mention the inevitable imperfection and subjectivity of my narrative in whatever I wrote. She hung up reassured. Or so I thought. In her very next call, however, she woke Alex and me around one in the morning. She was sobbing so hard that she couldn't speak. I had no way of knowing that she was on the other end of the line. Thinking it was my mother, who was eighty-four at the time and in fragile health, my heart seemed to leap out of my chest. I envisioned her bleeding from a bad fall, unable to lift herself up from the floor. I lurched as if thrown from a speeding car.

"Mom! Mom! What happened? Mom!"

Then Helena told me it was her.

I yelled at her for scaring me. She apologized and said, "I have to tell you a secret that I just realized I had been keeping. I was even more afraid back then, when we first talked, that you would get the story *right* and learn all our secret things – everything we'd ever wanted to keep back. It still scares me."

Plagued by her clinging doubts about me, Helena grew silent as we continued through the night-time streets of Paris. She was thinking that everything was going wrong and that she shouldn't have helped me. Then, to plant at least one solid flag in the midst of that confusion, she stopped me and spoke about how much Sana had meant to her.

"There are people who are so powerful that they orient us. Just knowing she was in the world – it was like I always had a central square in my sight. Do you understand? I could go anywhere, change jobs, do what I wanted, knowing she was where she was. Does that make sense?"

When I nodded, she asked me to turn on my recorder. She gripped it in both her hands. Speaking as though to the whole world, her voice crushed by sadness, she said, "Sana is the last person . . . the very last person I thought would die young. Though maybe fifty-three isn't young, I do not know such things any more. Her death has pushed everything from the center to the side. I don't know where I am half the time. I can't even walk from my apartment to the Metro station. Sometimes, I wake up at night and I think I'm in Haifa, in the House of Blue Hydrangeas. We both must be." Her eyes looked so weighted with despair when she glanced up at me that I reached for her. "But she's not there with me. She's gone."

She pushed the recorder into my hand as if it were a grenade and began to cry, her hands over her mouth. I took her in my arms and she shook. Speaking in a failing whisper, as if her voice were trailing forlorn behind her memory, she said, "I wake up and I can smell our old house and feel the dryness of the air. I can scent the sea in the distance. Sometimes I think that maybe I'm dead too. Oh, I know I'm still here with you – here now. I don't mean dead in my body. Not yet. But my spirit . . . sometimes I sense it is gone. And Sana's death has forced me to believe that it may not be long now before the rest of me is taken away."

Two people who really do not know each other – and who think they would never have met were it not for a woman's suicide – stand on the sidewalk as though between ticks of a clock. It begins to drizzle. The man opens his umbrella over them both. In this gesture, he hopes the woman understands that he means no harm. They walk off. As they near her apartment house, he begins to tell her of the American man made a widower by Abu Nidal and whom he refused to tape one August afternoon in 1982. She listens closely again. He is grateful. At the end of his story, he assures her that she will have a chance to cut out whatever she wants from what he tapes and what he writes – he will even change her name and Sana's. That's the point he wants to make, he says. He considers saying more, but he hopes that the umbrella over their heads, guarding them from the shuddering rain, makes her understand that he will protect her in other ways as well. He links his arm with hers again as they go inside. She does not reject him, so perhaps she understands. He thinks so, but he is wrong.

Chapter Six

Helena lived in a fourth-floor flat in the Marais. With its ancient cracked stone and shadows, the building seemed to draw in the cold and damp of the night. It was on the rue Vieille du Temple, just two blocks from Jo Goldenberg's. As we climbed up the stairs, I asked her if she'd lived there back in 1982, when Abu Nidal's terrorists shot up the restaurant.

"No, I was living then with a friend near the Bastille – in an apartment too tiny for us both – like a box. But you know, he thought we were only one person – and that we were both him! I tell you something," she said, sighing. "Women can be very stupid. Unlike men, we tend to see only what we want."

"Are you referring to Prince Charming?"

"Yes. And I will tell you another thing, when you are not so very beautiful, making love with someone who is . . . It took me two years to realize that my gratitude was not the same thing as love – it's an important lesson to learn, no?" Turning the key in her door, she anticipated my next question. "I didn't hear Monsieur Nidal's explosions or the shots, but I heard what had happened on the radio news and walked to the restaurant later that day. I saw all the police. My God, the Jews of Paris thought it was the end of the world. They bought guns and organized themselves. We had about fifty Yiddish John Waynes on our streets for a while – with pistols under their coats. I'm not joking. You would think no Jew had ever been killed before."

"But it must have been frightening."

"Look, I'm an Israeli – six Jewish dead is just a drop of blood for us. God doesn't even see just six dead. And if you think He does you're *meshugeh*."

"So how many does it take for Him to see?"

"He didn't see six million during the Holocaust – and who knows how many more Russians and Gypsies and everyone else. So it's some number more than that." She took my nod for silent disapproval and said with a shrug, "I'm sorry if I have offended you, but this is what I believe."

By now her bluntness seemed like an oblique form of kindness. I was grateful that she was not going to insult me with false cheeriness or put on any other sort of mask.

"On the contrary," I told her, "very little you or anyone else might say against God for all that's happened would offend me."

As we stepped inside, Helena reached up to touch the silver *mezuzah* on her doorframe and whispered a prayer in Hebrew. Looking back over her shoulder, she said, "It protects me against demons and ghosts and everything else that threatens me."

She turned on the lights. Books were piled on the wooden floor of her living room and teetering in stacks on her dining table. Her windows faced south toward the Montparnasse Tower, lit as though with hidden purpose – like a lighthouse at the edge of the world.

"I sometimes fantasize that I am a religious Jew," she said, putting her keys back in the front pocket of her jeans. "I know I can't be – I'm too chaotic. But it would make life easier." She designed a square in the air with her hands. "I would have a frame and I could live inside it." She leaned her head inside its borders for a moment, flashed a smile, then tossed away the make-believe frame. "Sorry," she said, taking off her coat. "I tend to act things out."

"Don't be sorry. Did you ever think of doing dance or mime yourself?"

"No, that was for Sana. She could explore that for the two of us. She freed me to do other things. Just like I freed her from doing the things I do."

She gestured for me to hand her my jacket. As I did, I said, "You mean, you didn't think you could keep up with her."

"Yes, in part. But I tried to perform myself, many years ago in

59

Israel – singing. But I was too nervous. I was sick in my stomach before every performance. I could not live like that."

Helena asked me what I wanted to drink and when I suggested tea, she said that I was being too American and insisted I have something stronger. "I have some very good brandy." She licked her lips with girlish delight. "It's delicious. I'll have some too. It will be nice. Please, you must have a glass with me."

She spoke like a little girl eager for a parent to join her in a game, and I agreed. While she was in her kitchen, I picked up some of her books on the history of music. Some of them were discolored, others charred around the edges. Helena said she'd had a fire.

"From a heater that goes mad and tries to kill me," she said, handing me my drink. "Probably works for Mossad – the heater, I mean. I didn't clean the books with soap. I was told that it would ruin the paper."

"Mossad? Why would Israeli intelligence be interested in you?"

"They have spies everywhere, and all of them need work – even if it's just to make life a little more difficult for Israelis living in other countries. And I assure you, they have ways of making even heaters blow up." She spoke to the Chinese rice-paper lantern dangling from the ceiling. "Hello Chaim, hello Moishe. How's work in the embassy going?"

She winked at me. I realized I would have liked to have known her and Sana as children.

At the corner of the room were half a dozen big brown boxes sealed with tape.

"More books?"

"No, clothing my father shipped over from Israel. He was cleaning up our storage rooms. I didn't want him to find my things, but he did. Dad is very, very . . ."

"Thorough," I suggested.

"Yes, and ruthless about throwing things out. Not like Mom and me. I bought many dresses when I was younger. They're all in those boxes." She gave me a small curtsy. "Back then I liked to look nice – I was a good little girl."

A shabby red velvet sofa and armchair were holding books as

well. Their cushions looked as though they hid colonies of moths.

"Should I clear a place to sit?" I asked.

"No, the books are all in order, though you'd never know it. I'll get you a chair. Just a second."

She walked the opposite way from the kitchen, into what must have been her bedroom.

"Who took the photos of you as kids?" I called after her.

"Mahmoud."

"He did a good job."

"He was very *competent*." She bit down on the word as though displeased.

"You didn't like him?"

She returned with a desk chair, which I took from her and put down at the edge of the small Persian rug centering the room.

"Did I like Mahmoud?" she asked herself. Her top lip curled into a theatrical snarl. "No, not much. Are we obligated to like the fathers of our friends?"

"Of course not."

"Or Palestinians? My God, just because they are oppressed must I like them all? I hope not. I've met some Palestinians who are not good people. Including Mahmoud. Except he only calls himself a Palestinian when he thinks he is being made a victim. The rest of the time, as he always makes clear, he is an Egyptian by birth – as if that makes him the favorite nephew of Rameses the Great."

Sensing wrongly once again that I was about to criticize her, she said, "Or don't Palestinians get to be human beings like the rest of us? You don't want them all to be Abu Nidal, do you? Or saints with little halos . . ." Helena hummed the first few notes Brahms' *Lullaby*, then snorted with contempt.

"Are you done?" I asked.

She grinned at that. I realized she'd been wanting me to fight back – probably all night. I concluded that Helena was one of those people who loved to keep pushing you until you gave her a sharp knock on the head.

"So why didn't you like Mahmoud?" I asked.

She started to give me a reply, then held up her hand. "No, let me tell you about Tia Zeinab – about her disappearance. And then you'll see why Mahmoud is not the favorite nephew of Rameses or anyone else."

Helena sat scrunched up in a corner of the sofa. I placed my recorder lightly on the arm next to her. She ran her fingertip over it as I pulled up my chair.

"Helena, if you'd prefer I can keep the tape off," I told her.

"No, it's okay. I was just thinking . . . The more you know about me the more you're not going to like me."

She spoke as though stating a statistical finding – one she was not happy about but had to recognize.

"Why would you think that?" I asked.

"That is what happens all the time. People like Sana more and more and me less and less. It's the way our lives go. It's our symmetry. 'No papers.'"

I started to say something encouraging, but she shooed my words away by flapping her hands. "Please, it doesn't matter. Sana helped free me from caring – her death, I mean. She ended the symmetry – at least most of it."

Helena pulled the recorder closer and took a long sip of her brandy. She told me that she and Sana were nine when Zeinab disappeared. She counted back the years on her fingers. "So it was 1955 or early 1956. Tia Zeinab simply didn't return to her house one afternoon. She would always be home before five to have tea with us and tell us stories. And no one in the neighborhood could say where she was.

"Mom, Dad, and Mahmoud searched across the city that evening, and during the next three days too. Then my father learned at a marketplace near the port that a woman who looked like Zeinab was arrested by the Israeli police a few days before. So he went to the local station and the police told him that they took her in a car to the Lebanese border and put her on the other side – with some other prisoners. But the policemen are very nervous. Dad thinks that maybe they are lying and that Tia Zeinab is still there, in a cell. But they tell him no, she is in Lebanon."

Helena tucked her legs under her bottom. "When Dad asks why she was arrested, they tell him that she caused problems at the marketplace. What problems? They don't know – just problems, they say. So the next day my father and Mahmoud go to the market again. An old butcher tells them that Zeinab was quarreling with a Jewish woman. She and Tia Zeinab pushed each other and screamed, so the police came. After he hears that, Mahmoud goes off in his old Ford with two other men to Lebanon."

"Who were the other men?"

"I don't know – probably men who worked with Mahmoud. Sana remained in Haifa with her aunt and uncle, of course. But she wanted nothing to do with them. She spent all her time at my house. She started crying from the first night and refused to take a step outside my room. My mother tried to persuade her to come out, to sit with us in the living room. She offered her bags of potato chips, her favorite food. Sana was tempted – she loved potato chips. But she wouldn't move from her corner of my bed. Her face was a little ball of fear. It was terrible – her eyes looked so bruised. There were dark shadows all around them. She cried and cried."

Helena reached for a cigarette. "When her aunt and uncle tried to go into my room, she shrieked like a tropical bird. Uncle Abu-ai-Rayhan sang to her through the door. It was like a film from Hollywood again – a musical, this time. But his singing didn't improve the situation. Sana went on strike – and not for the last time. The only power children have sometimes is not doing things."

"*Lysistrata*," I said.

"What about it?"

"That's the plot – the women go on strike for peace."

She lit her cigarette. "I thought of that too – as soon as she told me she would do that play. But back then Sana didn't want peace. She wanted everyone as upset as her. Not even the Prophet Mohammed was going to move that little mountain. And those stories of hers, they became scarier as the days passed. Queen Bee was after her all the time now. And me, I had to chase her away with more powerful magic than before. I had to make gestures in the air, in just the right way . . ." Helena imitated a tornado with her hands. "It was a sign language that only Sana knew. I once walked around her for an hour to keep her protected – and whispered Hebrew prayers. Then, when Queen Bee was vanquished, Sana asked me things like, 'What would happen if a girl were tied in a bag and dropped in the sea?' Or, 'What if the soldiers put chains on me and carried me to the top of the mountain and threw me down? Do you think my mother would come home and find me?' I cried so much and begged her not to say such terrible things, but she would not stop. She could not – her mother's disappearance untied a knot right in here." Helena tapped her head. "I told her she would be okay because I would follow her wherever she was taken by the soldiers or by Queen Bee. I would cut her ropes and chains with my magic scissors.

" 'But what if Queen Bee comes after us as we are running home?' she asks me. 'What if she forces me to climb on her back and carries me to prison?' "

"Sana always comes up with one more reason to be afraid," I observed.

"Exactly. But then I had an inspiration. I told her I would tap her on the head with hydrangea flowers from our garden and transform her into a tiny blue finch so she could fly away. She will be too small for Queen Bee to see, I say, and too camouflaged against the sky. And too quick. Her eyes . . . they opened very big when she heard that . . . as big as all the hope inside her. So whenever nothing else could calm her, when she was sobbing, I changed her into a bird with feathers the color of the sky."

I was thinking of Sana pretending to have a bird on her finger at the hotel restaurant in Perth. And the blue hibiscus flower behind her ear when I'd seen her at the bar – did it transform her into a finch when she was alone in her hotel room? But she'd been caught and made to jump – or maybe even pushed.

"I have a strange question," I told Helena.

"Then I will try to give you a strange answer."

"Do you think someone could be hurt – even murdered – by an imaginary being?"

"By Queen Bee, you mean? I don't know."

"Why a bee?"

She shook her head. "I'm sorry. There is so much about Sana I don't understand." She held up her empty glass. "I need some more. I'll be back in a moment."

While she poured herself another brandy, I considered that Sana's suicide might have been the ultimate failure for Helena; proof that she was not sorceress enough to save her friend.

When she had nestled herself back into the sofa, I asked, "Why do you think Sana was so frightened of being caught by a monster – of being murdered?"

She smoked thoughtfully. "I don't know. Maybe she was born like that. Maybe it was being an Arab in Israel – in a homeland that became a foreign country. Who can say? Anyway, Mahmoud finally brought Tia Zeinab back – in the same old Ford. At first, she seemed the same. She was smiling very big when she stepped out of the car. After all, this was a happy ending, and she was the star of our neighborhood mystery movie for two entire weeks! I don't think even *she* guessed that the ending wasn't truly so very happy – not at first. Or maybe she really was as good an actress as everyone in the neighborhood wanted her to be. Sana ran to her and hugged her. The two of them were all tears. They sat together in front of their house. When my mother and I ran to them . . ." Helena jiggled her fingers by her eyes to signify how they'd sobbed. "My mother loved Zeinab and that girl with all the life and ferocity the Nazis tried to destroy in her. She loved them with hugs and winks and kisses . . . That was my mother's victory over everything back there, you see. Thank God she never knew that Sana killed herself." Helena shook her head as though nothing good could be expected from the world. "I'll tell you something about my mother that is a secret. When she stood up with Tia Zeinab, she raised her hands over her head and gave thanks. You see, Zeinab coming back was the answer to her prayers. Yes, she still prayed, even after all that had happened in Europe, though she told everyone but me and my father that she didn't believe in God. No one even knew that she – and not my father – had put the *mezuzah* on our doorframe. I don't think she left Tia Zeinab's side for a week. But then we started to see that things weren't the same. For one thing . . ."

"Wait, why was Zeinab fighting at the marketplace?"

"The Jewish woman tried to cut in front of her. They argued and the stupid woman called Tia Zeinab *chametz* – you know, food that must be swept out of the house because of Passover. Tia Zeinab knew what that meant because she always helped my mother, my father, and me wash our house before Passover. And she ate the *Seder* meal with us, too." Helena's eyes hardened. "To say that a Palestinian woman is not clean . . . That is a very bad insult. Tia Zeinab went crazy and started to hit the other woman."

Helena stood up now to open the window to the street. We were being slowly roasted by the heating and I'd been progressively shedding clothing. She smoked for a time without speaking, pulling memories back from the past.

"And was it true that Zeinab had been taken to Lebanon?"

"Yes, but first she was taken to some building in Haifa. She couldn't identify this place. Maybe it was the police station my father visited. Other women were there. She said she was treated well, but bad things happened there. I am almost certain she was raped. She never said so, but . . . but I could see terrible worry in my mother's face when she looked at Tia Zeinab – and fear, too. She knew what had happened to her at the police station."

"Did she ever tell you?"

"No, she told me nothing was wrong – which was very strange because she would always tell me the truth, even when maybe I shouldn't know it. I think Tia Zeinab must have made her swear to keep silent."

Helena sat down again. "After Tia Zeinab returned home, she became nervous all the time. She began to sense problems that didn't exist. She believed she had special powers. She and Sana always wanted to have magic, you know – and unfortunately they wanted me to have it too. Now, when Tia Zeinab looked at you . . ." – here, Helena stared at me with a hypnotist's penetrating urgency – ". . . she was not looking at you, but looking for the crisis growing inside you. She thought she could see your future – fatal illnesses you were going to catch, a stone that would make you trip in the street . . . She saw bad things everywhere, in everyone. And everything was always talking to her. The walls whispered to her about roofs falling in. The wind told her about poison clouds from factories. She became Haifa's Cassandra. It was crazy! Mom began saying that when Tia Zeinab walked into a room a wave of catastrophe entered just before her. Me, I sometimes even have trouble remembering how she was before that. But I'm sure there *was* a before time. People change."

"Some people don't think they do – not really."

"They're wrong. In my experience people usually change for the worse."

Helena stood up again, made fidgety by her story. Carrying the tape recorder this time, she walked back to the window and leaned against the sill, framed by night. "Then, something even worse – we found out that Tia Zeinab's fear of what was about to happen was contagious. She made us all feel that we were going to suffer a tragedy at any moment. I remember she once shouted at me that I must move away from the window near Sana's bed because it was going to be broken by an explosion. I would be covered with glass. She slapped the top of my head when I didn't move quickly. It was the first and last time she ever hit me. She started to sob afterward and would not stop. I had to run to fetch my mother. The next time I went to Tia Zeinab's house, she'd put crosses of tape over all the windows, like we were going to be bombed. So you know what? I started to watch where I was sitting. And every little noise on the street made me imagine that Israeli soldiers were aiming their guns at Sana and Tia Zeinab and me. All that fear coming from her, it ruined everything – even the hours that Sana and I would spend in our hiding place."

"It never got any better?"

"Later, but not before it got worse. You know, Zeinab ended up putting Sana's bed in her room. She made her sleep there. And she made her promise not to leave the house except for school. She had to return home immediately. Though sometimes she stayed away, playing with me and other children. Mahmoud would spank her till she screamed for help. One day she closed her eyes and became silent – as if a door had shut inside her. She went on strike again. Even when her father hit her, she made no

67

noise. That should tell you something about the determination of that girl. And he hit her forcefully – strong enough to make marks. But she closed her lips like . . . like they were sewn together. Her silence, it provoked Mahmoud more. He'd changed, too, you see. After Zeinab returned, he could not resist the violence inside himself. Even I could see things were not right between Zeinab and him – that Sana was paying for their problems. Maybe Mahmoud thought that what the Jewish woman said about his wife was true, that Zeinab was *chametz* because the soldiers had raped her. If I had been older, maybe I would have understood him better – understood his guilt for not protecting his wife. But to me, he was just cruel. I hated him. Though Sana didn't. She feared him, but she loved him. She was very confused by all the changes. She wanted things to be the way they were before Zeinab disappeared. She wanted to go back to that time. But she couldn't. Sometimes she would not speak to me. We stayed in our hiding place for hours and she refused to say a word. I learned from her that people who are stopped from saying what they really think sometimes stop saying anything. They . . . they make believe they have no voice."

Helena whispered her last words with her hands over her mouth, as if she were breaking a taboo, then burst into tears. I stood up and kneeled next to her.

"The sadness comes in waves," she whimpered. "I'm sorry."

"You don't have to talk any more," I told her.

"No, don't you see? I am on strike, too, ever since Sana killed herself. I say nothing to no one. Nothing. But I have to tell someone these things. They are killing me. I have to get them out before they make me jump too."

Helena had put on a CD by Leonard Cohen when she'd gone to refill her glass, and while I held her hand he was softly singing: "But I swear by this song and by all that I have done wrong, I will make it all up to thee . . ." I would not have guessed she was aware of his voice, but when she had calmed she turned to the stereo and said, "So how do you make it up to a friend who is dead, Monsieur Cohen?" Looking at me, she added, "If you ask me, that's why she became a dancer and a mime – to say what she needed to say in the only way possible, because speaking about herself, out loud, speaking about what she felt, was always punished – and according to Zeinab might even create a tragedy in their family."

Helena went to the bathroom to wash her face. I began to wonder if she and Sana had become lovers. Weeks later, she would tell me on the phone, "Oh, we tried that once, in my Paris apartment. But we were so awkward that we just ended up giggling."

Now the phone rang. Helena darted back into the room and started a long conversation in Hebrew, smoking maniacally as she talked, as though enough nicotine might just carry her right across the Mediterranean to the coast of Israel. In the tumbling of her words I could tell it was someone she'd known for a long time and needed desperately to speak to. I liked the harsh, sandpaper sound of her Hebrew. Once, she spoke my name. Our eyes met and she swirled her hand in the air and pointed to a stack of books on her dining table, meaning I was free to look at them. "There are more in my bedroom," she whispered, holding her palm over the receiver. "Borrow what you want – don't worry about the order. It means nothing." Watching her talk on the phone, I realized that, despite what she'd said, I would end up liking her more and more.

After the phone call, which was from her father ("Dad sends his regards"), she said she couldn't speak about Sana any more that evening. Before leaving I asked after her father, and she told me he was retired now from the university. He had been living alone since her mother's death ten years earlier and spent most of his time gardening at a small house he'd bought in the desert near the Dead Sea. He was creating hybrid feijoas, a plum-sized fruit he'd first learned about from a botanist friend from New Zealand. His goal was a feijoa with golden pulp. He also taped a gardening program on Tuesdays at a television station in Ramallah and on Thursdays worked at the reference desk at a library in Hebron. It was a lot of driving, but it kept him busy. "If you ever want to check to see if there's an autobiography of Abu Nidal in Arabic or Hebrew, he's your man."

From the way she smiled when talking about her father I could see she adored him. I knew by now, as well, that she wanted to make her friendships and allegiances last for ever.

"He's not scared to work in the Occupied Territories?" I asked.

Helena would tell me later about his being attacked, but for now she merely replied, "Oh, please – who's going to make problems for an old Jewish man with hairy ears and tiny hands, just a little more than five feet tall, stumbling around with a cane like . . . like a Jewish Mr. Magoo."

"How do you know Mr. Magoo?"

"I watched too much television after I first moved to France. I love Mr. Magoo."

She sounded carefree and strong, but when we kissed good-bye her stance became awkward, as though she didn't quite trust her own legs and arms. By the doorway she touched the *mezuzah* again and brought her fingertips to her lips. To explain, she said, "You're leaving me alone now."

Chapter Seven

I spent the next three weeks working on my novel, giving my journalism classes, and transcribing Helena's tapes. I was struck by how dry and faded her voice sounded – like a furtive breeze across bare stone. Alex said she sounded very solitary, but not sad – as though she wanted it that way. I decided not to risk pressuring her – not to call for a few weeks. But she phoned late one night at the end of April, about a month after our meeting.

I'd been nearly asleep. After some small talk, she launched one of her odd volleys: "Who will save a girl who receives death threats?"

That sounded like a question Sana would have asked when they were little girls. I was reminded that the two of them had shared a language going back to childhood.

"Was someone threatening Sana – blackmailing her?" I asked Helena, believing I'd spotted another connection to *The Last Kabbalist of Lisbon*, in which Portugal's secret Jews – who must hide their faith from the Crown and Church – are always susceptible to blackmail.

"Me, not her," Helena replied. "They threaten me in letters."

"Who is threatening you?"

"I think you're going to have to tell me that, Sherlock. You see, they're not going to sign their names and write their addresses. Though that," she piped cheerily, "would be very, very nice."

"Why did they threaten you?"

"I'll send you the letters. After you've seen them, we'll discuss it."

"It's late – tell me now."

"No, you must wait. I'll tell you when you receive the letters."

"Helena, you got me out of bed. Tell me now."

She laughed. "Okay, okay . . . Sana's death – it freed me from my constraints and I began to write letters to the newspapers in Israel. The letters, they gain strength from my sadness and my anger. I can't help myself – she and I are writing them together."

"*Sana* is helping you write them?"

"Oh, please, I am not *that* crazy. But it's as if we are still together in our hiding place – all the time now. She looks over my shoulder when I write. She agrees with some things and disagrees with others. Three of our letters have been printed. Some readers must have found out where I live and have written to me. Maybe they work for the newspapers and saw my return address. Maybe they work for Mossad."

Being spied on by the Israeli secret police seemed very far-fetched and I made the mistake of saying so. She went silent, then said some things that didn't make any sense at all. I realized she'd been drinking. Finally, she told me, "They don't just hunt old Nazis and Palestinians, you know! They have files on all Jews with big mouths."

"Maybe so. Anyway, what do you say in your letters that might make Mossad so upset?"

"I'll send you the most recent one. I'll translate it into English as well as I can, though you'll miss some of what I say in the Hebrew original. It's a terrible shame you can't speak Hebrew. You're not such a great Jew, you know."

I laughed. "Don't worry, I'll assume your letter is much better in the original."

"No, you can assume it's much *worse* – it's always worse to be betrayed in your own language."

Nine threatening letters that had been sent to Helena soon arrived in the mail. All had been sent to her over the previous two weeks, after two newspapers in Tel Aviv, *Maariv* and *Yediot Acharonot*, had published a provocative letter from her. Five of them were in Hebrew, two in English, and the longest in a mixture of Hebrew and Greek, on blue-tinted paper.

She said that this last one had arrived from an Israeli man who claimed to have grown up in Salonika with her mother, though Helena had never heard of him and suspected he was lying. Among other things, he declared that her mother would never have forgiven her for what she'd written. That was what bothered Helena the most, even though she knew it was untrue. I told her that if we were to hire a detective, maybe the blue paper would lead us to a particular stationery store and the author.

She suggested that I'd seen too many episodes of *Columbo* and that finding some old Greek with a typewriter, a long but possibly counterfeit memory, and lots of free time would prove useless. "Unless you want to shoot him for me by any chance?" she added hopefully.

When I told her that if anything should happen to her I would indeed hire an Israeli detective to find her Greek enemy, she said, "Well, if I'm dead by then, tell Colombowitz good luck from me. If he finds the Greek, tell him I'm learning to make moussaka and all those other things I never had time for on earth."

When I didn't laugh she said, "I guess I am not very funny. Sorry. It's because I'm nervous."

The longest of the letters in English – a full handwritten page – was signed by "Judith," with thick quotation marks around her name. It was sent from England. She probably adopted that name to imply that she would defend Israel to the death; in one of the Apocryphal books of the Bible, Judith seduces an enemy general and chops off his head. The letter opened, "You must think you are very clever, but you are an anti-Semitic *hore* playing *write* into the Nazi hands." It went on to accuse Helena of treason and condemned her to death "at the end of a sword" for forgetting about the Holocaust. It ended, "I should pity you for *hateing* yourself, but there is no room for anti-Semites in a heart which has survived the death camps." The text contained numerous spelling and grammatical errors, from which it was clear that English was not Judith's native language. It was written in red ink.

The second letter in English was sent from Israel and had only two lines. A furious pen-point had pushed through the paper in various places. It read: "I have a very good gun, so watch where you walk around Paris because I will be following you."

Again there was no date, and it was signed illegibly over the line, "Righteous is the soldier who has spilled blood for the greater glory of God."

In the excerpts that Helena translated from the Hebrew letters she'd received, she was frequently described as a "bitch" and a "terrorist." But *zona*, meaning "whore," was the epithet most commonly used – twelve times in a three-page letter that was very neatly typed and signed by "David." If he was a madman, then he was a meticulous one, which made his threats to "carry her whoring carcass back to Israel in his suitcase" all the more chilling.

Quite apart from the threats themselves, I found it telling that nearly all the letter-writers viewed a woman who disagreed with them as a prostitute or an animal. Women who held divergent opinions could not apparently be human beings.

Despite my wariness, I agreed to help her translate into English the letter she'd written that had inspired such hatred. Our final version read as follows:

Dear Editor,

I recently read of the stoning to death of Yosef Ish-ran, 14, and Ya'acov Mandell, 13, two boys living in the Tekoa Jewish settlement in the Occupied Territories. Their bodies were discovered in a cave near their home and had been so badly mutilated by neighboring Palestinian Arabs that they had to be identified by dental records. I have also read that despite Yosef's mother's sorrow she is committed to remaining in Tekoa. She says she gets her determination from her son having once told her, "If you have to leave Tekoa, so be it – I will stay here. I love the place."

Various articles in newspapers and magazines that came out right after the stoning assured readers that until these killings Tekoa had been a model of peaceful co-existence between the 230 settlers and the 7,000 Palestinian Arabs living in surrounding villages. I had my doubts, but I accepted that – on the surface, at least – life was calm there. As we all know, however, "calm" is a word in Israel that implies no permanence whatsoever – a word always ready to be changed, so to speak.

Later came the reports that Arab snipers had indeed fired into the Tekoa settlement and had even set off roadside bombs prior to the murder of the boys.

The particular circumstances of these murders have forced me to come to a conclusion that I have been avoiding for some time, maybe my whole life. I also confess that two other events have prodded me to pick up my pen: an attack in the desert on my father Samuel, an eighty-year-old botanist who only wants to create beauty from out of the desert sands, and the death by suicide of a Palestinian friend who embodied all the creative power of both our peoples. It is in solidarity with her that I say the following: the Palestinians hate us, even in the best of circumstances. Even in Tekoa. And the truth that few of us will admit is that they are *right* to do so, because we have given them ample proof that we hate them even more.

Quite apart from the atrocities we commit against them and which are common knowledge, we show that hate every time a Jew says that our suffering is different and more important than theirs.

The three million Palestinians living in exile know we hate them. We should not forget about them and their brothers and sisters back home in the Occupied Territories, because they are equally capable of picking up stones. And make no mistake – there are stones enough in Palestine to kill every Jewish citizen of Israel.

We even show our hate in the most peaceful of settlements, in places like Tekoa, for the simple reason that these towns and villages are built on Palestinian land. Yosef's mother, good woman though she may be, is a representative of an occupying army. And let us not forget that she has come to us from America as well, since she and her family only moved to Israel seven years earlier. Surely every Palestinian around Tekoa has asked the question at least once: *is there so little land in the United States that these American Jews must take ours?*

So, let all those who praise Yosef's mother for her determination to remain in Tekoa know this: she allowed her son to become a target of hatred the day she brought him from the land of his beloved baseball stars to a new home where the games are much more seriously played. Do not ask me to believe that she is doing the right thing in remaining behind in Tekoa. Do not ask me to praise her courage. I will never believe that loving mothers allow their sons and daughters to live on land stolen from other people. Courage would mean recognizing her error and abandoning her new home. And until a first settler of Tekoa does that, or, better yet, gives it as a gift to a Palestinian whose home has been knocked down by our army tanks, do not ask me to believe they are people of righteousness and peace.

The brutal hate that characterizes both sides in this struggle will take many decades to subside, even if peace is established. And so, until such time as peace has accompanied at least two generations into adulthood, I call for an absolute separation of Jews from Arabs. All Jewish settlements in the Occupied Territories should be evacuated and closed, and all Arabs living in Israel should be deported. Let the Palestinians have East Jerusalem for their capital and let us begin to build the great barrier there – a wall moving north and south from the vestiges of Solomon's Temple.

When I hear our leaders tell us that the stones of the Western Wall are more valuable than the lives of Palestinians, then I know that the new wall must begin there. Let us begin its construction with the bloody stones that mutilated the bodies of Yosef and Ya'acov.

Know this: if the Wailing Wall could speak it would tell us this: "I would prefer to crumble to dust, I would prefer to vanish into nothing, I would prefer to be forgotten than to be used to justify the death of one more person. So blow me up if you have to and build a new wall, and let it run up and down Israel's border, let it carve its way into the sea, so that no more blood may be shed. Let there be neither gates nor doors

76

in this wall. Let words and even dreams be unable to pass through its stone."

Yes, let the separation between the two peoples be absolute – to protect us from those who would stone our children to death, and to protect them from those who believe that it is courageous to steal a homeland.

While Helena and I had been perfecting the English translation, I'd questioned her about the attack on her father, of course, but she'd always given me only the vaguest of replies. "When we're done with the letter, I will tell you all about what happened," she'd assured me.

Now that she was satisfied with our finished text, I called her and reminded her of her promise.

"Oh, it wasn't anything terrible. Dad was hurt by some Palestinian young men. They pushed him and made him fall. He had to go to hospital for three days."

"But he's better now?"

"He's just fine," she lied. "He's resting at home. Everything is calm."

"And the wall – are you really serious about the need to build one?"

"Absolutely. I no longer believe co-existence is possible. Even for those who leave Israel it does no good. In the end, they go out through hotel windows in Australia."

"So you think Sana committed suicide because she didn't see any possible way to escape her past?"

"Me? I know nothing," she replied resentfully. "Sana didn't trust me enough to tell me her thoughts. She only rarely said what she meant – she had a mother who heard whispers from the walls and a father who hit her so forcefully she would stay silent as her only defense. She had no government papers to live in her own home. Do you hear what I am telling you – in her own home?! My God, she spent years saving her cat from soldiers." Desperation burned in her voice. "If you don't write that . . . if you don't explain that in your story then everything will be wrong. Are you listening to me? Are you going to get everything wrong about her?"

"Helena, of course I want to get things right. I understand she must have been desolate."

"It wasn't just that! What she did . . . it was a last performance, with you as the audience. She waited till you were in the front row. Or do you believe it was an accident that you were there to see her death? You must have realized *that*, no?"

"But she couldn't have known I'd be there when she jumped."

"Hah! Of course she knew. She looked around and found you sitting at an outside table, sipping your tea, and she decided that the time had come." Helena gasped.

"What is it?"

"God, oh my God, even if she planned it, she must have been so frightened. If only I had been with her. I was such a fool."

"But why would she want me there?" I asked.

"Tell me, what is it that you do as a profession?"

"I teach journalism. And I write."

"Exactly. And she read a book you wrote. It made her trust you."

"You're saying she wanted me to write about her death? That killing herself was so I would pick up my pen? But I write fiction. It's insane."

"It may be, but if it was what she wanted then she got her wish, because you are talking to me now and you want to write something about her. You see? She knew that sooner or later it would mean that you would tell her story – how Zeinab was raped and how we lived in the House of Blue Hydrangeas and everything else. She couldn't write it, she didn't have that confidence – and maybe not the talent either. So she found a person who could do it for her. She knew you could make silence into something – into something with a life. If you want my opinion, that's why she told you she liked your book."

"But it would mean that . . . that in a way she almost –"

"That she used you."

"I can't believe that."

"You think she was a saint, don't you? Okay, maybe she was, but maybe saints are the most devious people of all. Sana planned everything inside the spider webs of that head of hers. And you, *mon cher ami*, were caught."

"Would she have sacrificed herself on the chance that I might write something? I don't think so."

"Maybe she was not thinking very right – something made her very emotional that week, very nervous. You told me she was miming with birds in the hotel restaurant. You still don't understand, do you? That didn't mean she was happy or having fun. It was not what you believed. It meant she was trying to flee from what was threatening her. And the flower behind her ear, it was tied to the end of a magic wand that you were not able to see – only *she* could see it. That bird that you caught and gave back to her – you thought you were just having good fun with her. But for her it was much more – it was a sign that you understood her and that you wanted to join her in all that she was planning. You agreed to become a part of her strategy. You entered into her fantasies. And let me assure you, she had much bigger fantasies than anyone you have ever known. You . . . you became like me, you see – a co-conspirator."

Helena whispered her last sentences, as if to keep them from eavesdroppers. But there was a tense force behind what she said. I pictured the white knuckles of her fist gripping the receiver.

"So she killed herself to get me to tell her story?" I asked. "Is that possible?"

"It *is* possible. I just don't know if it's truly what happened."

"You're not an easy person, you know. This whole story . . . everything that's happened since Perth – it's like you and Sana are turning my world upside down."

"I told you you'd like me less the more you knew me."

"That's simply not true and you know it. All this has just made me confused."

"We're all confused."

The hateful letters sent to Helena were spread in front of me on my desk. "Have you been to the police about the threats against you?"

"No, what should I say to the police? They can do nothing until one of the writers of a letter tries to hurt me. I will tell you something – at this point, I think I would like someone to try, just to end my waiting."

"Aren't you frightened?"

"Of course I am. Do I not sound frightened to you?"

"No, you sound angry. Maybe even a bit amused. I think you're much stronger than you think."

"That's a good one! You haven't guessed yet that I'm an actress, too? Sana and I aren't friends for nothing. We are two little *démonettes* hiding in the dark and making believe all the time. You know, if you ever go to Israel, you will find that most Israelis are very good actors. Rabin and Sharon and Netanyahu – always acting in plays that they think are written in the Torah. Those fools don't even know they are writing them all by themselves! You say precisely that in your book, too – about Jews having to wear masks to keep themselves safe and how that will make them the best actors in the world. Sana must have loved that when she read it. Your book was perfect for her. You really should try reading what you write sometime."

"That's amusing," I said in an irritated voice.

"It was not meant to be. What I am saying is that you should read what you wrote and not trust any of us."

Helena went off to get her cigarettes. When she got back on the phone, she said, "So what do you think of my letter?"

"Maybe you should stay out of politics."

"No, I stayed out for my whole life. Sana's death makes me go in. You agree with what I wrote, don't you?"

"I don't know anything about solving the problems in Israel and Palestine."

"So let me guess – you, as a good American . . . you think that if everybody just sits together and discusses *how they feel* then the fighting will disappear – one-two-three? Or maybe if Monsieur Arafat and the Israeli leadership appear on *Larry King Live* together, they will go home as friends. Let me tell you, you believe in magic wands with blue hydrangea flowers at their tips more than Sana."

I'd promised myself at my brother's deathbed – watching him fade away despite all our wishes to the contrary – that I would never believe in magic ever again.

"Look, Helena, sometimes you go too far," I told her. "In your letter, you make it sound as if Yosef's mother was responsible for his death. Don't you see how that could make people furious at you? It's a terrible thing to say – hurtful and mean."

"Oh, is it? Is it really? Then you tell me what kind of good American mother brings her family to a settlement surrounded by Arabs – by seven thousand fucking Arabs! She is not right in the head. She is a criminal!"

"But maybe things really were calm in Tekoa. The stoning might have been simply an aberration. Things like that happen."

"My God, you weren't lying, you *really* don't know anything. Read my letter again. In Israel, *calm* is a codeword meaning things are not yet exploding but might at any moment. The only way to live there is to make yourself forget that – forget what can happen at any time. And people do. We are very good at pretending, like I say. We even believe the roles we are playing. But I assure you, when an Israeli or Palestinian is *calm*, that's the time to watch out!"

"Still, you don't always have to push so hard. Ever heard of the word *tact*?"

"I was tactful for fifty-three years! When can I say what I really think? After I'm dead?"

"Still, all these threats . . ."

"Well, I'm not going to kill myself and make it easy for them. That Greek son-of-a-bitch who has the *chutzpah* to talk for my mother . . . He can wait for ever if he's waiting for that. And Sana can wait a little while longer, too. She can go fuck herself!"

"You think she's waiting for you?"

"Of course she is. She'll wait as long as she has to for me. She is the most patient person in the world. Wherever she is, she's on strike until we reach her – not moving half a centimeter." Holding the receiver away from her mouth, she shouted, "But you *are* going to have to wait, Sana, you hear me?"

"We? Who's the *we* she's waiting for?"

"Me, I mean."

"No, tell me, who else?"

"My father for one. She loved my father. She thought he was the cutest man in the world – a Jewish elf. When she was twelve she was already taller than him. And she liked to play with his eyebrows – they are furry."

"Who else?"

"I don't know. But she must have had close friends in Brazil. And maybe . . . maybe she's also waiting for you."

"And if you were killed for writing your letters, what would she think?"

"Sorry, my pasta is boiling on the stove. I must prepare supper. It's calling me." She held the phone from her mouth again and made believe she was being summoned. "Helena . . . Helena . . ."

"Bye," she said.

"Listen, you think she'd be pleased if you were killed, don't you?"

"Richard, you are very clever, but you don't know when to keep quiet. If you will excuse a small criticism, I think you need to learn some tact yourself if you are going to write Sana's story."

She hung up before I had a chance to either scream at her or apologize; I was not sure which was the more appropriate reaction.

The next time Helena called, it was again late at night and she had clearly downed one too many brandies. She even started speaking to me in Hebrew. I was beginning to believe that drinking was doing her real damage.

She was desperate now to tell me about the attack on her father. "I must," she said. "I cannot hold secrets inside me any more."

"So he's not fine?"

"No, not at all."

Helena explained that Samuel had been driving from his home in the desert to the library in Hebron at seven in the morning on March 12th, and he had just crossed over into the Occupied Territories when four young men stopped his car. They were standing in the middle of the road, their beat-up white Fiat on the shoulder. He recognized one of them, slender, nearly six feet tall, with beautiful eyes the color of olive leaves. His name was Ibrahim and he'd come to the library two years earlier to ask about universities in Australia; his uncle in Melbourne had suggested he try to win a scholarship. He'd told Samuel that he wanted to be an engineer. He'd built bridges ever since he was little, with wire, nails, and spokes from rusty bicycle wheels.

Samuel had gone on the internet to order prospectuses from Australian universities. When they arrived, he'd put them in a large envelope and left them at the reception desk with "Ibrahim" written in Arabic on the front. The boy had picked up this package on a day when Samuel wasn't working.

Now Ibrahim pointed his automatic weapon at the old man's chest. He and the other young Palestinians had tangled, dusty hair. Whiskers bristled on their chins. They looked as if they'd been up all night. Samuel thought Ibrahim would not want to admit he knew an old Israeli man in front of his friends, so he said nothing. Maybe that was a mistake. Maybe the young man got angry at the tiny Jewish botanist from the library who didn't seem to be able to distinguish one Palestinian from another.

In a despairing voice, Helena told me, "My father should have said, 'Shalom, Ibrahim, any news from those universities in Australia? And how's your uncle in Melbourne?' Sometimes I think that common kindness has been trained out of us."

A stocky young man wearing a San Francisco 49ers T-shirt then ordered Samuel to hand over his keys. The four hopped into his Peugeot. They might have left him there without hurting him, or even returned his car after taking it on an adventure, but the old botanist's second mistake, at least according to Helena, was to say in a pleading voice that the Peugeot had carried him safely all over Israel and the Occupied Territories for seventeen years and that it meant a great deal to him.

"Men who want trouble do not like to be asked to have feelings," she told me.

One of the youths pointed his gun at Samuel's right leg, just above the knee. He pulled the trigger. The old man tumbled over and cried out. His white sun-hat went flying. He felt a sharp pain in his arm and heard a crack like snapping wood; he'd fractured his right forearm in his fall. "*Gott helf mir!*" he called under his breath in Yiddish – "God help me!" Before he lost consciousness he thought of Rosa telling him his Olympic career as a discus thrower was over. He heard laughing. Hers? The young men's?

When a first car whooshed past him he awoke in its trail of dust and smoke. Samuel tried to stand up but failed. Two more cars sped by. Recoiling from the pain, he entered a dark and prickly silence. He was sweating so much he dreamed about melting into the desert. When he awoke again, he leaned up on his good elbow. A fourth car had stopped. It was long and green and shiny. He remembered a man with sagging jowls eating an apple and peering at him through his open window. The man threw the core on the ground by Samuel's feet. Then he sped off.

An old Polish Jew was lying by the side of the road in a puddle of blood and four motorists went on their way . . . A fifth car finally stopped and the driver called for an ambulance. Samuel was taken to a local hospital, where the bullet was removed.

He was home now, and a nursing assistant was caring for him during the day. Though he could still only hobble around, he was cheerful.

"After all that he has suffered in his life, he's either become extremely resilient or simple in the head, depending on your viewpoint," Helena observed. "In any case, he doesn't want to consider his future. But I have to. If he can't walk again, what are we going to do?"

We talked about her father's options for a long time. Helena grew glum and diffident. Then, with renewed vigor in her voice, she mentioned she'd had a new letter printed.

"Not again!" I moaned.

She said she just couldn't stop herself. "If I love Israel but hate what is happening, then what should I do? You tell me."

She'd used the translation we'd done of her previous letter as the basis for a follow-up – her debut effort in English. She'd sent it to the *New York Times*, the *L.A. Times*, the *Guardian*, and the *Daily Telegraph*. She was both thrilled and frightened by the possibility of gaining a wider and ever more irate audience. She even asked me if I knew of any Jewish weekly or monthly in the United States that might publish what she had written.

"I wouldn't tell you even if I did," I replied. "You want to get hurt, don't you?"

"Look at it this way – if anything happens to me, you can hire Detective Colombowitz to investigate. You and he will have some fun. Besides, my family had so many troubles back there that I am vaccinated against murder."

I let my silence imply that, once again, I did not find her amusing.

"Look, I do not want to be attacked," she rushed to assure me. "But I also do not want to keep quiet. You understand?"

I pleaded in vain with her to withdraw her letters from consideration; most readers would believe she was just a harmless kook, but a few might think she was dangerous.

Luckily, no American or English editor ever published what she sent.

"I'm not sure I should have translated that letter of yours," I told her.

"I take full responsibility. And nothing's going to happen, I promise. You know, you are sounding a little like Tia Zeinab – I think you've caught her catastrophe sickness. In any event, I stopped leaving my home during the day a long time ago. I'll be okay."

"So what makes you so afraid of going out during the day?"

"If I tell you, you'll think I have only half a head."

"You don't really care what I think, do you?"

I expected Helena to laugh, but she snapped, "That's not a very nice thing to say."

"I'm sorry," I said. "Look, all I want is for you to talk about your fear. I'm not going to think badly of you."

"A while ago," she replied, "I began to see a man following me when I left my apartment."

"Who?"

"I don't know. It began maybe three years ago. There were really two men – they took turns. One of them was so obvious I'd have to have been blind not to see him. I think he wanted me to know he was following me – I always saw happiness in his eyes. But I have not seen him since I stopped going out during the day. I even talked to him once. He denied that he was following me. We spoke in French. But when I yelled in Hebrew that I would call the police, he cursed me back in Hebrew. *That* was a mistake."

"Was he Israeli?"

"Of course – who else speaks our language? But it's not so very important. He never did anything to me."

"I hate to say this, but maybe he and the other guy are still following you. They would be harder to spot at night."

"I don't care. Going out only at night isn't for them. The night makes me feel better – more hidden and protected."

"You don't think someone can hurt you just as easily at night?"

"You'll be happy to hear, Sigmund, that I do some thinking about that. It's inherited from my mother. In the camp, my mother only felt safe at night. To wake up in the morning was the hardest thing for her. During the night, in her dreams, she sometimes escaped over the barbed wire and ran all the way to Salonika. During the day, she could be chosen for the ovens."

"How long have you felt like that?"

"Maybe for ever. I knew I wanted to pass through life without being seen as soon as Sana and I started to enter our hiding place. Then, after Tia Zeinab began to see catastrophe every-where, I said, 'Who needs to live like this?' Of course, from my mother, I knew that if they saw how thin and pale I was I might be chosen for the ovens. Queen Bee might just point her finger at me and say, "Too skinny – *Krematorium*!"

"And you still feel all that?"

"I might."

"Did Sana really believe there was some sort of monster after her?"

"Do you believe in God?"

"On bad days."

"Good answer! Well, Sana believes in Queen Bee on bad days, too. Even more important, Queen Bee believes in her. Me, I look at it this way – as my mother's only child, I have the number eighteen tattooed on my arm as well. It's invisible, but it's there. So I'm safe." Helena was silent for a moment, then added, "What would you think if I suggested to the Israeli army

86

that they put tattoos on the Palestinians, to keep them under control? I could add that to my letters."

"Helena, I've got an important question to ask you," I said, wanting to change the subject. "Now don't get mad at me, but when did you last see Sana?" I hadn't dared ask this before because I suspected there'd been a big fight between them.

"Look, I have to tell you our story the only way I can," she replied in a voice requesting patience. "It's like the books in my apartment – maybe you can't see an order, but it is there. Maybe it's not perfect, but it's all I can do."

"You don't have to tell me what happened, just how long ago it was that you last spoke."

"Five years ago – four years before she died." I thought she was going to explain a bit more, but she simply added, "Though I still speak to her, of course."

On June 3rd, I flew to Paris for two days to tape her again. After checking in at the Hotel Villa Modigliani, I took the metro to the Marais. It was three in the afternoon when I arrived at her apartment, but she was only just finishing breakfast and came to the door carrying her steaming coffee mug.

She had straightened out her living room and put all the stacks of books behind the armchair. A stunning bouquet of pink and white carnations blossomed in a glass pitcher on her mantelpiece. The Persian rug was now a vibrant brown and black.

"I *aspirate* the entire apartment," she explained, fidgeting with her hair, embarrassed to be drawing attention to herself. "I will not tell you all the missing things I found."

"It looks great," I said, not wishing to correct her English.

Once she'd finished her egg and toast, she grabbed my recorder and said, "I'm beginning to like this talking. It is almost like I am an important person."

She dropped down on her plump sofa and rested my tape recorder, her cigarettes, and a ceramic ashtray on its arm. We talked about Paris for a time and she told me that two or three times a week she had begun walking several hours at night with no particular destination in mind. Sometimes she thought that if she walked long enough she'd come right back to where she started, as if the city were a circle – or even a planet. "I know of no other place like that," she said. "I think it is why I stay. I mean, I can get lost without getting really lost. Anyway, it's good for me to be going for walks again."

I pulled my chair opposite her. She re-entered her story by telling me that everything had changed again for Sana a couple of months after Zeinab's return. At that time, Mahmoud received an offer of better work in a bank in Italy. He took a ship there – to which city, Helena wasn't sure. She also didn't know the bank's name but believed it had been headquartered in Egypt or Saudi Arabia. Sana had been nine. Her father used to send money home every month.

"From where exactly – what return address?"

"Rome, I think – I'm not sure."

"Do you have his current address by any chance?"

She stuck out her tongue as if that were preposterous. "Look, when I was a kid, I didn't care where he was. And I still don't care. For all I know he may live at the Vatican."

"After he left, what did your parents say about where he was?"

"They just said *Italy*. They were also very happy he was a thousand miles away."

"Did Sana ever indicate to you he might still be living there?"

"She didn't talk about him. She knew I didn't like him. But she gave me the idea that he was dead."

Helena said that with the money Mahmoud sent home Zeinab bought an ice-box, good shoes for Sana, and a purple couch with green pillows.

"Purple and green?"

"Zeinab was ahead of her time," she laughed. "The rest of us had to wait a few years for the 1960s to come."

"Did she still see catastrophe everywhere?"

"Yes, though she improved a little after Mahmoud left. At least, her predictions of tragedy became less frequent. And they no longer made people angry – except for maybe my mother. Sana never got hit any more, which was a blessing."

"So everything was a bit better?"

"Not everything. Tia Zeinab would complain to my mother that Mahmoud never wrote to her more than a few lines. She, on the other hand, sent off pages and pages every week. She told him everything about the neighborhood – births, deaths, accidents . . . She hoped her letters would make him love her again, I think. Sana wrote too, and we would send some of the pictures we drew in our hiding place by the light of a little candle. Even then I sensed that Zeinab was trying to make up for being raped by Israeli soldiers. Now I think that maybe Mahmoud believed she was responsible. Probably she did too."

"He never came back?"

"No, but after two years of separation – this was around 1958 – Tia Zeinab announced one day to Sana that they were going to Italy. They would be gone for a few weeks. When Sana heard this, she went on strike again. She sat in my room like she had been condemned to death."

"Wait, you said she still loved her father – even if she was frightened of him."

"But Sana thought her mother had other intentions – that she wanted to convince Mahmoud to let them stay in Italy. And Sana didn't want to leave Haifa for ever. Before going, she gave me her favorite pin. She told me to hold it for her. It was a butterfly – a big one in bright blue, red, and green enamel, with glass stones for eyes. She thought that if the pin remained behind with me, it would pull her home again."

"Do you still have it?"

"No, I sent it back to her a few years ago."

"That must have been exciting for her – to have it again," I said.

Tears flooded Helena's eyes. When I stood up to go to her, she said, "You have an astonishing way of saying the wrong thing at the wrong moment, you know that?" She reached for a cigarette and did her best not to look at me.

"I'm on your side, Helena – yours and Sana's."

"They were not always the same, you know."

If I'd have kept silent, perhaps she'd have gone on to explain what exactly had gone wrong between the two of them. Instead

I said, "Even if you disagreed at times, at least you had a shared past. No one could take that away from you."

"Oh, would you please stop trying to encourage me!" She pounded the arm of her sofa, then jumped up and went to the window. Her lips were trembling.

"You didn't kill her," I said.

"Keep your analysis of me to yourself, Sigmund."

"You don't like people helping you, do you?"

With an outraged face, she said, "Is that what you are doing? Thank you very much for telling me. *Merci beaucoup!*"

She stared at me hard, her eyes now rimmed in red, then gripped her hair with both her hands and tugged it back. I saw that she had on her pearl earrings again.

"Those are lovely," I told her.

"What are?"

"Your earrings."

She sighed, her anger breaking. "It's very fortunate for our relationship that you have a perverse sense of timing." She wiped her eyes, then opened the window a crack. She hit me playfully on the top of the head before sitting back down. Pulling her hair back again, she said, "You really like them?" When I nodded, she added, "My mom gave them to me. She always adored pearls."

"So you think Sana knew she was going to stay in Italy for a long time?" I asked.

"Maybe she heard her mother talking to my parents – maybe Zeinab told them."

"And how long *did* they stay?"

"Two years." She lit her cigarette. In a resentful voice she said, "You know half the people in Paris live alone. What do you think of that?"

"I think you're not particularly pleased about being one of them. And that Sana broke your heart."

She considered her words carefully. "No, I'm just angry at her – and at everything that happened. It's incredible, but I'm still furious about things that happened forty years ago. Isn't that crazy? I should probably take Prozac. Or maybe heroin."

"It's very bad for your teeth."

"Excuse me?"

I told her that a friend who had been a junkie had once told me that when you get off heroin your teeth begin to crumble.

"It'll be worth it if it makes me forget." Helena squinted from the smoke. "You know, I always thought that Tia Zeinab had lied to Sana. But then, after Sana killed herself, I started turning the past around and around in my head. Now I think that maybe Mahmoud was the one who wanted his wife and daughter to remain in Italy. He may not have told Tia Zeinab at first. Maybe staying more than a few weeks was a surprise to her as well."

"When did you find out for sure that they were staying in Italy for a long time?"

"I never did – not officially." Helena took off her pullover. She was wearing a pink sleeveless undershirt. Her shoulders and arms were so skinny – like coat hangers. I realized then what should have been obvious – she was starving herself.

"You live mostly on brandy and nicotine, don't you?"

Her eyebrows arched up defiantly. "I hope you are not going to say that's a bad thing!"

"Why don't I take you for a big lunch today? You choose the place."

"That is a very nice proposal, but I have not been hungry for many months."

When I insisted we have a proper meal together, she said that her father had been after her for years to change the way she lived. "He will not succeed, so you will not either."

"I'm very persistent," I observed. "So don't bet against me." She started to protest, but I interrupted her, "So what happened next with you and Sana?"

"Next? Nothing – no letters from Tia Zeinab or Sana. *Poof*, they vanished!" She stood up again and leaned back against the wall by her window overlooking the Montparnasse Tower. "My father was given a job at the university. He was happy. But Mom was lonely. So we moved to a house in the suburbs. Mom kept chickens in the garage – like we were still living in the House of Blue Hydrangeas. Our neighbors were embarrassed – they were *Herr Doctors* and *Monsieur Professeurs* from Europe, and you could see the way they looked at our house . . . like bad smells were coming out. But the kids all loved the chickens. I made new friends – kids who had bicycles and Barbie dolls and fancy shoes, with accents from Bucharest and Munich and Odessa. One French family from Algiers – the Hadjenbergs – they even had a swimming pool. Can you imagine! My eyes looked like bugs' when I saw it. This new neighborhood – it was all Jewish. It took me years before I realized that *that's* why it seemed so very odd. In our games, some of my new friends shot Arabs and took them prisoner. I wanted to be accepted, so I played with them. But I never thought of Sana as an Arab. She was just Sana. We were very young and we were always too busy hiding from soldiers and Queen Bee and Tia Zeinab's predictions to think about things like that – things that meant absolutely nothing."

Helena picked up a book from one of the piles behind her armchair and opened it at the middle, drawing her finger from top to bottom. "Though maybe I could not read Sana well enough – not all the way to the end. You see? Maybe she was always aware she was an Arab and I was a Jew." She closed the book and hugged it to her chest. "I remember our first day together after she came back from Italy. We stood in front of our new house in the Jewish suburb and I showed her the blue bicycle my parents had just given me."

"Wait – had Sana moved back to her house in Wadi al-Nisnas?"

"Yes. Her uncle and his wife had gone by then, so it was just Sana and her mother."

"Why did her uncle move?"

"His wife had given birth. They needed more space. So listen – I was showing Sana my bicycle and a small Jewish man walked past us. He was one of our new neighbors, a Hungarian Jew who was saved by Wallenberg during the war. I said hello. We were both looking at him – we were curious. Why not? He was wearing a big dark suit in that dry Haifa heat! He was not right in the head. But he must not have liked us looking at him. He said to Sana, 'What is the matter, Fatima, did you never see a white man before?'"

"That's awful. Was Sana very upset?"

"She didn't show it, but she must have been terribly hurt. I made believe I didn't know what he was talking about – to spare her from being embarrassed. I said he was just a crazy Hungarian in an ugly suit and that his Hebrew was no good anyway. I was in my thirties before I thought about it again. I realized he meant that Sana was a different race – not just to him, but to me too! That had never occurred to me. Can you imagine a Jew saying such a monstrous thing – a Jew saved by Wallenberg? I think of it all the time now. Because I realize he was like so many people who had not learned what they should from all that had happened. You see, I grew up thinking everyone was like Sana and me."

"Did Mahmoud come back from Italy, too?"

"No, he stayed." Helena gazed down sadly. She let the silence of her disappointment in the world lead her thoughts away, then said in a shamed voice, "When Sana and I first saw each other after her stay in Italy, we laughed and jumped around. But we soon saw that everything was wrong between us. She was taller and skinnier, and she stayed even more in her own world – all alone. She did crazy things. I was scared of her. And my anger at her leaving, after my initial joy, it made me cold and distant."

"What kind of crazy things did she do?"

"She would pass hour after hour just playing by herself, gesturing with her hands, telling stories to herself, moving her lips to say things I could not hear. She did not want to be interrupted by me or by anyone. It was like she was living in a universe where no one else was welcome – like she was deaf and dumb. A little like Farid in your book."

"Did she ever speak to you about the stories she was telling herself?"

"She only told me that Italy was not safe. Queen Bee was not there, but there were other monsters. I didn't know what she meant or what had happened to her there. But not being able to speak Italian and not having any friends . . . And her parents not being able to find their love . . . She must have felt she could only count on herself. In the end, it maybe was not enough."

93

Helena stubbed out her cigarette vengefully. "If you want my opinion, it's not enough for any of us."

Helena excused herself to go to the bathroom. She bent down and kissed my cheek on the way out, which she'd never done before. I was touched.

"Thank you," she whispered.

A month later she would tell me why she had suddenly felt affectionate toward me. "Giving you part of the story made me so much lighter and able to go on. I was feeling more free than I had in an entire year."

When she returned, she said, "I told you that most people in Paris live alone because that is another reason why I live here. I am not unusual in France. In Israel, I am. People there want to know why I have no children, why I am not married – and why I live in Europe. 'Do you believe in God?' they ask me. 'Are the French still anti-Semites?' They want to know everything. But I have no answers that satisfy them."

"Surely your father isn't like that."

"No, not him. But he is just one man. And more and more frail. He still can't walk very well. Soon he'll be gone too."

She sat on the sofa again. A remoteness in her eyes made me think she was remembering her father as he had been years before. I wondered if she'd be living in Israel if her mother were still alive.

"After Sana returned from Italy, we went to visit her and Tia Zeinab every six months or so," Helena began again. "Usually on our mothers' birthdays. The last time we saw each other was for Tia Zeinab's funeral. That was in October of 1963. Sana and I were seventeen. I remember the date very well because it was just before the assassination of Kennedy. Zeinab . . . her death was terrible, maybe the worst moment in my young life."

"How did she die?"

"She became sick and was sore all through her body. She could not eat. Many years later, my mother told me it must have been breast cancer that killed her – that had spread into her stomach and other places. Mom visited Zeinab in the hospital every day while I was at school. She never missed a day."

"You saw Sana at the funeral?"

"She was with her aunt and uncle. Mahmoud did not come. I don't know why. And she was sad – so sad. Her face had so little color. It was gray. We talked and I hugged her, but it was like hugging air. I begged her to stay with us in our new home, to live with us, but she said it was impossible, that she must stay with her aunt and uncle. I could see I was not going to be allowed behind . . . behind that shield she made inside her head. I was banished. It felt so unfair. You know, I think sometimes she and I have been angry at the world for all its unfairness since we were little girls. What neither of us could ever say is that we were also angry at each other."

Helena pressed a hand to her chest and took a calming breath. "After that, we did not see each other till the spring of 1996. No cards, no phone calls – nothing."

By the time Helena moved to Paris in 1974, she was sure she'd never see Sana again. She'd fallen in love with and married a French Jewish botanist who looked like Alain Delon and who'd been doing a post-doc with her father in Haifa. She left him four years later when she discovered that rhododendrons were not the only things he pollinated freely.

"It was not the other women," she told me, "but the cologne he put on himself to cover their smell. Men who smell like lilies make me pity them, and the last thing a woman wants is to feel sorry for the man she has in her bed."

Out of the divorce she received their apartment near the Sorbonne. She returned to school and earned a master's degree from the University of Paris in Middle Eastern Studies in 1982. After graduation, she worked as a clerk in the Israeli embassy for six years. She quit the day her boss told her he didn't like her wearing jeans to work.

"He was very conservative, and he was telling me in his personal Hebrew code that I would never receive a promotion."

Unemployment – and the clinging depression it provoked – triggered her first bout of terror of going out in the daytime. Seven months passed without her poking her head out of her apartment except to go to check her mailbox and pick up essentials once a week at a small produce store nearby. On learning of her plight, an acquaintance who managed a nearby pastry shop began delivering her lunch every day. Later, after they'd become friends, this woman offered Helena work as a sales clerk. Helena realized it was probably her last chance to resume her life. A year later, still working there, she sold her apartment and used the proceeds to help pay for a small tearoom to be added to the shop, becoming co-owner in the process. She managed the tearoom from 1988 to 1997, during which time she overcame her fears of going out during the day. In fact, she traveled extensively around Greece, Morocco, Turkey, and Albania in order to record old Jews who could still sing the traditional songs of their particular communities. This fieldwork led her to investigate the influence of Muslim and Christian cultures on Sephardic music. Curiously, she discovered that the lyrics of specific Jewish songs tended to remain the same no matter where in the diaspora they were sung, but the melodies generally moved closer to the dominant musical styles of the region or country in which the Jews were living as a minority. She referred to this flexibility as "melodic adaptation."

Helena knew nothing of Sana during this period. She was curious the whole time, but thought it best not to tempt the past. "We both knew it was better to have wonderful memories than to risk spoiling them. But then," she added, her eyes beaming, "in 1996, in June, I was walking down the Boulevard St.-Germain, right in front of the bookstore La Hune. And I saw this beautiful woman doing mime. She had short hair and was so elegant – like a ballet dancer. She was wearing long black pants and a bright pink T-shirt. She was thin but strong – very strong. A crowd was around her. She was imitating a group of dogs that was being walked by a man who was too small to control them. All the dogs had their own personality. When I saw she was Sana, it was like . . . like a building fell on me – things were very dark and I was dizzy. After my balance returned, I wanted to run far away. My heart . . ." Helena pounded her fist into her chest. "Then she saw me. But she didn't stop miming. I only saw the recognition in her eyes – like she was saying *so there you are, you little démonette . . . I knew I'd find you someday.* My tears were blocking my sight, which made me furious because I could not see what she was doing. Watching her – it was like I'd come home. Like the world had regained its original order. When Sana stopped, she took a flower out of the air and brought it to me. She walked through the crowd like Moses, bouncing on her heels like she might jump high into the sky and fly. When she handed the blossom to me, she whispered, 'No papers, Helena.' Well, that was too much for us both. We sat down right on the sidewalk, sobbing and laughing."

Helena fetched herself a small glass of brandy and carried it to the windowsill, staring out at the landscape of Parisian façades and rooftops. On my request, she showed me what she meant about Jewish music's "melodic adaptation" by singing a brief ballad about Queen Esther. She closed her eyes as she sang, and her voice wove each of the different melodies in a hushed voice, as if they were all too delicate and ancient to sing any other way. When she was done, she said, "Thank God I had an opportunity to see Sana again before . . . before she died. I should have recorded her too." Her voice was fragile with regret.

"How long did you spend together on that visit?" I asked.

"Just three days. Look, would you mind terribly if we did not speak any more about her for the moment?"

"No, of course not."

She smiled gratefully. I was hungry by then and told her I'd get us some Chinese food at a take-out near the St.-Paul metro station that I'd been to before. I also wanted to give her time to be alone. She warned me she wouldn't eat with me, but she did end up picking at the rice noodles and having a bowl of won-ton soup. Over jasmine tea, we agreed to meet the next day.

"But really there's little more to say," she told me, shrugging. "Nothing important happened after that. We came to know each other again. We found out we liked each other – not as children, but as adults. That's all. She only stayed three days. I didn't see her again after that. She mostly talked about Paris and how pretty the buildings were, how fast the people walked . . . To her, the whole city – it was like the circus doors had opened and she could look inside. You see? I remember she said that she wished she could paint it. That's all she said – nothing more. You know almost everything I know by now. Maybe why she killed herself is there, maybe not."

On my way out, she embraced me hard. Again I was very moved. Later she told me she meant it, but that this time her gesture of affection was also intended to convince me that she wasn't holding anything back.

When I arrived at her apartment the next afternoon, she had puffy eyes and a red nose. She looked like she hadn't slept at all and was coming down with a cold. When I asked after her health, she replied, "Oh, please, there are few things in the world less important than that."

"But you didn't sleep."

"I was thinking too hard."

"About what?"

"Many things – everything. I can't understand how I came to be where I am."

I could see she needed a day without speaking too much about the past, so I asked if she would take me to the places that she and Sana had visited together back in 1996. "You don't have to talk about anything bad that may have happened," I told her. "Just show me some of what you did together in Paris. We'll go slow. We can have some fun for a change."

"But you know I can't go out during the day." She spoke as if she was disappointed in both of us.

"Okay, we'll go out tonight."

"That would be useless. In the darkness, you will not see what she saw."

"Helena, you have to come out during the day sooner or later."

"I do? Why is that?"

"To see that nothing's going to happen to you – that Tia Zeinab was wrong."

"No, she was right. Death was growing inside Sana all the time we were children."

"She didn't need special powers to know that her daughter wasn't going to live for ever."

"But what if something happens now? And not just to me, but to you too?"

"Then you can say 'Hah, I told you so!' Wouldn't that give you some pleasure?"

"No, I don't think it would."

I continued to insist and she finally said, "Listen, I will kill you if you leave me alone even for a second – even just to buy a postcard."

"Agreed."

She got her coat. "I'm only going out to give up ownership of what Sana and I did together. After today, all that will be yours."

Helena tiptoed down her stairs, her fingers tracing along the wall. Once she was on the street I offered my hand, but she said she wanted to try walking on her own. She refused to look anywhere but straight ahead as we started off. Near the metro station she hooked her arm in mine. A tremor – like a spasm of cold – shook her.

"It's when I think of turning around," she explained to me. "I may see one of the men who used to follow me, and I'd prefer not to see anyone from Israel today."

I looked around and saw no one trailing us. But she had her tremors all the time. On the rue Saint-Antoine we had to stop because her pulse was racing so fast I feared she was about to have a heart attack. I ran into a café and got her a glass of water so that she could take a Valium. She told me she generally took half a pill on getting up and another half to go to sleep.

"Then you probably shouldn't be drinking brandy or even wine," I pointed out.

"No, probably not," she agreed matter-of-factly, shrugging off my implication.

I wanted to sit with her for a while and rest, but she insisted on starting off again before she lost her will. I realized I hadn't understood anything about the depth of her terror – or her courage.

We began our tour at the Church of St.-Julien-le-Pauvre. "It's my favorite in Paris," she said. "It's like a country church – like all churches can hope to be if they live long enough. So I took Sana here first."

The nave, enclosed in sand-colored stone, seemed heavy with unspoken wishes. The air smelled of centuries of stale darkness – as though sunlight was never permitted through the doors. Like a happy little girl Helena motioned me over to the arch-ways at the side to show me an icon of St. George. He was killing the dragon with his needle-like lance and looked quite dashing in his long red cloak. I told Helena his expression was very determined.

"No, not determined," she corrected. "He's sad."

"Why sad?"

"It is his only destiny to kill the dragon. Now that he is doing it, there's nothing left for him to do in life. His own life ends with the dragon's death." She stared at St. George as if trying to read his mind. "I told Sana he was sad, too, and she said, 'You're right. They're like us – twins who don't look alike.'"

"I guess I don't have to ask which one of you was the dragon," I observed.

Helena pounded my shoulder.

We huddled together on the cane-work chairs, where she and Sana had sat five years earlier. I put my arm over her shoulder. She closed her eyes and breathed in deeply – as though she could still scent Sana sitting beside her.

On the way out, I read a panel on the wall about the church's history and discovered it had become the chapel of the Hotel Dieu hospital in 1658 – the very hospital where I'd visited the American victim of the attack at Jo Goldenberg's in 1982. I felt as though everything in my life had drawn me to this moment – that destiny had led me here.

When I told Helena that I sometimes sensed invisible connections between my past and present, she said she often felt that way. "That's one of the reasons I take Valium," she observed with a wry smile.

She motioned me to the door. "Come, I'll show you what Sana did next."

We stopped nearby, on the rue Galande, in front of an Egyptology store called Cybele. An ancient wooden bust of a pharaoh gazed out from the window, regal and serene.

"Sana started miming here. She did the dragon that St. George kills, up and down the street, swinging its tail, biting. She chased some people. A crowd came to see."

I traced my gaze up the façade of the stone building across the street into the dome of blue sky. Had Sana felt the impermanence of her own small life as she stood here? Did she already sense the gravity of her personal history pulling her toward suicide?

"She enacted the battle," Helena continued. "It was fierce. St. George and the dragon became one being – one goal, one death. She conveyed this by making their movements more and more similar – as if they were in a dance." Helena pointed up to some metalwork balconies down the block. "People were watching from their apartments. What they didn't realize was that Sana . . . that she was very upset. They didn't see that she was expressing something terrible about herself. No one ever knew this about the way she did her mime. It was like when you misunderstood her invisible birds in Perth. She was so good at what she did – so very astonishing – that people didn't see the substance of what she was saying. When she finished with St. George and the dragon, she did not wait to hear the applause. She just ran away."

We went to many other places that Helena and Sana had visited over their three days together – the Eiffel Tower, the Picasso Museum, the Café de la Paix, an Alsatian restaurant near the Trocadero, the Village Voice bookstore, the FNAC on the rue de Rennes . . . I bought Helena lunch at a small Thai restaurant near the Montparnasse train station that Alex and I had discovered a few years before. She ate all her duck in coconut milk, some sticky rice, and even stole a spoonful of my coconut ice cream. She was more playful – fully at ease with me for the first time, I think. I didn't want to spoil it by asking why, but I hoped it was in part the triumph of going out with me during the day.

Our eyes met just before we got up to leave and she did not try to escape our intimacy. She said, "I did not become the person I thought I'd become. And I am only now starting to get used to that idea."

We ended our tour by a wooden bench on the Boulevard St.-Germain. "Sana sat here for two hours while I did errands," Helena told me. "She said to me, 'Don't worry about me, watching people is my food.'"

Dropping down on the bench, I wondered what it was like for a girl from a dusty old alleyway in Haifa to grow up into a woman performing on the streets of Paris. I felt her need to reach out to other people – and her fear of speaking. Thinking of Zeinab, I felt a tiny twinge of the pride she would have taken in her daughter. Yet if Helena and she were really twins of the spirit, then coming out during the day to perform – or even just to observe people – must have required a great effort of will. Every day could have been a struggle for her to step outside her own universe and join ours – to keep from disappearing entirely.

As we walked to a Metro station to continue our tour, Helena felt strong enough to tell me the little that Sana had divulged about her adult life.

After leaving Haifa in the late 1960s, she'd studied and performed with dance troupes in Rome, Bologna, and London, choreographing pieces for small groups in other European cities as well. In 1994 she moved to New York and began dancing and acting with an ensemble based in Manhattan. Helena said she'd jotted down its name on a scrap of paper and would try to find it.

"The thing is," Helena told me as we were walking by the Pompidou Center, "Sana said almost nothing about herself. We talked about the things we saw in Paris – about the present. I remember I asked if she'd ever fallen deeply in love and she said no. We got drunk one evening and started kissing. But it was no good – we just ended up giggling. I thought it was a shame we were not lesbians."

"What was she doing in Paris?"

"She had never been more than a day or two here, so she came for a week just to take a look around. Her group had been at a street theater festival in Germany, I think. And that . . . that is all I know about her life since she lived in Haifa."

Sensing my disappointment, she added, "How can I explain? I wanted to know all about her – I *did*. But I didn't want to push her to tell me things. Sana was very vulnerable, though you would never know it. You understand? It's like I told you about sometimes keeping quiet and not asking – that was essential with Sana. I wanted to let things come out at their own rhythm. I thought we had time to let things proceed slowly. Now that we'd found each other, we'd never let go again. Besides, we knew so many of the important things already . . . I knew how the skin on her shoulders became all covered with tiny bumps when she was afraid. And the little animal noises she made when she was sleeping. She knew . . . she knew the feel of my hair moving through her fingers when we were lying in bed. And the completeness we made when we sat together in the dark. So why would I need to rush?"

A few days later, while I was transcribing the latest tapes I'd made of Helena at my desk in Porto, she called to give me the name of the ensemble that Sana had performed with in New York.

"It was the Soho Dance Theater. But I have no address or phone number."

"What was Sana's home address?"

"I don't know. She was moving at the time. She said she would write me to give it to me."

"And did she?"

"No. I never received any letter."

I knew that was a lie because she'd mentioned a letter from New York that Sana had signed, "Love – Lone – Lane – Sane – Sana." But I decided not to confront her yet.

"All right, but one other thing, can I have your father's phone number?"

"Why do you want to call *him*?"

"He knew Sana when she was a child and he may have things to tell me." In the ensuing silence, I sensed her preparing an excuse. "Look, Helena," I added quickly, "it's just that you've told me what you could. I need to speak to your father now."

"He's an old man, you should leave him alone. You can't call him."

"Helena, I'm not going to hurt him."

"His memory is no good. He gets confused easily. A few weeks ago he told me how he saw on the news a story about a whale eating a boy in Australia."

"A whale?"

"Yes, it's crazy. He said the boy's father and uncles pulled the whale out of the water and killed it. Twenty minutes passed before I realized he meant a shark."

"Then I'll write to him. He's less likely to get confused that way. If you're worried about what he might tell me about you, I promise to ask only about Sana."

Helena relented and gave me his address. Much later, I would find out that after I hung up, she had called her father and asked him not to say anything bad about Sana's family or reveal anything about her brother. And under no circumstances was he to speak about Helena's relationship with Sana.

Chapter Eight

I wrote a brief note to Samuel, explaining myself and asking him to send me his phone number so we could talk about Sana's childhood. I also searched for information on the Soho Dance Theater on the internet, but only turned up a brief reference to the group's production of Dostoevsky's *The Grand Inquisitor* at the Joyce Theater in 1996.

I got the Joyce's phone number without any difficulty, but the person I spoke to at the box office didn't remember anything about the ensemble. I decided to go there in a few weeks, when I would be in New York to visit my mother.

Over the previous month I'd written e-mails to Mário, Ana, and several other performers in the mime troupe to ask if Helena's characterization of Sana as a girl – particularly her tendency to retreat into her own walled universe – was true to her adult life. Yes, they all agreed, she would sometimes vanish into herself without warning. While eating lunch, for instance, she could simply go quiet for ten or fifteen minutes. Her eyes would focus on something inside. Then she'd suddenly come to herself and start conversing again, as if she'd never been away. Or during a rehearsal she might leave for a half-hour to sit by herself in a back row of the theater. They had learned not to bother her at such times. Mário said he used to call her "Mrs. Snapping Turtle" because she could be pretty nasty if you disturbed her at the wrong moment.

"Nasty how?" I asked him.

"She would shout at you to leave her alone. Or she'd shake her hands at you as if you were a major nuisance."

"What do you think she was thinking about when she was by herself?"

"New dances – ways to do things differently. You have to understand, ideas for choreography and movement were always coming to her. It was as if colored sparks were always going off inside that head of hers. She needed to be by herself to see how they could be used in a controlled way."

He told me she never once seemed frightened or troubled during her moments of quiet. She'd never spoken of needing to hide. That struck me as odd. Either she had changed a great deal or – as I was beginning to believe – had learned to mask her feelings more brilliantly than ever.

By now, I was sure she wanted nothing more than to communicate with people at a deep and intimate level, yet she could never reveal her feelings openly. Maybe that was the dilemma that pushed her to kill herself.

Mário had never questioned that she'd been born in Italy, especially since she'd demonstrated fluency in Italian while performing in Milan. On the two or three occasions that she had mentioned her parents, she had said they were both Italian as well. Her father had been born in Egypt, she'd said, and had picked up the nickname Mahmoud there. His real name was Marco. Her grandfather, she explained, had been in the diplomatic corps and had moved his family around the world – from Rome to Cairo to Asmara. His final posting was in Canberra.

Before the troupe's first trip to Australia, Sana implied to Mário that her father was no longer alive. She told him that *he would have been* so excited by her performing there.

Mário and Ana both found it impossible to believe that she was a Palestinian from Israel. Ana even went so far as to say it couldn't be true, that she would never have lied to them all.

"Sana *was* the truth as far as I was concerned," Ana wrote me in an e-mail.

Mário said she had mentioned Israel only a few times, and always in relation to *Lysistrata*. She had told him once that "it was essential for the men and women to be well balanced, with neither side able to win a clear victory. Whoever wins must also lose."

When I asked what such an equilibrium in ancient Greece had to do with Israel, Mário said he'd send me the video of their dress rehearsal and it would become obvious to me.

No one in the troupe could say anything more about Mahmoud.

When I asked about Sana's kinship with birds, they told me she'd often choreographed them into her works – in fact, in *Waiting for Godot* she'd created a role for a parrot that follows Estragon around and acts as a kind of witness to his bewildered clowning, sometimes even mimicking what he says. Mário also said she had spoken of someday adapting Farid ud-Din Attar's epic poem, *The Conference of the Birds*.

By this time, I was beginning to understand that Sana had created a new past for herself. Had she told me the truth about being from Israel on a sudden whim? Maybe she'd already decided she was going to jump from her hotel room, so that revealing her real background to me no longer mattered. Yet if Helena was right – if she'd choreographed everything to seduce me into telling her story – then she'd told me the truth in the hope that I would get her story right.

A few hours later, it occurred to me that maybe the people in the mime troupe had their facts right: Sana had been born in Italy, after all, and to Italian parents. Helena might have made everything up. Why, after all, did I trust her version of events more than theirs?

I rushed to my desk to look at the photographs she'd given me. Maybe these two girls conspiring together in front of the camera weren't Helena and Sana. Was that possible?

I urgently wanted to speak to Helena's father to get a confirmation of her account of their life in Haifa. After two weeks of waiting to hear from him, I telephoned friends in Jerusalem to see if they could find a phone number for him, but only one Samuel Verga was listed in all the Israeli phone books, and he lived in Tel Aviv. I called anyway and spoke to him in a mixture of Portuguese and Spanish, since he was conversant in Ladino. He was happy to try to help, but he was not Helena's father – nor did he know any other Samuel Verga.

In a frantic mood, I then called Mário to beg him to try to look through the troupe's files to find me a phone number for Mahmoud. I reminded him about sending me the tape of *Lysistrata*.

A few days later, the video arrived by express mail. Sana had moved the action from ancient Athens to Haifa in the 1950s. The women all wore Palestinian headscarves. Additionally, the chorus and Lysistrata – played by Sana – wore black veils that covered all but their eyes, which were heavily made up. From what Helena had told me of Zeinab, I imagined that Sana had made her eyes look like her mother's.

The men all wore Jewish prayer shawls. The Commissioner sported a white yarmulke.

Instead of Hermes standing in each doorway, as in a Greek city, a Jewish star crowned all the roofs. Besides being a celestial messenger, Hermes was also the Greek God of Thieves, and his statue was used as a protection against robbers. I would guess that the six-pointed stars Sana used instead were meant to imply that the Jewish God protected these Israelis because He was a greater thief even than Hermes – the greatest thief of all!

The video was poorly focused on occasion and was unable to catch the sweep of the stage, so it was difficult to get a true idea of the performance. From what I could tell, however, Sana had given all the graceful movements to the men, who executed balletic jumps and raced about with great bravado. By contrast, the women moved as though carrying great weights around their necks – or fearing every movement – except for Lysistrata, who darted around the stage, outdoing the men with her acrobatic feats. At the point when she declares a strike, for instance, she bursts through the chorus of women and leaps – exultant – off the roof of her home to the ground, surely ten feet or more.

Sana executed this astonishing stunt with the compact sureness of a cat.

The most dramatic moment occurred when Lysistrata

removes her clothes and dashes across the stage to the Commissioner. After tying her veil around his head (as in the original play), she clothes him in her dress (an addition Sana must have made). The Commissioner – now a Palestinian woman – joins the strike.

This moment of triumph for the women soon becomes their undoing, however. Now playing the role of a matron with broad, comic gestures, the Commissioner sneaks off to the men's chorus under cover of darkness and informs them how and when to rush the women's fortress. The men murder all of the strikers except Lysistrata, who – bloodied, beaten, and still naked – is caged at the center of the stage. The Commissioner, smiling with satisfaction, covers her head with his veil so that she is unable to see. Each time she breathes in, the fabric is drawn torturously over her nose and eyes, giving her face a cadaverous appearance.

Alex had heard my stories about Sana by now, and on watching this scene he said, "Like a bird with its wings broken."

The feeling of crippled suffocation Sana inspires is unbearable.

At the very end, the male characters – including the men's chorus – all gather around Lysistrata's cage and extend their arms through the bars, their worm-like fingers straining to reach her. It is unclear whether they seek to console her or kill her.

The curtain falls.

I decided to visit Helena in Paris again before my annual summer vacation in New York with my mother, and to bring her the video. She warned me that she would not watch it in my presence and would have to pick a moment when she was feeling particularly strong to see it.

On July 1st, the day before my departure, Mário called to tell me that Sana's doctor had relented and had given him Sana's father's address and fax number, which were both in Bologna. Sana had not provided any phone number for him.

I started a letter to Mahmoud that very night. When I met

109

Helena at her apartment the next afternoon, I told her the good news about finding him and asked her to take a look at what I'd written.

When she finished reading, she frowned. "Great," she said sarcastically. She handed my note back to me. "But if you talk to him, don't tell him anything about me."

"Why?"

"I told you, I don't like him."

"If he asks, can I just tell him you're in Paris?"

"No. Besides, he believed I was a terrible influence on Sana, so he won't ask. He has probably forgotten all about me."

That was the reply that someone who had invented the stories about Sana would have given me – in case Mahmoud truly didn't remember her. An ache opened in my gut at the possibility that she had offered me nothing but fabrications and falsehoods from our first moment together.

"What's wrong?" she asked.

"I'm just tired," I lied.

Helena began to make us tea – in an old ceramic teapot in a chessboard pattern of blue and white. "It's what Tia Zeinab gave me in her will. It's the one she would use to make tea for Sana and me – when she would tell us her stories. I've always loved it."

"Do you have any photographs of Zeinab or Mahmoud?"

She shook her head. "*Tiens!*" she exclaimed suddenly. "You know what you should do? You should lie to Mahmoud and say that Sana left him some money in her will. That way he'll agree to talk to you."

"You don't have much faith in him."

"If he'd been driving the fifth car he'd have let my father die in the desert."

"Or much faith in human nature either."

"I don't believe that people have a human nature. Speak to your good friend Colombowitz – he'll agree with me."

"Still, Mahmoud must be grieving terribly, and it would be an insult to . . ."

"Grieving!" She slammed down her tin of tea. "He didn't even come to Tia Zeinab's funeral."

110

"So that's what you're so enraged about."

"No, I'm enraged, as you say, because he used to hit Sana – hit her hard. He left the shape of his hand on her skin – all red and painful. You know what it's like to carry your father's hand around with you everywhere you go?"

Later that evening, I described *Lysistrata* to her in detail, since she wanted to be prepared for it. She took the video to her bedroom and hid it in her closet.

I told her then how Sana had told her fellow dancers that she was from Italy.

"It's just what I would expect," she replied, pouring two glasses of brandy.

"Why?"

"Look how much time it has taken me to tell you about us. You have twenty hours of tapes. Sana isn't going to invest all that time in people she doesn't trust. It is easier to invent a simple past – with nice Italian parents and a grandfather who's a big diplomat. It's all lasagne and Chianti and 'O Sole Mio.'"

"But it's deceitful, don't you think?"

"What does that have to do with anything? Sometimes I tell people that Haifa is all toys and ice cream and swimming in the warm Mediterranean. I certainly never say my mother was in Auschwitz. Why do people need to know that?"

"Are you embarrassed your mother was in a camp?"

She gave me a disbelieving look. "Embarrassed? My mother was the bravest person I ever met! Look, do strangers have a right to learn about her personal life? Or mine? I'll tell you something . . . After the Six-Day War, Mom heard a friend say that we had the right to kill Palestinians and take their land because of all that the Nazis did to us. At that moment, she invented a new past too. Would you want to be another person's justification for stealing a country? Would you want your friends to use your past and your grief to justify their political goals? So she began to tell people she spent the war on a beach near Smyrna – making her skin tan, eating baklava, and learning to drink Turkish coffee."

111

Helena laughed. I didn't. "What, you don't find that funny?" she challenged. "Mom and I thought it was very amusing."

"I guess my sense of humor is different."

"My father didn't think it was so funny either. Maybe you're like him."

"I just don't think it's funny to tell people you didn't suffer when you did," I observed.

"Oh please, people aren't interested in how anyone else feels. You're how old?"

"Forty-five."

"And you haven't understood that yet? Look, if it makes you feel better, maybe Sana really believed she was from Italy. When she was a kid, she lived there for two years. And when she was an adult, she went there again. We choose a profession and friends, why can't we choose what happens to us in our past?"

"If we do, then we aren't who we are."

"Is *who we are* only one thing? Can't it be two? And anyway, is it really so very sacred?"

I almost accused Helena of lying to me about never getting a letter from Sana. But I decided to get in touch with her father before confronting her. Maybe we did share the same sense of humor, and maybe he'd tell me things that his daughter wouldn't – or couldn't.

Four days later, while at my mother's house in New York, I wrote another note to Samuel, explaining myself further and begging him to please get in touch with me. Then I finished my letter to Mahmoud. I said I wanted to talk to him to find out more about his daughter's life. I would be happy to fly to Bologna at a mutually convenient time.

I had it translated into Italian at a nearby travel agency specializing in tours to Italy. Faxing it seemed too intrusive, so I sent it off by express mail. I gave both Mahmoud and Samuel my phone numbers and addresses in New York and Portugal.

I heard nothing from either of them over the rest of our stay with my mother, however. And when I arrived back in Porto, no letters were waiting for me. I still didn't know about Helena asking her father not to talk to me about Sana, so I figured he wanted nothing to do with the past. As for Mahmoud, maybe he'd moved or died.

While in New York, Alex and I went to the Joyce Theater. A lighting technician who'd worked there for a long time was the only person who remembered anything about the Soho Dance Theater's *Lysistrata*. He recalled that the opening night had been well attended, but that the production had closed almost immediately. He couldn't say why. He gave me the phone number of a friend of his who'd been a dance critic in New York at the time. His name was Mark Fleisher and he was now living in San Francisco. I called him, but his message machine said he'd be away until September 1st.

On returning to Portugal at the end of July and finding no response from Mahmoud, I wrote him again. This time, I sent along a copy of the Italian paperback edition of *The Last Kabbalist of Lisbon*. Near the end of my letter, I tried to put my feelings for Sana into some written order for the first time:

> *I'm not sure why I felt such an immediate connection with your daughter. It's odd how a virtual stranger can have such a tremendous effect on your life. I write about that in my novels on occasion, probably because I've always felt we're so lucky to be able to feel deeply about people we don't even know very well. If we didn't have that capacity, I suppose we wouldn't even be able to fall in love.*
>
> *I would like to have known your daughter better and would be grateful for the chance to talk to you about her.*

Once again, I had the letter translated into Italian, but I faxed it this time. To my astonishment, whoever received it sent me a reply only ten minutes later. I called Helena right away.

"It's here, it's here! A fax from Mahmoud – I'm holding it in my hand."

"What's it say?"

"I have no idea. It's in Arabic."

"Arabic? How could he be so stupid?"

Helena's Arabic was very rusty, so I faxed Mahmoud's reply that afternoon to a friend of hers at the Sorbonne who was a specialist in Egyptian and Middle Eastern literature. Helena called me that evening with his French translation and we soon finished an English version:

> The office is temporarily closed and will reopen on the 12th of August. Send your name and phone number, and we will get back to you. Be advised that it can take up to a week before your birthday present arrives, so if you need it to arrive before the 19th of August, please contact another agency.

Helena had no idea what this message meant and began to laugh. "Mahmoud probably works for a big toy shop."

I dashed off another fax – asking that he write to me in English, French or Italian – but, after another ten-minute wait, the exact same Arabic reply slid through my machine. I realized then what should have been obvious – it was just a standard letter.

Chapter Nine

Since meeting Helena, I'd begun cutting out articles from the newspaper on suicides. I suppose I was hoping to find some clue to Sana's motivation. Yet keeping them all together in an envelope in my desk drawer became oddly important to my sense of security as well, as if I needed them for my protection.

While my brother was dying he kept a stash of medicines in the night-table next to his hospital bed. His small leather bag contained anti-depressants, tranquilizers, and God knows what else. Neuropathy had crippled him, and he couldn't use his hands except as flippers, so I would drop a pill on to his tongue and then help him take a sip of apple juice to wash it down.

I often thought of his stash when placing a new article in the envelope because when my brother had confessed his agony to me one morning, I'd told him that no one would think any worse of him for ending his own life if that was what he wanted to do. My implication was that I would help him.

The first article that had caught my attention was published in the *Expresso*, a weekly Portuguese newspaper. It was only a square inch of copy:

Young Man Hangs Himself

A young man committed suicide yesterday, by hanging, in the Boys Home, a social welfare institution in Barreiro that provides shelter to orphaned and abandoned boys. The youth, 19, was found at about 7 a.m. in the playground.

On the night after I read the article, I had my dream again about being trapped at the bottom of a well, birds with human faces dropping out of the sky on to my head. When I woke, I could feel death – heavy and cold – buried deep in my gut.

Over time, my collection grew to seventeen articles. The method of suicide was only mentioned in three of them, which I found strange, until I learned that such information is omitted to deter copycats. Apparently, desperate people are extremely suggestible.

One case in particular troubled me. The suicide of a fifteen-year-old girl from Lisbon had been met with stunned surprise by her friends and parents. "She never seemed depressed to me – she was a carefree girl," her mother had told reporters.

In all the other articles, "prolonged depression" was cited as the reason for the suicide. Yet the more newspaper copy I clipped, the more obvious it became to me that that phrase meant different things to different people. Was the young man who hanged himself depressed in the same way as the mother of four whose son had died from an overdose and who slit her wrists on his birthday? Was the torment they suffered the same as that of the father of three implicated in a pedophile ring in Madeira?

Did their feelings overlap on one specific emotion that prompted them to seek a permanent escape?

In the article about the fifteen-year-old girl, I often returned to a quote from one of her friends: "Once, we were walking home from school and she suddenly started to run. When I caught up with her, she wanted to give me her ring, but I refused to take it. That was the only time she seemed upset to me."

I remembered Sana tossing me her invisible finch. Was that the gift she bequeathed to me? I *did* take it from her. So maybe Helena was right – I became part of Sana's plan at that moment.

Was she good enough an actress to hide her depression from everyone? "She would have seen it as part of her performance," Helena told me when I asked her.

"But this was her *life* – not a performance."

"I've recently realized that for Sana it was the same thing."

The most famous suicide I came across was that of Hannelore Kohl, the wife of the former German Chancellor, Helmut Kohl.

116

An article from the July 6th edition of *O Publico* said that she had been plagued by an allergic skin disease that prevented her from ever going outside during the day or, in its later stages, even turning on a light bulb. She lived as though sealed inside a tomb.

Then, on June 14th, 2001, the suicide of the daughter of the long-deceased Shah of Iran made the news. Leila had taken her own life in her London hotel suite. The article I cut out was entitled "The Mysterious Death of Princess Leila." But there seemed little mystery to it. She'd suffered dangerous mood swings in recent years and had been prone to prolonged melancholy. Over the previous two decades, her emotional life – like that of many Iranians – had become entangled in a hopeless symmetry: hundreds of thousands in their own country desperately wanted to escape, and hundreds of thousands of those overseas – like Leila – longed to return home.

Might it be the same with Palestinians? I wondered. Had Sana wanted to go home and felt she couldn't – that it would have been a dead end?

Then I realized that neither the West Bank nor Gaza held a single memory for her. Whatever the Palestinian nation's future borders, that country would never be her home, since she had been born as an Arab in Haifa – in Israel. In a sense, she was stateless – which might have been why she insisted she was from Italy. In her case, the tragic symmetry was that if she went home it would be to a place where she would always be a foreigner.

Over my summer vacation in New York, I'd bought a book by Theodore Zeldin called *An Intimate History of Humanity*. One chapter was entitled "How the art of escaping from one's troubles has developed." In it, Zeldin mentions stress experiments done by the French scientist Henri Laborit, who discovered that tormented rats allowed to run away and find shelter regain their normal blood pressure after a week. Those prevented from escaping lose hope, however. They keep their high blood pressure, develop ulcers, and suffer extreme weight loss.

When their cage door is opened, they're too traumatized to escape.

In discussing the implication of these findings for human beings, Zeldin writes: "When circumstances do not permit you to escape physically, you can do so in your thoughts. The imagination is the only part of you which nobody and no group can touch. You may be powerless, but in your imagination you can transform the world."

So it was that I began to believe that an inner universe – a place where she could create her magical dances and gestures – had provided Sana with sanctuary since she had first crawled through a wardrobe into hiding. It also seemed clear to me that something in Australia had threatened the very existence of this life-saving refuge. Even her mime had failed her.

She ought to have told me or someone else that she was in trouble, I thought. She should have shouted for help, as loud as she could. But then I realized that raising her voice was the one thing Sana had been prevented from doing since she was a little girl.

Chapter Ten

On August 2nd, Mário called from Brazil and said, "Things are getting weirder."

He told me then that he'd just met an ex-boyfriend of Sana's he'd never heard of. This man was going to call me soon, having just flown to Portugal to visit his sister in Lisbon on his way to Vienna, where he had an exhibition opening. He was an abstract painter. He claimed to have gone out with Sana for six months. Mário thought that sounded fishy, so he wanted to warn me that he might try to trick me in some way.

A few days later, the ex-boyfriend telephoned from Lisbon. I'll call him Júlio, since he later confessed to me he was embarrassed about some aspects of his relationship with Sana and wished me to withhold his name.

Curiously he used the expression *Sana went out with me a few years ago* in telling me why he was calling, as though it had been her choice and not his, or as if she had grudgingly consented to be with him.

He said he would talk to me about her if I came to Lisbon. He suggested that we meet two days later, at 8 a.m., as he would be busy with gallery owners on the previous day and had his flight to Vienna that afternoon.

Meeting him so early in the morning would mean me staying over a night in Lisbon, so I asked for a later meeting. Apologizing, Júlio said it was the only time he had, so I caught a flight to Lisbon the night before. I decided on a hotel on the site of the 1998 World Fair, near the river. Flopping down after my shower, I gazed into the mirror opposite my bed. Past the length of my feet, legs, and chest, I could see my eyes as though they were closed, my lashes pressed to my cheeks. It was as if I were looking at myself lying on a mortuary shelf. I didn't move for a long time, remembering Sana and my brother and all the people I'd known who'd died young.

I took the subway the next morning and met Júlio at the Café Mexicana, in London Square. I'd picked him up some tiny almond cakes at Astro, a wonderful bakery not far away that I'd discovered a few years earlier. He thanked me with a grateful smile, adding that his sister was *gulosa* – sweet-toothed.

"She'll devour each of them in one bite," he added with a laugh. His Brazilian accent made serpentine twists around his vowels.

Júlio steered me inside, suggesting we sit inside rather than on the outdoor patio. "I get enough light back in São Paulo," he told me.

He was tall and gangly, and he leaned forward as he walked, as if he was always having to duck. He had short unkempt hair and hadn't shaved. I liked his American-style informality.

A cook in a white apron, carrying a huge two-tiered cake, solid and white as plaster, with silver ball-bearings at its circumference, almost bumped into him as we passed by the cookie counter, and he and Júlio shared a laugh about the near-miss. Júlio put his hand on the man's shoulder for a moment. He seemed completely at ease with himself. Was that what Sana had found so attractive about him?

I excused myself right away to go to the bathroom – I've inherited my mother's need to pee every half-hour when I'm nervous. On the way there, I noticed the aviary at the back of the café. Green and blue parakeets were sitting on the bare-branched remains of a long-dead, six-foot-high tree, eyes closed, still as statues. At this hour, they were undoubtedly hoping for a few more winks of sleep.

As I sat down opposite Júlio, I pointed out the aviary to him.

"Yeah, it would have given Sana the creeps," he told me.
"Why?"
"The poor things are trapped."

Later in our conversation, he added: "She and I walked into a church in São Paulo once and there was a dove inside. She nearly had a fit. She started sobbing because the bird couldn't get out. I had to find the priest, who assured her that when he opened the doors in the morning he would gently encourage it to leave. This had happened before, he said, and no dove had ever been injured."

We were seated at one of the square marble tables. The dim lighting gave the place the sleepy feel of an aquarium.

After ordering his coffee, Júlio told me he'd seen Sana for the first time at a Turkish restaurant in São Paulo. "She was eating alone at the next table. At some point we started talking. I thought she was stunningly beautiful."

He added that after sharing some baklava for dessert they'd returned that night to his apartment and made love. Over the next six months, they'd seen each other two or three nights a week. He would have preferred living with her, but she wanted to take things slow.

"She said that women have to move slower than men or everything goes wrong."

"Is that why you said that *she* was the one who went out with you?" I asked.

He smiled. "I was wondering if you'd catch that." He scratched his hair in a comical way, as if to dismiss the importance of what he was about to say. "I always had the feeling I wasn't quite right. It's what finally broke us up. It's hard not being good enough."

"Did she ever tell you why?"

"No, she denied that that was what she felt. She said that she just needed a lot of time by herself. She was busy with her choreography and had to rehearse many hours a day. She must have been feeling very pressured. Anyway, she always made me feel as if I was something on the side, like a . . . like a country home you go to only on weekends. It made me frustrated beyond belief. I couldn't ever seem to really reach her."

"Did you two ever go out with other members of the Paulista Troupe?"

"Never."

"But you must have gone to their performances."

"No, Sana didn't want me going."

"But you know Mário a little bit."

"I only met him recently, after one of their performances. After Sana died, I started getting curious again about what she did. I introduced myself to him at a bar where he and the other dancers were celebrating. We never met while I knew Sana."

Responding to my puzzled expression, he said, "She wanted to keep me separate from the rest of her life. When we were together, it was like we were in a castle. She didn't want anything getting inside with us."

"What did she tell you about her childhood?"

"Just that she grew up in Israel. And that her parents were from Europe – her father from Poland and mother from Greece."

"You're sure she said that – Poland and Greece?"

"Absolutely."

"And what city was she from?"

"Haifa. She grew up in a mixed neighborhood – I forget the name of it. I mean, mixed in the sense of Jewish and Palestinian. It wasn't much of a problem back then, she said. She even had a best friend who was a Palestinian."

"Even that?" I nodded with admiration at Sana's reinvention of herself.

"Yeah, her name was Helena. Sana used to talk about her sometimes. Hey, you should probably talk with her! I don't have her phone number or address, but you might be able to get it from Mário or someone else in the group. Sana said they had been very close – like twin sisters. They used to go to the movies a lot with their mothers."

"And Sana said Helena was a Palestinian?"

"Yes. They were born almost at the same time. Helena had to hide sometimes from Israeli soldiers because her parents didn't have official papers for living in their house. Sana used to go with her into hiding. They'd even take Helena's cat with them. It made them very close."

"Sana told you she was Jewish?"

"Of course. I don't know about Portugal, but being Jewish

isn't a big deal in Brazil – São Paulo has a huge Jewish community. My father's family is Jewish. No one cares – no one I know at least."

"What else did she say about her parents?"

"She said her father was a botanist. He made hybrid citrus fruits, I think. And her mother was a Holocaust survivor. I don't know what kind of work she did. What else . . .? She said her father was very small. His eyebrows were like tufts. She used to play with them."

"Did she mention if her parents were still alive?"

"No, she said they were dead. I guess that's why she didn't want to talk about them all that much. It was painful for her."

"Did she ever mention Queen Bee?"

Júlio's eyes opened wide. "How'd you know that?"

"Know what?"

"That's what she used to call me. 'You're my Queen Bee,' she'd say to me sometimes, usually when she was frustrated with me. It was odd – I mean a Queen Bee should be a woman, right? How d'you know?"

"I've spoken to Helena – the woman you mentioned. Apparently, it was a kind of nickname they used back in Haifa."

"A nickname for Helena?"

"No, for someone in Sana's head. For a person she imagined."

"Imagined how?"

"Like an imaginary friend, I guess. Kids have them."

"Well, I guess she found Queen Bee for real when she found me."

Júlio went on to tell me stories about how Sana behaved when the two of them were alone, and I was impressed by his fierce loyalty to her. He seemed like a sweet-natured man to me. He told me they'd broken up a little more than a year before her death. They'd had no fight. One evening, as she left his apartment, she said she'd call him the next day. But she never did. He decided not to chase after her; even though he still loved her, their relationship seemed hopeless.

What I remember most was Júlio opening his hand to me and saying: "Sana was like an opal – with so many beautiful colors deep inside. But hard, too – as though you could never quite make a lasting impression no matter how much you tried."

Then he closed his fist tightly, as though he'd never open it again.

Chapter Eleven

T wo nights after meeting Júlio, Samuel called. He apologized for not getting in touch with me earlier, but his health hadn't been very good. "Also," he confessed, "my daughter asked me not to speak to you."

"She did, did she!" I replied, declaring war in my mind.

"Don't be angry with her. She's very protective of Sana – and me too, for that matter."

"It's just that she could have been honest with me."

"That's true, but it makes no difference now. I'll talk to you about whatever you want."

Samuel's accent was a mixture of London public school and Hebrew. I told him it sounded very sophisticated.

"Thanks. It's from my days at the University of London. Quite a number of the English despised Jews back then, so I tried to fit in as best I could. At some point, of course, I realized that even speaking like Laurence Olivier wasn't going to be enough – not with the way I look."

I insisted on calling him back, since I knew we were going to talk for a while. Then, to start things off, I asked him about his attack. He told me it wasn't important and that he could hobble around well. "I can care for my feijoa bushes and flowerbeds without anyone helping, and that's all I really need to do for now," he said.

He told me he was going to buy a new Peugeot as soon as he felt confident enough to drive again – an automatic so he didn't have to step on the clutch. On my insistence, he then spoke at length about what had happened to him in the desert, adding a great many details that Helena had left out, most lamentably that he'd lost control of both his bladder and bowels when he was shot and was a sorry mess the whole time cars were passing him.

"I smelled like the cat house at London Zoo," he confided with a little laugh. "You know, the only really upsetting thing – after the initial pain and shock – was those four cars passing me without stopping. It makes you wonder."

Later, when I told Helena that, she said, "My father's parents and sisters were killed in the camps and he still wonders about human cruelty? Excuse me, but his being shot by those boys and passed by those cars just proves what we've always known – no one cares about anyone else. There is no such thing as solidarity."

While lying on the road, Samuel had thought about Helena and Rosa. He felt they'd be very disappointed in him for dying, but he had no strength left with which to fight. Then he was standing outside his old wooden synagogue in Lodz, and Marlene Dietrich was singing "Lili Marlene" from inside the rabbi's house. He was thinking that he might not be able to create his golden feijoa if she ever stopped singing, though how the two were connected he didn't know.

Despite everything, Samuel was flowering with comic joy. "Other dying people get to see winged beings and luminous tunnels. Me, I get a synagogue burned to ashes sixty years ago and a time-traveling Marlene Dietrich. Hah!"

I knew then where Helena had gotten her quick laugh.

While lying wounded on the road, he simply shut his eyes and said goodbye to the world. When he opened them again, he saw a woman's face leaning toward him – the driver of the fifth car, a Palestinian schoolteacher.

"An angel calling for help with her cell phone," Samuel said. "She was so beautiful."

He was rushed to a hospital in Hebron. "The Palestinian doctors there were wonderful," he told me. "They saved my life. And such good Hebrew they spoke – better than mine."

"And what's your prognosis?"

"My doctors say that I'll be able to walk pretty well in another month or two. Of course I'll need my cane, but I needed that before, so everything will be more or less the same."

I broached the subject of Sana – asking what he'd thought of her as a girl.

"Oh, you can't imagine what a good, sweet-natured child she was!" he told me in a voice warmed by affection. "And so much energy! My goodness, you could hardly keep up with her. So talented, too. She even had a very nice singing voice, you know. I taught her and Helena 'Lili Marlene.' They were such good companions."

When I asked why he thought Sana had killed herself, he said, "Oh, life takes you places, some of them bad, who can know? Maybe . . . maybe the fifth car never came along for her and she just gave up."

He did not know anything about Mahmoud's current whereabouts or if Queen Bee represented anyone real in Sana's life; in fact, he'd forgotten all about her. He did tell me that part of the reason that he and Rosa had left the House of Blue Hydrangeas was that relations with Mahmoud prior to his departure for Italy had not been nearly as friendly as they'd once been. Mahmoud had concluded that there could be no future for Palestinians as long as Jews lived in Israel. Overnight, he shut Samuel and Rosa out of his life.

"The future of Palestine came to him as a revelation," Samuel told me. "He was praying and it just hit him."

To explain the depth of Mahmoud's new belief, Samuel told me about a Palestinian legend that three burning coals fall from the sky during the winter, the last marking the onset of spring. Mahmoud had said he had seen two blazing coals fall in a vision, and that it had been revealed to him that the third coal would never fall as long as Jews lived in Israel. Eternal winter was the destiny for his people. The land, and with it the hearts of the people, would grow barren as stone.

"Helena probably never realized it but Zeinab wouldn't come to our house if Mahmoud was at home. He didn't even permit her to talk to Rosa. And I know it for a fact that Sana often got punished for disobeying him and continuing to play with Helena."

"If he really thought that way, then why did he move to Italy?"

"I think he wanted to escape his bad marriage. It was killing him. Or maybe Zeinab finally got up the nerve to tell him to go. I think he was an essentially good man, who found himself under way too much pressure – after what happened to Zeinab, I mean."

"Was she raped? Helena wasn't sure."

"I don't know quite how to reply to that."

"I'm sorry. It's a terrible thing for a stranger to ask. You don't have to answer."

"It's just that it was a secret for so long. Yes, Zeinab was raped. And by more than one soldier. God, it was terrible. For someone who grows up in Europe or America it's bad enough. But let me assure you, it is even more devastating for a Palestinian woman. And Mahmoud, he believed he'd lost everything – his wife, his honor, his place in the world. I think that he believed that only if he left could he become the good man he'd been – and save Zeinab and Sana. He could find his honor in another country. In a strange sense, leaving was a very responsible thing to do, since it meant that life was more calm and stable for his wife and daughter. Also, to tell the truth, he never had much patience for Jamal. So when the chance came up to work in Italy, he went off. He did say to me once that when the next war started, he'd return. He called it the Springtime War, because it would mean the end of the spiritual winter that had gripped his land. He once told me to my face that he hoped he wouldn't have to kill me, but that he would shoot me and Rosa and Helena if he found us living in the House of Blue Hydrangeas during the Springtime War."

"What did you say?"

Samuel sighed deeply, and I understood that all this talk about Mahmoud and the past was draining him.

"I said I was certain he could never shoot us," he replied. "But I moved us to a Jewish suburb the first chance I got. Mahmoud's change seemed a sign that life would become more hostile between the Jews and Muslims in Haifa."

"Samuel, just one more question – who was this Jamal you mentioned?"

"Helena hasn't told you about him?"

"No."

"He was Sana's younger brother."

"Why the hell didn't Helena mention him to me?"

"I don't know."

"How can I get hold of him?"

"You can't – he's dead. But listen, before I say anything more, I think you should speak to my daughter. She knows what happened to Jamal a lot better than I do."

I was furious that Helena had lied to me. I called her the moment I hung up on Samuel, but she wasn't in – or refused to answer. I slept as if on broken glass that night and only reached her the next morning. I was glad I'd woken her and started hollering right away.

She acted cool at first. "I'm sorry, I didn't think Jamal was very important."

"Oh, come on, Helena. I know you can lie better than that."

"You hate me," she moaned. "I knew you would."

"Please stop that. I don't hate you. But why did you lie if it wasn't important?"

"Because . . . because it was all so complicated with him. I don't know how to talk about what happened. And Sana – she made me promise never to tell another person what she told me about her brother."

"But how can I talk to you if you are going to lie?"

"She made me swear that I would never say anything – don't you understand?"

"But she's dead!" I shouted. "She can't be mad at you any more."

Helena let the silence ring with my anger – and maybe with the falseness of what I'd just said; after all, Helena had spent most of the last year keeping Sana alive.

"If you come here," she whispered, "I'll tell you everything."

"Helena, I can't afford to fly to Paris every time you lie to me. I'd be broke in a month." She had no answer to that. "Didn't you think I'd find out that Sana had a brother?"

"Yes, but I tried to wait as long as possible. I was frightened. I suppose . . . suppose I've ruined everything. I'm so sorry." She started to cry then as if life were spilling out of her.

I reassured Helena that I wouldn't stay angry at her, and after she'd regained her composure, she began to tell me about Jamal. He'd been born six years after Sana and had been a sweet and contented baby – Mahmoud's pride and joy. But by the time he was three, Zeinab had begun to suspect he was deaf. That turned out to be untrue, but he was diagnosed as developmentally disabled – "retarded," as they called it at the time. He was the boy with the gaping mouth in one of the photographs I'd kept with me.

"Did Mahmoud hate him because he wasn't normal?" I asked. "Your father implied it wasn't an easy relationship."

"That's one of the complicated parts. Look, this is no good on the phone. I'll pay for your trip to Paris if you can come here to talk to me about this. I won't lie again."

Exactly a week later, on August 18th, I flew to Paris. When Helena opened her apartment door, I saw that she had cut her hair and dyed it chestnut brown. Straight bangs curtained her forehead, making her eyes seem larger and more aware. Her skin was darker, as well – almost olive. She looked starkly beautiful and alive, as though ready for her portrait to be painted. "Wow!" I said, which only made her groan. I kissed her cheeks and told her she was beautiful.

Anxious to remove my gaze from her, she quickly offered me tea and, without waiting for my reply, darted into the kitchen to fill her kettle.

"I stayed with my father for the last two weeks of July," she explained as she spooned tea leaves into Zeinab's pot. "I could take walks there without worrying – without feeling watched. The land there is just rocks and sand from the time of Moses. All those feijoa bushes he's planted . . . they are very beautiful. And we were alone, just the two of us. Under a sky that is so very blue. It is like nothing in Europe – you can't have a sky like that with cities and people."

"And now? Are you able to leave your apartment during the day?"

"No, not yet. Not in Europe – Europe is still back there."

"Maybe you need to move home to Israel."

She gave a snort. "All of Israel isn't my dad's house and farm."

"You don't need all of Israel. You only need one place."

She thought about that. "If you walk far enough into the desert you don't come back to where you started – not even if you follow your steps to where you began. You risk getting very lost. And I don't want to. You see, I learned that I don't want to join Sana." She gazed at me hard, determined not to cry. "I whispered goodbye to her there – with my father. Nearer to our home in Haifa. But it didn't make me feel any better. I thought it would, but I was wrong."

Sitting with her feet tucked under her bottom on her sofa, sipping her tea from a mug, she said that Sana – during her brief stay in Paris in 1996 – had woken Helena one night and spoken to her of what had happened to Jamal over the years. "She told me not to switch the light on," Helena recalled. "So I got out a candle and we sat in my bed, under the covers. She said she had to speak to me about her brother or she would go crazy. The words rushed out of her like . . . like they were on fire. When she was done, she said she had to go out for a walk. I said I would go with her, but she said no, she had to go alone. It was after three in the morning. She didn't return until dawn. She scared me. I made her a cup of coffee and sat down by her feet. She brushed my hair and told me one last thing. Maybe it was the thing that made her think for the first time about jumping."

Chapter Twelve

If animals hadn't liked Jamal as a boy, then maybe he would not have ended up in prison. But they *did* like him – the shadowed quiet of him standing on the street under a scraggly palm, or sitting in the old bathtub in the courtyard, ear to a transistor radio, listening to some nasal tune he'd picked up from Beirut. Dogs in particular were awed by the boy with the radio. Maybe it was because only the black box by his head ever seemed to speak. He hardly said a thing, looking more or less like just another puzzle piece of the natural world, not so different from a pomegranate tree or winter rainstorm, or one of those other thousand odor-infused curiosities that just were what they were and couldn't ever be figured out or changed, though one could lick and scratch and sniff them. Or maybe it was him just standing there so still at times, his mouth wide open, that made him so right for creatures with snouts and floppy ears, like a memory-image they couldn't quite get rid of and wouldn't want to even if they could.

When Sana was a girl, she used to tell Helena that if you bent real low and looked at her brother from a certain underneath angle you could just about think that he was standing there opening his soul to the workings of the world – listening for creaks in the earth's crust or feeling the bend of gravity under his feet. Maybe that was what the animals saw in him. "Do you think so?" she'd ask Helena.

"Maybe," the other girl would reply, but she didn't think so at all. She imagined that the inside of Jamal's head looked like white smoke.

Sometimes the hope in Sana's voice would rise into her eyes as tears. She loved the boy as if she had given birth to him herself.

And she felt her being normal had somehow made him come out not quite right. The two children were on a see-saw together, Zeinab used to say. But it wasn't fair – not for her and not for him. Everyone knew that.

Her uncle Abu-ai-Rayhan believed that when Jamal went all quiet he might even have been listening in on the verses Allah spoke to Mohammed fourteen centuries earlier in the Arabian desert and which were always being whispered if only we had the prophet ears to hear them. And it was true that the boy sometimes had that mystery-solved look on him, of hearing a melody playing inside himself that put everything into a sensible order.

"But he was probably thinking of nothing more than the radio vibrating in his hands," Helena told me.

Sometimes Sana and Zeinab admitted to themselves he might only be as holy or gifted as a brick. But they never said so aloud.

Helena told me that the first animal Jamal befriended was the she-goat belonging to Murta, the rumpled old fruitseller who always seemed covered with a dusting of fine sand as old as Mesopotamia, so that he was more like an old sepia photograph than a live person. Aisha was the goat's name, like the heroine of the famous – and eponymous – Egyptian movie, and Murta had bought her because she had those Hollywood-on-the-Nile eyes he liked so much. But the poor little creature was timid and skittish. Murta had just about given up on getting her to give any milk or even venture beyond the corner of the scruffy courtyard where she stood shivering night and day. If his world had been more modern, he might have taken Aisha to a veterinarian, but, this being Wadi al-Nisnas in the 1950s, he got the imam to whisper a few prayers over her, draped prayer beads around her neck, and resumed selling pomegranates, pears, and carob juice on the street.

One day the old fruitseller woke up to find Jamal – who couldn't have been more than seven at the time – leading Aisha down the street by her frayed rope. It was the first time she'd consented to leave her courtyard.

"How'd you get that pitiful beast out there, boy?" Murta asked.

But Jamal just shuffled off with Aisha loping happily behind him, scratching his rear like he was always doing, until he reached the small rough triangle of grass by the marketplace, where he kissed her right between the eyes and left his lips there for a length of time most people would consider dangerous to one's health. Likely that hypnotized the beast, because she immediately got down to the long-neglected business of filling her belly with grass, her molars grinding in top gear to make up for all the nutrition she'd missed out on over the previous months.

She gave quarts of frothy milk after that and lived a long life of neighborhood adventure, complete with rides in the back of trucks and even a bath in a public fountain, all thanks to Jamal introducing her to the world.

Maybe she regarded the boy as another goat – or perhaps as God. Who knows, after all, what a creature like Aisha thought when she got over her agoraphobia and found a boy's lips pressing to her forehead?

After Jamal's success with Aisha, neighbors began inviting him in to look after their pets while they were out at the market or down by the port, dropping coins into his hands to tend their chickens, or take their cats out for some exercise, or even give their parakeets some flying time around the kitchen. It was their way of doing two good deeds at once – for Jamal and for their animals.

When Sana went off with Zeinab to visit Mahmoud in Italy, Jamal remained behind. Mahmoud's proud love for him at birth had turned to disappointment and then a frigid distance. He never laid a hand on the boy, but did not want to see him.

"Jamal could be sitting in the room playing his radio and Mahmoud didn't even know he was there," Helena told me. Frowning, she added, "He took out his anger on Sana instead."

The boy remained in Haifa with his uncle and aunt after his mother and sister had left. Jamal knew they'd gone, but even when they came back he never asked why. As he grew older, Sana realized the obvious: he would never have a profession, or even a way of earning his keep. And he'd just get in trouble if he had nothing to do. This dilemma kept her up at night. She felt his future lodged inside her gut.

Sana tried teaching him to count so that he could work at a store, or even sell candles and matches on the street, and though he even learned his multiplication tables in the end, coins in his hands only confused and frustrated him. She taught him to read all the letters in the Hebrew alphabet so that he could begin to decipher the street signs, and though she was sure he would be able to find work one day as a delivery boy, he would make fists and clout himself in the head if she tried to make him leave the neighborhood.

She gave up. Or maybe she was only biding her time, because ten years later she came back from a summer at a dance school in Rome with new ideas on how to help her brother. She was twenty-four by then and Jamal eighteen. He was still living with their aunt and uncle. It was 1971, and Zeinab had been dead for eight years. Mahmoud was still living in Italy.

In Rome, Sana had occasionally seen students in blue jeans being tugged down the street at the end of a half-dozen leashes – walking rich people's dogs. She had the idea that Jamal might do the same thing for the frail old Jews and ambitious young couples living in their villas and apartments up on Mount Carmel. To anyone walking a dog in one of the hilltop parks she would hand a photocopied sheet that read in Hebrew:

Dogs walked. No charge for the first month. Good rates. Expert care.

People sometimes looked at Sana and Jamal as though they'd just landed from a flying saucer. Two or three times she was cursed. But Sana knew her brother needed steady work if either of them were to have a chance of happiness, so after three weeks of accosting pet owners she had received agreements from four. Once in the morning and once again in the late afternoon, her brother sat on the bus that zig-zagged up the hill from Wadi al-Nisnas to Mount Carmel and took the dogs out for walks, thereby earning some money and getting himself a profession at the same time.

The hardest part in all this was training Jamal to use the bus alone. Sana had to ride with him at first, all the way up to the commercial district at the top of the mountain, where they'd get off by the Leumi Bank. From there, she taught him the way to the Jewish homes where his dogs were waiting for him. The first time she asked him to ride alone he cried, however, and beat his fists against his own head until he got a nosebleed. But she wouldn't take no for an answer.

"One stop, Jamal, just one stop alone, that's all I ask," she begged, tilting his head back and wiping his nose with a tissue.

He wouldn't do it, so she ordered him to sit there by himself and not move. He cried with his face pressed to the window. She had a taxi waiting for her and followed him. At the next stop she helped him get off, but he refused to talk to her or even look at her for the rest of the day.

It took a month of tears but she finally had Jamal trained to get to the top of Mount Carmel and back all by himself. He began to look forward to these trips. Pretty soon he had another three customers.

A young husky with one blue eye and one of chestnut brown loved him more fiercely than all the other dogs and sometimes knocked him down with licking. People were nice to him on the bus too, and he was learning more than just the most basic Hebrew words for the first time. He could say "dog," *celev*, and "is this my stop?" *ze hatachana sheli?* He even conversed sometimes with perfect strangers. The people whose pets he walked served him bowls of ice cream – his favorite thing in the world aside from his dogs and his sister – and he would sometimes come home all sticky, much to Sana's adoring annoyance.

That was pretty much the way things stood for seven more years. Until the wrong person noticed that Jamal could come and go inside the houses of rich Jews just by knocking on their doors. One day, this man approached Jamal on the street and asked his name. All the young man could later remember about him was that he was short and heavy, and smelled like gasoline. Maybe he worked as a mechanic. Whoever he was, he must have told another man named Hamid about Jamal because Hamid spoke to him several times as he walked his dogs. This man had long hair and big dark eyes, and calluses on his hands. He smoked cigarettes one after another. He bought Jamal little gifts – cookies, T-shirts, magazines with pictures of animals. That's all the police ever knew about him because that's all that Jamal ever knew.

Jamal was twenty-five now, a big, loose-limbed, sun-darkened young man with his hair combed back off his forehead by his aunt every morning, then mussed up along the course of the day so that he looked as though he was always playing in the wind. It seems that Hamid's original idea was for Jamal to leave the bomb he gave him in the home of the owner of four stationery stores on the morning of May 20th, 1978. This elderly man's name was Rosensweig. His wife, Miriam, always gave Jamal vanilla ice cream when he returned their collie after their morning walk. All this came out later during the trial, though it took hours to get the details in any sensible order, since it was Jamal who was doing most of the testifying. He spoke as clearly he could, in the local Arabic dialect, but he got his days and times and nearly everything else confused. Some people didn't believe a single word he said. They were sure that his slowness was just his attorney's clever strategy. The lawyer, Suleiman Tamari, was a Palestinian Israeli who'd been a *kibbutznik* in his youth, so he was considered doubly suspect by more than a few officials in the courtroom.

Hamid's plans changed. Why, no one ever found out. He told Jamal to leave the bomb on the bus riding up to Mount Carmel on the morning of May 19th. He didn't tell the young man he was carrying an explosive device, of course. No, he said that the rectangular package wrapped in brown paper contained a silk dress from Paris that would be picked up by Mrs. Rosensweig, who would get on the bus after he – Jamal – had gotten out. She was expecting it to be there. Hamid even wrote her name on it – Miriam Rosensweig. Jamal remembered the blue color of the writing when he came to testify; he liked to sniff fresh ink.

Hamid told him he was to sit alone and leave the package on his seat when he got off the bus. Investigators speculated it was to be set off by remote control, since Jamal didn't have to twirl any dial or push any buttons. Hamid never said that Jamal shouldn't speak to his aunt or uncle about the package for Mrs. Rosensweig, probably because the boy hadn't mentioned them, but he did instruct the young man that he mustn't tell his sister Sana. Jamal had told Hamid that his big sister called from Rome every two weeks to speak to him. She was studying and performing dance all year round by then.

"Jamal probably adored having his own adventure, with no one knowing," Sana told Helena. "We all need secrets, after all."

That tragic morning, Jamal got all excited about being able to walk his dogs – as always – and forgot that he was to leave the package on the bus. At least that was what he told Mr. Tamari. Maybe he had second thoughts about doing something so secretive, without even his older sister knowing about it.

Jamal didn't know what to do with the package once he stepped off the bus, however. Mrs. Rosensweig would be expecting it. In a panic, moaning to himself, he left it on the bench of his usual bus stop in front of the Leumi Bank and rushed away. He was sure someone would see it and give it to Mrs. Rosensweig.

Later, an eyewitness named Mordecai Gerber would say he saw Jamal walking away and picking his nose. That was often what he did when he was nervous, particularly if he thought people were looking at him.

After Jamal had three of his charges in his care, at precisely eleven o'clock, the bomb exploded. By some minor miracle, no one had been waiting at the stop. Even so, the force of the blast sliced the left arm off a nine-year-old Persian Jewish boy named David Mizrahi who had been winding his new watch on the sidewalk. His arm was found fifteen feet from his fallen body. The watch was still around the wrist. Shrapnel also lacerated the chest and legs of a seventy-seven-year-old survivor of Bergen-Belsen named Edith Brauner, who had been crossing the street, and the thrust of the explosion was so strong that she suffered two broken ribs as well. Several others were injured less seriously. The windows of the Leumi Bank were shattered.

Mordecai Gerber gave the police a description of Jamal. The old man had been carrying a loaf of rye bread to his car when he was knocked against the wall of a jewelry store by the blast, but his memory was good.

The police picked Jamal up less than an hour later. After hearing the big noise and running to see what had happened, he'd sat shivering at the base of a pine tree in a nearby park, his blue- and brown-eyed husky sitting beside him. He'd let go of the two other dogs' leashes and they had dashed away.

Jamal's aunt and uncle were frantic for the next three days, thinking he'd been kidnapped, or had become disoriented and was lying somewhere at the bottom of a canyon. Sana flew home. She rushed to the homes of each of his clients and asked after him. They were worried too. The husky had been found in the park, but the two other dogs had been discovered roaming the neighborhood. Maybe poor Jamal had been hurt in the bomb blast and was in an emergency room. A few well-wishers had made calls to hospitals and clinics, but they hadn't located him. A young Jewish pharmacist drove Sana to four different hospitals, but Jamal wasn't at any of them. They went to local police stations as well, and finally learned – five days after the police had picked him up – that he'd been arrested. The police captain would not tell them where Jamal had been taken. The young man was suspected of being a terrorist. He was being questioned.

Sana fainted on hearing the news.

She hired Suleiman Tamari the next morning – he was a friend of the pharmacist who'd taken her to hospitals and police stations. Ten days later, they were able to learn that Jamal had been subjected to prolonged interrogation in Haifa but was now in Ashkelon Prison, just north of the Gaza Strip. They were not allowed to visit him.

It came out at the trial that during the first stage of inter-rogation in Haifa men from the General Security Service, the Shin Bet, had sat Jamal down, handcuffed his hands behind his back, and tied his ankles to the legs of his chair. They asked where he'd gotten the bomb and the name of his organization. Jamal told them about the package for Mrs. Rosensweig and how he was supposed to leave it on the bus. He said he'd sniffed the blue ink with which her name had been written. He liked the smell. He hoped that was all right. He told them how Hamid had given him presents and what he looked like and that he smoked cigarettes all the time. No, he didn't know what brand, but it was a red package. He couldn't think of anything else to say, so he brought up the subject of his dogs. In a trembling voice, he asked if the men could tell him if the two who'd run off had been found by their owners? They were going to be so angry with him. He said he was sorry. He began to cry.

His interrogators had had enough. One of the men tied a canvas hood soiled with shit over Jamal's head and then they started asking everything all over again, whacking him with a billy club across the top of his head after each answer, harder and harder, since what the young Palestinian said made no sense. Then they left him alone. His whimpering didn't subside even after twenty-four hours, so on the second morning another man took the sack off and stuffed a urine-soaked rag in his mouth, then covered his head again. Jamal told Sana later that he tried to scream but nothing came out. He was worried he might die. Then he'd never know if his two escaped dogs were all right.

That afternoon, someone came up behind Jamal and tied his hood so tightly around his head with what felt like wire that he passed out from lack of air. When he woke up, he was lying on the ground, on his side. He was still bound to the chair. His whole body ached, and his throat was as dry as sand.

A balding man asked in Arabic if he was all right. Yes, Jamal replied. The man righted the young Palestinian's chair and gave him a drink of water. Jamal thought he was safe now. But then the man tied the hood back over his head. It now had two small air holes so that he could breathe. Jamal howled until he was hit with a club across the face. That night, lit cigarettes were stubbed out into his neck, cheeks, and back. A man prevented him from sleeping by clouting him with a club every time he slumped over.

Medical evidence that came out at the trial also indicated that Jamal had been raped, but it could not be proved beyond doubt that this was done by a member of the Shin Bet and not by a fellow prisoner or a guard at a later date. Jamal would not speak about it.

At the trial, his interrogators denied beating him, or even treating him roughly.

This struck me as impossible, given the extent of his injuries, but a year after Helena first told me about their denials, Suleiman Tamari sent me an Israeli government report produced in 1987 by a special judicial commission that concluded that interrogators routinely lied to the courts with regard to even the most horrendous torture. Headed by a former Supreme Court Justice, Moshe Landau, this Landau Commission stopped short of recommending criminal prosecution of the Shin Bet interrogators, saying that they "were just carrying out orders."

Sana told Helena that she saw cigarette burns on Jamal's neck the first time she was allowed to see him. "You understand – it was four months after he was arrested and they were still torturing him."

Apparently, the Shin Bet thought that the gangly young man with the vacant look was acting, that he'd known exactly what he was doing. In fact, few Palestinian militants ever admitted wanting to kill Jews, but everyone knew that they took pride in having Jewish blood on their clothes – and that martyrdom meant an early entrance to heaven. The young fanatic who blew up the Haifa bus stop may have been a bit slow, but that was precisely why he and his colleagues thought he'd get a light sentence if he was caught – and maybe never even be put on trial.

At Ashkelon Prison, Jamal developed an ear infection from his beatings. Handcuffed, he was driven north to a clinic at Ramle Prison for treatment. After he recovered, he was put in solitary confinement there, in a three by five foot cell, and fed through the door, like a rabid animal. For breakfast he was given an uncooked egg, two olives, and a crust of old bread. Lunch was a fish put whole through a grinder and cooked, and a tablespoon of raw rice. Dinner was a bowl of bean soup, a teaspoonful of yogurt, and another egg.

Only once did a guard enter his cell. This man had blue eyes and short gray hair. He didn't like that the young terrorist was playing dumb and hardly touching his food. He stood Jamal before him, took out a knife, mumbled some Hebrew words, and slit open one of his nostrils. He was probably imitating what he'd just seen in the movie *Chinatown*, in which Roman Polanski did the same thing to Jack Nicholson.

Jamal had to go back to the clinic to get four stitches. Prison officials said that a fellow prisoner was responsible and had been punished with solitary confinement.

"When I saw my brother for the first time," Sana told Helena, "he looked like he'd been run over by a truck. There was crust all around his nose and lips. And those burns – I remember flies feeding at them. For me, he was like a tortured saint. I couldn't bear it."

Jamal asked his sister when she would take him home. He begged her to take him back to his dogs. Was he in prison because he'd let go of their leashes?

"He told me he'd find a way to make it up to his clients," Sana told Helena. "He'd walk their dogs for free, for as long as he lived. That's when I lost my mind. I shouted for help, but all they did was grab me and drag me away from Jamal."

At the trial, the prosecutor surprised everyone by asking the judge for mercy. "By then, after hearing Jamal testify, even he understood that my brother could not have known what he was doing," Sana said. "Anyone with ears or eyes knew that he had been used."

The judge asked Jamal if he wanted to make a final statement on his own behalf.

Very likely to impress the old Jewish judge, he spoke a few words in Hebrew for the first time – "Is this my stop? What a good dog you are!" After looking back at Sana, who lifted her hands over her mouth and nodded through her tears that he was doing well, he asked the judge if his sister could take him home now. "She's a dancer!" he announced in Arabic.

He was sentenced to twenty-eight years in prison.

*

It was after three in the morning when Sana finished this part of her brother's story. Shaken, too upset to continue speaking, she rushed outside to go for a walk along the Seine, refusing Helena's company. Returning at dawn, she slipped into her friend's bed and added the following.

All the years Sana danced overseas in Rome, London, and Bologna, Jamal lived at Ashkelon Prison. He'd get up every day at five in the morning and work in the kitchen till six in the evening. He loved opening the cans of vegetables and kept a collection of labels taped over his bed. Most of the guards and other prisoners considered him their little brother. He was even allowed to wheel the special meals for sick prisoners to the clinic. Jamal loved the rubbery smoothness of the trolley wheels going over the floor. A doctor named Tannenbaum gave him picture books every Hanukkah. Once, he also gave him a red radio. He was permitted to keep it in his cell and to tune it to any station he wanted. Sometimes other prisoners would read to him.

In June of 1993, Sana received word from her uncle and aunt that Jamal had appeared at a special hearing and was to be let out of prison. Dr. Tannenbaum had somehow arranged things and even called them to tell them the good news. Jamal was now forty years old.

Then, the evening before Jamal's release, a fellow prisoner – a Hamas militant, it was rumored – asked him to put a capsule in his mouth containing a message and swallow it. Once he was free, he was to defecate into a plastic bag. A man would come to see him in two days at his uncle's house in Haifa and ask for it.

Jamal didn't want to, but when he was threatened with a beating he did what he was told. Maybe his cell was bugged. Or maybe there was an informer among the prisoners. Jamal was moved to the clinic in the middle of the night and his release was cancelled. The message was retrieved the next morning from a chamberpot. Jamal was never told what it said.

A few days later, according to what he would tell his sister, he was taken from his cell, again in the night, and interrogated by two men he'd never met before. Furious and impatient, they demanded to know all about how he'd gotten the capsule. Where had he met the man who'd given it to him? Who else was friends with this militant? After Jamal told them what he could, they tied a hood over his head. Two other men entered the room. One of them carried something heavy, judging by the dry thud it made when he put it on a table. Jamal began to beg to see his sister, but was silenced by slaps across his face. He heard arguing in Hebrew and decided to go as quiet as possible. He pledged to Allah never to talk again if only they'd let him be.

One man tugged Jamal's right arm out straight and pressed it down on to a table, so that he couldn't move it. Jamal knew something terrible was about to happen. He told Sana later he smelled the danger around him. Despite his pledge, he started shrieking. Another man lifted up what must have been an ax – though Jamal never saw the weapon – and chopped off his hand.

Nine weeks later, Jamal's aunt and uncle received written notification that their nephew would be exchanged for an Israeli reservist who'd been kidnapped near Hebron six months earlier. They were never told about Jamal's severed hand.

On the appointed date, August 14, 1993, he was driven to Gaza City and let out in front of the Majlis, the former seat of the Israeli military. He was not brought back to Haifa because his parents had never obtained proper papers for living in their own home. As far as the Israeli government was concerned, Jamal Yasawi was a foreigner who'd been mistakenly allowed to spend his youth in Israel.

His aunt and uncle had told Sana about the exchange, and she was there to greet her brother. Sana fainted when she saw the tulip bulb of flesh sticking out of his coat sleeve. She hit her head hard on the ground and suffered a nasty gash. It was the scar below her hairline that I noticed in Perth.

Jamal explained what had happened to him as they walked to a pharmacy to buy a bandage. A month or so later, Sana asked Mr. Tamari to investigate, and they were informed that his hand had been cut off in a brutal fight with other prisoners. According to the warden, some Palestinian militants had wanted revenge against him for telling the guards all he knew about the man from Hamas.

Sana wasn't sure what she was going to do with her younger brother. Maybe she could smuggle him back into Israel, to their aunt and uncle's house in Haifa. But that would be pointless; sooner or later, he'd be hunted down by the police and deported. Or worse, they would arrest him and send him back to Ashkelon. This time, he'd be killed – whether by a guard or a fellow prisoner it made no difference. She certainly couldn't bring him to Rome – he had no papers. And anyway, what would he do in a foreign country where almost no one spoke Arabic?

For several days Sana and her brother slept at an acquaintance's apartment. She took the floor and Jamal the couch. Their host, Ali, taught geography at a high school in Gaza City. He told Sana that Jamal could stay with him as long as he wanted. She was touched by his kindness and by the gentleness with which people in the neighborhood treated them both. Jamal's stump made him a kind of celebrity, especially among the street children. They followed him around and asked to look at it. Some raced away hollering and giggling after touching it.

Sana wondered if there might be dog owners in Gaza City who'd want his help walking their pets. Or now that he knew a little about working in a kitchen, he could maybe find a job in a restaurant. Though with only one hand . . .

One afternoon, while Sana was going around restaurants to ask about employment, Jamal ventured out alone. She couldn't, after all, keep him locked up. He was a grown man. His body was found two days later in a garbage dump just outside the town of Dir al-Balah a few miles south of Gaza City. She insisted on an autopsy, and it was discovered he'd been shot twice in the head from very close range, with a 22-caliber pistol.

She never found out who did it, though Suleiman Tamari speculated that the local leadership of Hamas was angry that he'd answered the guards' questions. Or maybe some militant thought that Jamal might – even if by accident – reveal important information about the prisoners he'd met to the wrong person.

"Even today, my rage at what he was made to suffer is so strong that it makes my bones ache at night," Sana told Helena.

Back in Porto, I managed to get a phone number for Suleiman Tamari's office in Haifa. When I reached him, I explained my interest in Jamal's case. We spoke in French, the only language we had in common. He dug out his notes and told me that an unidentified man with a Russian accent had called him shortly after Jamal's release and claimed to know the two guards responsible for slicing off his hand. To Tamari's astonishment, the caller even named the man who'd held down Jamal's arm, identifying him as N. (I've used only the initial letter of his first name on the advice of my publisher's lawyer.) The anonymous caller then said that N. wished to pass on his apologies to Jamal's family. He added that he did not feel at liberty to reveal the identity of the other guard.

Tamari later questioned a former prisoner who'd known Jamal, and he was able to learn that the other culprit, the man who had wielded the ax, was probably S. This was the guard with blue eyes and short gray hair who'd slit open Jamal's nose. Apparently he liked to quote the Old Testament before brutalizing a prisoner.

Had S. believed in an eye for an eye and a tooth for a tooth? Would he have preferred to hack Jamal's entire arm off so as to make up for nine-year-old David Mizrahi's loss – the arm blown off by the bomb Jamal had left at a Haifa bus stop?

Tamari believed it was N. himself, suffering pangs of conscience, who was the anonymous caller.

"But wouldn't he fear prosecution?" I asked.

"You're joking, I hope?" the lawyer replied in his precise but heavily accented French. "Even if I had in my possession a video of the guard and his friend cutting off Jamal's hand, nothing would ever be done to them."

"Do you know if they're still at Ashkelon?"

"No."

"Can you find out?"

"I can try."

"And if they're not there, can you try to find out where they are?"

"Why?"

"I want to talk with them."

He laughed. "Fine, but I don't think they're going to want to talk to you."

Chapter Thirteen

On August 21st, I sent another fax to Mahmoud. The next day he called. I jumped up from my desk when he identified himself. He spoke English quite well, which surprised me. I commented on it right away.

"When I was very young I lived in England for a time," he explained. "And later I visited Sana in London. You knew she lived there for a short time, didn't you?"

"Yes, but I didn't know for how long. And I didn't know you . . . you were in such close touch with her."

"She was there a year."

"How long ago was that?"

"Oh, goodness, let me see . . . It must have been 1988 or . . . maybe 1989. After that, when she moved again, we used to meet in London at least once a year. We always stayed at the same hotel. We have many good memories from there."

"I don't know where to begin," I confessed. "I have so many questions. I didn't think you'd really call. God, it's amazing to finally speak to you."

"Why wouldn't I call?"

"You don't know me. And I'm sure . . . I'm sure her death has been very hard."

"Look, I loved Sana. It's no trouble talking to you about someone I loved."

He asked me then to go into more detail about how I'd met her, and I spoke for a time about Perth. When I'd finished, he said that I should come to Bologna if I wanted to hear more about her. "But it has to be soon," he warned me.

"Why's that?"

"I'm scheduled to go on a business trip to the Orient next month. I'm not certain when I'll be back."

I agreed to come that weekend if I could get a flight. We'd meet on Saturday morning and I'd stay through Sunday night. He said he didn't mind being taped. "You can even send the cassettes to Mossad, I don't care."

I found that a strange reply, but didn't make any comment.

I tried to reach Helena but couldn't get her. I called her father, and he was worried for me. "Just be careful. Remember, Islamic nationalists sometimes want to hurt people like you. Not that I'm saying he's one of them, but there's always been more to Mahmoud than meets the eye."

"What do you mean?"

"The way he found religion so suddenly. I always felt that that was more a political decision than anything else – as if he were using the Koran as an excuse to hate us. Or maybe someone important told him to stop seeing us. I mean, why was it that he and his brother moved from Cairo to Haifa in the first place? They were Palestinians, but his family had lived for generations in Egypt. They weren't so very poor. They didn't need to move. So why did they?"

"Helena mentioned something about there being a big quarrel in his family – with his father or something."

"That was what *I* told her when she asked me. I just invented that. I had to say something when she got curious. I was worried she'd get frightened if I told her what her mother and I thought."

"Which was?"

"Well, ask yourself what started among the Palestinians in Egypt."

"I don't know."

"That's where they became politicized – in Cairo. Many people forget, but as far back as the 1920s there'd been Palestinian national movements there. Mahmoud and his brother moved to Haifa sometime in the late 1930s or early 1940s. Was moving to a new country when they were so young their own idea? We never found out. I think they probably traveled back and forth between Haifa and Cairo until Israel was founded in 1948. There were Palestinian student movements by then – and big demonstrations against Jewish immigration. It was in places like Cairo that people like Mahmoud started dreaming of their own country. It was from there that they carried that message back to Israel."

"Are you saying that Mahmoud was involved in politics?"

"No, I'm saying much more than that. I think he was working for one of the nationalist organizations from the start. Later, sometime in the 1950s, I think maybe he was recruited by Fatah. He and his brother both. Rosa thought that even before me. But it was just a hunch – we'd no evidence to prove it."

Samuel added that there was nearly always something reticent in Mahmoud's manner. It made him think he had lots to hide. Laughing, he then said that maybe it was just his overly suspicious mind. He hoped he hadn't frightened me. Mahmoud was really not a bad person – just someone in the wrong place at the wrong time. I was to give him his best regards and tell him that he was very sorry to hear about Sana. If he was ever in Israel, they should have a reunion.

"You want to see him even if he's been working for Fatah all these years?" I asked.

"Of course! I've got no quarrel with his goal – I've always thought there should be a Palestinian state. I just don't like their methods. I don't want anybody killed or hurt. You have to remember, our families were so close. I have so many good memories of Sana and Zeinab and Jamal."

I agreed to pass on his message. As soon as I hung up, I realized I'd forgotten to ask an important question and called right back.

"Did Sana suspect that her father was a member of Fatah?"

"I wouldn't know."

"Did Zeinab?"

"This is mostly just speculation, so I'm a little hesitant to tell you."

"I want to hear anything – even just rumors."

"Well, it could be one of the reasons they argued so much – why Zeinab didn't leave with him for Italy right away. With her catastrophic way of seeing the world, she would have seen disaster at the end of that road. As for Sana, I don't know . . .

She was a bright girl, and she talked a lot with her mother, so maybe she suspected something too. Though Zeinab was surprisingly good at keeping secrets if it was necessary."

"Do you think Mahmoud's political activities might have had anything to do with Sana's suicide?"

"I can't see how they could. Helena said they hadn't seen each other in many years. She told me Sana spoke of him as if he was dead."

"But Mahmoud said they'd seen each other very frequently around 1988. Sana was living in London then. Even after she moved away, they would meet there on occasion."

"I'm surprised to hear that. They weren't close when Sana was a girl."

"Samuel, do you think Mahmoud really went off to Italy to work for a bank?"

"Now that's a question I've been asking myself for forty years! Why don't you ask him when you see him? I'd love to hear what he has to say."

I'd told Samuel that I hadn't had any luck yet reaching his daughter and he'd told me to just keep trying. But as we were about to say goodbye, he whispered conspiratorially, "She's here with me, you know."

"Who?"

"Helena. She was in the room so I couldn't say anything before, but she's gone out now."

"She doesn't want me to know she's there with you?"

"No. She's hiding – she wants to escape everything and everyone. But I didn't want you to keep wasting your time calling her in Paris."

"How long is she going to be with you?"

"A few weeks, I believe."

"She's okay?"

"She could be better. I worry – but then I've always worried about my daughter."

He promised he'd try to convince her to call me. Later that night, when I was already in bed, she did call. She was only slightly annoyed that her father had told me where she was. "I should have known he couldn't keep a secret. He lost that ability when he stopped working for the British as a professional eavesdropper."

She said she was simply trying to help her dad with his feijoa bushes and to forget Sana for a while. "I don't know if I should tell you this," she added, "but I'm also trying to stop drinking."

"That's a very good idea. Why wouldn't you want to tell me?"

"Because the last thing I want is praise for an effort that is probably going to fail."

"Or praise for anything else, for that matter."

She sighed as if I were being impossible. When I told her what Mahmoud had said about Mossad, she replied, "Dad mentioned that to me. Mahmoud was just trying to be macho."

I tried to get her to talk more about him, but she didn't want to. She said she only called to tell me about her last quarrel with Sana. "In case Mahmoud brings it up, I want you to know how it is from my point of view."

"One minute. I'll call you back." I slipped on my pajama bottoms and phoned her from the phone downstairs so as not to bother Alex. I also grabbed my tape recorder and plugged it into the telephone.

"Okay," she began, "we had a great time over her stay in Paris in 1996. I told you that already. We laughed and cried and everything else. We sang old songs from films. Doris Day – 'Que Será Será.' You know it?"

I sang a bit of the chorus.

"Not bad! So we were like an old Hollywood movie together. But she had to go back to work. Me, I had an idea. I told her, 'I will come to New York with you and stay there for a few weeks.' Sana danced me around my apartment in a tango when she heard that – an invisible flower in her mouth. I called up the airlines and made a reservation. Everything was perfect. Then, one thing I forgot . . ." She paused dramatically.

"What?"

"Guess."

"Money?"

"No, my passport! I couldn't find it anywhere. Not in the drawer where I kept my important papers, not anywhere. I was very upset. I cried. And I couldn't take the flight. Sana was very sweet. She said, 'Don't worry. You'll come next week.' She even said the delay would give her time to buy an extra futon and some furniture for her new apartment.

"So I made a reservation for a week later and rushed to the Israeli embassy for a new passport. No problem, they said – it would be ready in three days. I called her up to tell her the good news. No answer. I called again. Nothing. I tried all week at the number she gave me. On the night before my flight, a man answered who had never heard of Sana. I thought that by accident she had given me the wrong phone number. I cancelled the trip again and wrote to her care of a good friend of hers. She'd told me to write to her through this man because she wasn't sure of her new address."

"Who was the friend? Why didn't you tell me?"

"Wait – it makes no difference."

"Why?"

"Patience, please. My letter came back without being opened two weeks later – there was no person with that name at that address. So I tried again, and the same thing happened."

"But she wrote you a letter."

"How do you know that?" Helena asked, stunned.

"You once told me she signed a letter to you from New York, 'Love – Lone – Lane – Sane – Sana.'"

"*Merde*, you don't forget anything that could make trouble for me, do you? A letter came four or five months later. It said, 'Forgive me – it is all too complicated to explain right now.' I heard nothing more from her. Not until your book arrived from Perth more than two years later."

"That's very weird."

"Who cares about weird! It was such a betrayal. I was so angry that I sent her back the brooch she'd given me as a girl . . . our beautiful enamel brooch. She knew that meant the end between us. Oh, I wish I still had it!" she said bitterly. "What a fool I was."

"How did you send it back to her if you didn't have her address?"

"The stationery Sana used was from a theater in New York. I realized it must be where she performed. I sent it there."

"The Joyce Theater?"

"I don't remember."

"Did you keep the letter?"

"I burned it and threw the ashes out the window."

Chapter Fourteen

I arrived in Bologna on the evening of August 24th. I'd booked a hotel over the internet, which turned out to be a big mistake. The "pleasant, bustling shopping street near the university" turned out to be shabby and depressing, with dirty metal grates slammed down over the shop windows at night. And instead of students wearing backpacks, I had heroin addicts guzzling beer and spraying foam on each other just outside the front door. True, it did have a sweet little garden, with pink and white azaleas, but my "clean, comfortable room" was dingy and dark, and smelled of mildew, as though it had been recently flooded. On taking a shower that night, I discovered that my towel was little more than a dishrag woven of rough cotton and didn't absorb any water.

After drying myself with my T-shirt, I sat on the bed to watch TV and at least refresh my Italian. By default I chose one of those variety shows with a buffoon-like little man as host – always laughing – and several Amazon-legged blonde women introducing each new guest. It was grotesque, but I didn't want to be alone.

The next morning I woke early and climbed out of the marshmallow mattress. At the brass and glass café next door I drank a cappuccino and ate several almond cookies. A friendly girl at the tourist office near the medieval towers that dominate Bologna's skyline gave me a good map. I headed off toward my destination slowly; it was only just nine and we were to meet at ten sharp. I knew if I were early I'd only get more jittery. As I neared Mahmoud's address, I seemed to recoil deep inside myself. I was swimming inside my own heartbeat and could hardly hear anything else.

The churches I passed were all constructed of sand-colored brick, very soft to the eye. A man on a brown horse was talking to a priest outside one of them. That's the only observation I scribbled in my notebook all morning, since I was too nervous to write any more, but I also recall that the tiny priest was holding the end of a green hose. Since there were no plants in sight, I guessed that there must have been a grand garden in the church compound. I realized that much of the city must have been kept behind high walls. All we outsiders saw was what the city allowed us to see.

The via Capramozza was a narrow street in a quiet area south of the main square. Over the rooftops the green hills in the distance hoisted up needle-like cypresses toward the sun. The handsome old residences around me were painted that deep dusty orange that I've only ever seen in Italy. The south-facing windows were glinting like mirrors. It was going to be a scalding day.

I'm way over my head, I thought as I rang the bell.

"Are you Richard?" a woman's voice asked through the intercom in a strong Italian accent.

"Yes, it's me."

The buzzer sounded. I climbed the stairs to the second floor. I didn't have to knock. A woman of about fifty, holding a red and white hand towel and smiling pleasantly, was already standing in the doorway. She had shoulder-length gray hair and wore jeans. Her feet were bare.

"Welcome," she said.

We shook hands. Hers was cold. "My name is Carlotta. My English is not good. You must forgive me."

I apologized for speaking Italian so badly. We entered a cluttered living room. A silver racing bicycle was leaning against tightly packed bookshelves, and a huge box of clothing sat under one of the windows.

"We run out of places to keep the things . . . the things for the children. Mahmoud will be with you in a *momento*. May I get you a coffee?"

I settled on tea with milk. Carlotta invited me to sit on a red velvet couch with yellow cushions and went off to the kitchen.

Black-and-white photographs covered the walls – mostly land-scapes of Israel and Palestine. I recognized the Dome of the Rock, Masada, and the Wailing Wall. I stood up to examine them, then walked over to the bookshelves. Nearly all of the authors were Italian, and many of them were familiar: Primo Levi, Italo Calvino, Ignazio Silone, Natalia Ginzburg . . . There was also a small section in Arabic.

Carlotta came back in with a black ceramic teapot, two matching cups, and a plate of biscuits that looked like shells covered with powdered sugar. I told her she was being way too kind to me. She said, "No, you are a friend of Sana's. So you are much more than a guest."

That touched me greatly. And the maternal tone she used made me believe that Sana had been able to count on her.

"These are *sfoguatelle*," she said, pointing to the biscuits. "From Bologna. A *specialitá*. I buy them this . . . *mattina* . . . what's the word?"

"Morning."

"Morning, yes. You must have one."

They tasted like cheesecake.

"It has ricotta inside," Carlotta told me. "Good, no?"

"Delicious."

"Sana eats them when she comes here. She likes them so much." Carlotta tried to say more, but failed. She smiled as if she were about to burst into tears.

"I'm sorry," she said. "Thinking of Sana . . . it takes my thoughts and makes them in *un nodo*." She raised her hands and tied an invisible knot.

"I understand," I said. An awkward silence descended between us. "Are you the reader or is Mahmoud?" I asked, gesturing toward the bookshelves.

"Most are mine." She frowned and shook her head. "Mahmoud . . . he only reads the newspaper. He has no time."

She gazed around the room as though displeased with something. She pointed to a darkened area of the wooden floor. "We had a piano there." She pointed to the window. "The sun – he makes the rest *piu chiaro*."

"The sun bleaches the wood."

"Yes," she smiled.

"Who plays?"

"Me. But I am not so good."

Footsteps came from down the hallway. Mahmoud stepped into the room, his hand already out to shake mine. He was tall and slender, had dark, vibrant eyes and soft gray hair that twisted up behind his ears. He was dressed in a light blue cardigan sweater and very neatly ironed jeans. He looked professorial, which surprised me – and younger than his age, which he told me later was seventy-six. I believed I could see something of Sana in his posture, which was very stiff, as though he were compensating for a shivering timidity.

He took my hand in both of his and shook it firmly. His eyes radiated pleasure. "Thank you so much for coming at such short notice. Sit . . . sit . . ."

He gestured me back to the couch and sat next to me. His British accent seemed more pronounced in person.

"So, you live in Portugal," he said. "That is unusual for an American."

He had long hands, and he moved them elegantly. I thought maybe Sana had inherited that as well.

We talked for a time about how I'd ended up in Porto and then went on to discuss the difficulties I'd had learning to teach in Portuguese. I wasn't sure if I ought to mention Alex, but he wasn't fazed. He thought it wise that we were not in the same profession. "Two writers might kill each other," he laughed.

I found Mahmoud calm and friendly, which surprised me after all I'd heard.

"Thank you for sending me your novel," he said. "I have not read it yet, but Carlotta has."

I looked at her and made the grimace I make when I'm embarrassed.

"I have some questions I would like to ask you," she said. "Later . . . we talk about it later."

"Of course."

I gave Mahmoud regards from Samuel. He held both his hands on top of his head, as if his thoughts were flying away. It was a sweetly comic gesture. "Oh, my goodness, that was a century ago. I'm surprised he remembers me. Tell him I hope that he is well."

"Helena remembers you too."

"Oh, Helena! Sana always spoke so fondly of her. What crazy girls they were!"

Mahmoud picked up a pack of MS Italian cigarettes from the coffee table. I turned down his offer, which he thought was a very good idea. He used a slender silver lighter pulled from his sweater pocket and gripped it in his hand as we talked. He questioned me about meeting Sana in Perth. He wanted to know everything – if there were other people I'd seen her talking to, what her mood was like, even what clothes she'd been wearing and if she'd had any other books with her. He seemed particularly interested in how sensitive I'd found her – at her bursting into tears after I'd signed her book for Helena. His urgency in wanting to know every detail seemed odd to me until I realized I was one of the last people to see his daughter alive. That must have been behind his willingness to see me. So I answered his questions carefully and told him all I could remember – even about the soaps she'd given me and the other people in the mime troupe.

"Where are the soaps now?" Mahmoud asked.

"At the bottom of a drawer. I don't want to look at them, if you know what I mean."

"Unfortunately, I understand very well."

After he was finished with his questions, he smiled and opened his hands. "And now it is your turn. I am at your service."

I took out my recorder. "May I really tape you?"

"But of course."

I placed it on the table between us. He and Carlotta had put me at ease, but I still swallowed deeply before asking my most important question: "Do you know why Sana might have wanted to end her own life?"

Mahmoud shook his head, then looked at Carlotta. She said, "We think about that so much – all the time. We do not know."

"Had she been depressed?"

Mahmoud stood up and walked around the coffee table to

where the piano used to be. He swirled his foot across the floor, smoking thoughtfully. "Sana – how can I say it?" He inhaled too deeply on his cigarette and coughed. Carlotta told him in Italian to put it out, but he just waved her away. "Sana was a complex girl," he continued. "She had many interests – and too many things to do. But it never seemed that she couldn't . . . couldn't move past her problems." He shrugged. "I just don't know."

I told him that I was missing a good deal of her history, ever since she'd first moved to Italy as a girl.

"It's simple. We were living in Bologna then. She came from Haifa with her mother and enrolled at school."

"Did she like being here?"

"No, not much." Mahmoud turned away as if he'd heard something far in the distance. "One moment, please," he said, then walked purposefully into the kitchen.

He returned with a glass of water and sat down next to me again. In Italian, Carlotta asked if he'd taken his pill. He said he had.

"Anyway," he began again, "life was difficult for her here. I mean, a new country, a new language . . ." He took a long drink. "It took months for her to make friends. But she did. Then she was happier. And in the end, it worked out well, because she could get Italian citizenship."

"Did she give back her Israeli citizenship?"

"No, she kept both. But having an Italian passport was useful for her traveling overseas and for earning money here. It was good security, too. I didn't want her to be stateless – not ever."

"What do you mean stateless? She was born in Israel."

"Who knows what the Israeli government will do. They might one day decide that Palestinians born in Israel are no longer citizens. They might round us up and send us off to Syria or Jordan. Don't think it can't happen."

"You must really hate the Israelis after all that has happened."

"Maybe so. But I do not think of it like that. I only want things to change there."

"So Sana was, in a sense, Italian?" I was thinking of what she'd told the other members of her troupe.

He tilted his head, pondering my question. He patted his chest. "I'd prefer to say she was Palestinian in here, all the time, and Italian only sometimes."

I wanted to talk about Zeinab and Jamal, but I thought he might not like it. Mahmoud noticed my hesitation and asked what was wrong. I said, "And yet she and her mother moved back to Haifa after two years. Why was that?"

"That was what Zeinab wanted." He knocked his fist against his forehead. "We had a big quarrel. I got too angry. I was young – a different man than I am now. I turned away from her and didn't say what was in my heart. She screamed, then I said things I shouldn't – you know how it is when you are not in control. Zeinab went back home. She was right to go. That is all – she just went home. Nothing more happened."

"When did you next see Sana?"

"Oh, she was much older. Let's see – she must have been eighteen or nineteen. I was living in Rome then. She came there to study dance. She stayed with me. We were better together by then. She was older. And I was older, too, and more patient. Not so quick to be angry. We understood each other better."

"That would be about 1965 or 1966?"

"Yes, that's about right. She found herself an apartment soon after she came. I was not in favor of it – a young girl all alone in Rome." He shook his head. "But Sana always knew what she wanted and always told me, 'I don't need you! I can do everything by myself.' That was true! So she found a small apartment in the Trastevere. She was very happy and proud – her first home all by herself!" He turned to Carlotta and smiled. "The apartment was so small." He stepped his fingers through the air. "Two paces and you crossed the bedroom!" He laughed.

I remembered that Sana had made a similar gesture with her fingers in Perth. My heart began racing. "I can't help thinking that her death wasn't meant to be," I said. "That she jumped at a moment when God was looking away."

Mahmoud's eyes moistened. For a second I thought he'd be all right, then he hid his head in his hands and started to cry silently. Carlotta came to him and whispered something in his ear. Looking up at me with troubled eyes, she said, "We return in a minute." She tugged on Mahmoud's arm to get him to stand, but he wiped his tears and said in Italian that he wanted to keep talking. Looking at me, he said, "I'm sorry. I try to not make it happen again."

"It's all right."

He stubbed out his cigarette, then immediately took another one from his pack. Carlotta lit it for him. He wiped his eyes again with the smoke swirling around him. "You can go on. You can ask me more questions."

Carlotta sat opposite us again, the coffee table separating us. She leaned forward, protective of Mahmoud.

"So Sana started living in Rome and studying dance. When did she begin performing?"

"A few years later. She makes her own group. It is small. But she has not so much patience for ideas from the others on how to dance. So it is better for her to decide all the details."

"And you saw her perform?"

"Many times."

"Did she ever go back to Haifa?"

"Yes, but not very often. There was not so much in Haifa for her after her mother died."

"There was her brother."

Mahmoud turned away as if he'd been slapped. "Yes, Jamal." He gave me a hard look. "You know, when you get to be old like me, you will realize you have made many mistakes. But what do you do? It's too late. Life is very unfair."

"How often did Sana go to visit Jamal when he was living at your brother's house?"

"She saw him once or twice each year. How can I explain to you? She needed time away from him. She needed to make her own life. She was always too responsible for him – too much on the . . ." He held out his arm and made it rock up and down.

"A see-saw," I said. I remembered Samuel telling me that Zeinab had used that metaphor. I felt as if a door had just opened – that I had entered their shared history. I knew I would write a book about Sana and Helena, and what had happened to them, at that precise moment.

"Yes, but it was no good that the two of them went up and

down. It was mostly my fault, of course. For not being with Jamal. Anyway, he was with his uncle and aunt. He was okay. He was more okay than all of us."

"But then he got in trouble."

"That had nothing to do with Sana. Although she thought that finding him his work with dogs – that it led him toward prison and death."

"Do you think that might be why she killed herself? I mean, Jamal being murdered?"

"No, we talked about Jamal many times and that was not the reason. What happened made her very angry but not depressed. It made us *all* very angry." Mahmoud's eyes were flashing.

I told him I'd spoken to Sana's lawyer and learned the names of the men who'd cut off his son's hand. "Do you know, by any chance, if those guards are still at Ashkelon?"

He shook his head. "I tried to begin an investigation, but the authorities refused."

"I'm going to ask another personal question that's none of my business, so please don't get angry."

"I might cry again," he said, smiling gently, "but I do not expect I shall become angry."

"Why didn't you go to your wife's funeral?"

"Because before she died she made it very clear she did not wish me to be there. She wrote me a letter and told me that."

"She said that she didn't want you to come?"

"Yes. And I thought, too, that Sana might not want me to be there. We were not the best of friends then. I thought I could be . . . be kinder to them by staying away."

"Are you retired from the bank now?"

"Yes."

"What bank was it?"

"A private one, from Egypt. It is for business investment. What do you call it in America . . . ?"

"A commercial bank, I think."

"Yes, that's right."

"When I faxed you, I got a note back saying your office was closed and mentioning something about birthday presents."

He looked at Carlotta and raised his eyebrows. After she

shrugged, he replied, "How can I explain? The machine works automatically when I'm gone. It sends you the message like it sends to everyone who faxes me."

"But what about the birthday present?"

"Who translated the letter for you?" he asked, worry seeming to deepen his voice.

"Someone from the Sorbonne in Paris. A friend of Helena's."

"I sometimes arrange money transfers for people. Through my banking connections." He spoke more easily now. "But it's safer that I keep that information to myself. So I say 'birthday present.'" He winked at me. "You understand?"

"Not really, why is it safer?"

"It is a long story."

"I want to hear – please."

"Because I am retired. The Italian government does not want me to earn commissions. But I need to support my children. I have a second family as you see, and I must care for them. You do not know the tax system here. They are like the secret police, like Mossad, like the KGB, except they are much worse! For all I know, the walls are listening to us even now. The tax officials in Rome give me nothing but problems."

"And who sends these money transfers?"

"There are Palestinians all over the world who need help sending money to relatives in Lebanon, the Occupied Territories, France, Italy – even in Michigan. I had one for a place called Lansing just a few weeks ago. Where is Lansing?"

"I'm not sure, but it's got to be somewhere near Detroit. Why don't these people just go to their bank?"

"You have to understand, many of them don't speak the language where they live. They have no accounts. The whole world is not Italy or America. So I make it possible. If I didn't, they would have to send money through the post. It could be stolen." He leaned across to me and patted my leg. "If you ever need money sent anywhere, I shall send it for you. You will see how good it works. No charge!"

Carlotta told him in Italian she had to get going on an errand.

"I'm sorry," she said to me, "but I go now to fetch our daughter from her school. It is time soon for her lunch."

"But it's August. How come she has school?"

"It's just half a day – the classes are mostly art and sports," Mahmoud replied. He turned to his wife. "Why don't I go with Richard to get her?" he asked in Italian.

"Yes, if you do not mind, Alice would be pleased," Carlotta told me, smiling.

Mahmoud had an old blue BMW parked in a garage around the corner. There was a big dent in the door. He apologized. "A long time ago I learn I can either fix my car every time an Italian hits it or live my life. There is no time for both."

We drove on a broad avenue that circled the city. He had a thin ring with a tiny turquoise stone on the little finger of his left hand, next to the wedding band. It looked very feminine, and I liked the contrast with his strong fingers. I asked him where he'd gotten it.

"In Lebanon. On a business trip." He pointed to his eyes. "I saw it in a shop window."

We were silent for a time. He looked irritated about something. Then he asked me if getting a novel published was difficult.

I gave him a brief and rather cynical primer on the intricacies of the publishing industry, and he listened patiently. When I was finished, I asked if he was thinking of writing a book.

"Oh, not me! I've no talent for that. No, I am curious, because Sana sometimes said she wanted to write."

"What would she have written?"

"Maybe a play. She told me once she wanted to write something about her past."

"An autobiographical play?"

"Maybe just some scenes from her life."

"Which scenes would be most important, do you think?"

He glanced at me quickly and turned his bottom lip out. "Our childhoods mean the most, no? So maybe about hiding from Israeli soldiers. Or maybe . . . maybe when I left for Italy alone."

"Did she ever talk to you about me or my books?"

"No, I'm sorry. Look, I'm an old man, so maybe you will forgive me. But will you let me give you some advice?" He spoke in a grave tone.

"Of course."

"I think maybe that after you leave Bologna you should forget about Sana. It's not good to remember too much. Forget us. Forget Haifa. You are in Portugal. You have Alex. That is good. Go on with your life. Just write your novels. That is more than enough."

"But what if Sana didn't feel she could write those important scenes in her own life the way she wanted. What if she wanted me to do it?"

He looked at me tenderly, as though frightened for my destiny. For a moment I thought he was going to pull over to the side of the street, but he just asked if I would get his cigarettes from the pocket of his coat in the back seat and hand him one.

We didn't speak again until he'd finished smoking. He touched my shoulder then and said, "I lied about the ring. I'm sorry. It was from Zeinab – her last present. Sana gave it to me after her mother died."

Just before parking at the school, I asked about Júlio.

"I don't know much about him," Mahmoud said. "I think he was the one who hit her."

"Júlio hit her?"

"I think it was him. I never met him. She came to Italy once with a bruise on her neck and another on her cheek. He was not a good man."

He backed the car into a parking space in front of a large brick building.

"She didn't show you a photograph of him, by any chance?" I asked.

"No."

Mahmoud must have sensed me wondering how Sana could have stayed with a man who was physically violent. He gave a shrug and said, "The heart sometimes makes a mistake and, as

166

we know, it is not always easy to free ourselves." He turned off the engine. "But I made her promise not to see him."

Alice was already waiting at the gate to her school with two friends. Her father had warned me not to speak of Sana – they'd been close and Alice was only now coping better with her death. "It's been hell," he said. "So I'll just tell her you knew Sana and we'll say no more. You don't mind?"

"Of course not."

Alice was twelve, but she looked a couple of years older than that, with big knowing eyes and an adult way of crossing her arms over her chest. She was tall for her age and endearingly gangly. She looked as if she had secrets too. She wore a head-scarf, as did her friends, but she was also wearing flashy gold and blue sneakers.

Mahmoud told me it was an Islamic school founded fifteen years earlier by an Italian convert who'd gone all the way to Isfahan to study the Koran with an Iranian imam.

"Not with the Ayatollah Khomeini, I hope."

I'd intended this as humor, but Mahmoud replied seriously. "No, Khomeini was too important, too . . . I'm sorry, I've forgotten the word I want."

"High up," I tried.

"That will do."

When Alice saw us approaching, she waved quickly and said goodbyes to her friends, then walked to us, bouncing, her feet pointing out. With a pang of joy twinned to sadness, I realized the obvious – Sana must have influenced her to begin dance lessons. Later, I confirmed with her mother that the girl was taking classical ballet.

Her father bent to kiss her cheek, holding her shoulder tenderly. Then he took her backpack. We shook hands when Mahmoud introduced us. As she walked with his arm over her shoulder, I wondered what it was like to have a father who was in his seventies and who adored her. Did she know her luck?

I got in the back. From the front seat, Alice turned to me, all eagerness.

"*Lei è Americano?*" she asked in Italian.

"*Sì.*"

"*Da dove vieni?*"

"Stop!" Mahmoud ordered. "Alice," he said in a monumentally frustrated tone, "your teacher has come all the way from the North Pole to put some English in your little head, so no more Italian." He turned and winked at me.

"From where do you come?" she repeated.

"New York."

She said something in rushed Italian to her father, then pushed him on the shoulder playfully.

"She says she wants to spend all of next summer in New York."

"If you go, you can stay with my mother for a long weekend," I told her.

"Oh, that would be good, wouldn't it!" Mahmoud smiled. He gazed at me in the rearview mirror. "But your mother would have to be careful, this one here is nothing but mischief – just like . . ."

Mahmoud was about to say "Sana," but caught himself in time. Alice knew, however, and turned away. She leaned her head against the window and only gave distant replies to her father's attempts to tug her thoughts back into the car with us.

Back at the apartment, violin music was coming from down the hallway – a high quick melody. The notes came at us like sparks.

"It's my mother," Alice said to me, taking off her headscarf. She had long brown hair. She shook it down her back.

"My wife plays in the Bologna orchestra," Mahmoud said.

"How long has she played with them?"

"Oh, goodness, twenty years."

We sat again on the couch to listen while Alice went to shower and change. "About fifteen years ago," Mahmoud said, "I am visiting here on business – with the university. And I –"

"What did you do for the university?" I interrupted.

"I arrange loans for Palestinian students – and Arab students from other countries, as well."

"Are there many in Bologna?"

"Some – it is a big university. The oldest in Europe, you

168

know. So, I am here, and I go to a concert because . . . because I am lonely. I don't like Western music then, but they are playing Beethoven and I have never heard anything composed by him. You can see how ignorant I was – and still am. I see this woman on stage and I can't look away and I don't know what's happening to me because my chest . . ." – he tapped himself over his heart – ". . . I can't seem to breathe."

"Did you introduce yourself after the concert?"

"No, I am too timid. A beautiful Italian woman and me, an Arab immigrant? No, I say nothing. But I come to Bologna every weekend I can. I go to more concerts. It is so expensive, but what other choice do I have? I should say something to her, but I can't. Then, one day . . . Bologna is not a big city, so you see people you know all the time. And I see her when I pass a bookstore." He gestured toward the window. "A bookstore not far from here. And I go in." He stepped his fingers in the air. "I pretend I'm reading, but I . . ." Mahmoud made sneaky glances to the side. "She sees me looking and smiles. She smiles! So that's when I go to her and say how lovely she is. By some great luck, I am able to keeping my heart from exploding and she does not think I am crazy."

"And that was that."

"Yes, that was that."

"And you moved to Bologna right away?"

"Not right away. A year later I was able to establish an office here – Carlotta cannot move to Rome, of course, because her job is here."

"Do you ever miss Rome?"

"Never. Bologna is very central – between Milan and Rome. It's easy going back and forth."

"Are you in Milan a lot?"

"Yes, we have a Muslim Cultural Center there. It's very important for my business. And I take Alice sometimes. She must learn about her heritage."

Carlotta and Mahmoud invited me for dinner that night, and would not hear of me refusing.

"It is no trouble," Carlotta assured me. "Only pasta and salad. Do not worry. You eat meat?"

"Yes, even pork and shellfish."

"You are not a terribly good Jew," Mahmoud joked.

"Helena tells me that all the time."

Carlotta suggested I take advantage of the sunny day to go sightseeing, then come back before supper, which is what I did. I managed to make it to the Morandi Museum, one of my goals, but inside the artist's cups, vases, and pitchers were all my daydreams about saving Sana.

That afternoon, I began to wonder how I would have tried to paint her, and how her face ought to appear in a portrait, and about eight months later, I found out . . . At that time, in April 2002, two close friends from London, Judith and Tim, sent me a beautifully printed monograph on the English contemporary artist Ken Kiff, whom I had tried to convince to illustrate some stories of mine before his death. In studying a self-portrait of his one lazy Sunday, I saw how he kept half his face in deep shadow, only vaguely formed. That half might become absolutely anything he – or the viewer – wanted.

I returned to Mahmoud's apartment at seven that evening, carrying a small bouquet of red, pink, and white sweet-pea flowers I'd found at a glorious florist's shop near the central square. Carlotta beamed at me when I handed them to her and, after holding them to her nose, told me they smelled *divinamente*. She put them in a slender amethyst vase at the center of our table.

Tomasso, their fifteen-year-old son, only stayed for a few minutes, as he was going out to the movies with friends. I had no chance to talk with him. He had Mahmoud's dark eyes and his mother's round face. His thick black hair was long and fashionably mussed, as though he'd spent an hour getting it to look unstyled.

Tomasso stomped through the house before he left, looking

for a letter he'd misplaced. He was very angry about something. Mahmoud was furious with him, too, and though he said nothing, he smoked vengefully and squinted at the boy. The walls seemed to sigh with relief once he was gone.

"Your son seems to be at that age when nothing is right," I said to Mahmoud, as he carried a bottle of sparkling water in from the kitchen.

He just shrugged with irritation.

"I only hope it continues not for so very long," Carlotta replied.

She'd made pasta al pesto, with a large tomato and mozzarella salad, on to which Alice drizzled balsamic vinegar. Over supper, we talked about the girls' basketball team. She was playing center at the moment, because the only team member taller than her couldn't dribble and look up at the same time. "She always runs into other girls and loses the ball. One time she dribbled out of the lines and hit a wall."

Alice made her father smile all the time. After we talked about her classes for a little while, we moved on to Carlotta's career. She said that the only problem with playing in an orchestra was that it forced a prolonged adolescence on her. She felt like Tomasso sometimes. "Seeing the same people every day, and always everyone quarrels, about the most little musical nothing, until . . ." – here she pulled at her hair – "until you want to make a murder. I think maybe I need some time with no playing – a year or two. We shall see."

After dinner, while I was carrying plates into the kitchen, Carlotta took my arm. "The violence in your book – was it really so bad for the Jews in Portugal?"

"At that time, I'm afraid it was."

"Terrible. It takes me much time to read that violence. The thing is – the book makes me feel I am there. I see it all. But I don't want to." She smiled. "You understand?"

We continued taking dishes and silverware off the table and moving them to the kitchen. "What do you think Sana saw in my book?" I asked.

"Saw in it?"

"Why might it have been important to her?"

Carlotta gave a quick squeeze to my hand, then tapped her temple. "Give me time to think about that."

About a half-hour later, while I was seated on the couch, sipping my tea, she began to look at me purposefully. Alice was telling me about a hiking trip she had taken with some friends to the mountains near Como and how one of the girls had lost her sneaker down a ravine. They'd tried unsuccessfully to reel it in with a fishing pole. Alice and I enjoyed laughing together. When she was done, Carlotta asked me into the kitchen.

"Two things I think," she said. "First . . . your narrator, Berekiah, he talks with Farid in sign language – talking with hands, no? Like dance or mime. But he also talks in spoken language – in Portuguese. He moves between worlds. I think that is what Sana wants. She wants to dance and to mime, but she also wants to talk – with words that we can hear, you understand? She wants to write. Berekiah, your narrator – she wants to be him."

"Mahmoud also mentioned Sana wanting to write. Had she ever showed you anything she'd completed – or was working on?"

"No. She says she thinks it is the next thing for her – her next *passo*."

"Step."

"Yes, step. But it can mean she must abandon dance. So she is worried. It is a risk."

"What would she write?"

"She never say. But there's a second thing. Berekiah must live in a foreign country – to escape all the violence against the Jews. He takes a boat to Constantinople at the end, no? Well, this is like Sana, too. She comes to Italy. She is *esiliada*."

"Exiled."

"Yes, and at the finish of the novel, you say that Berekiah will go home. Or at least he wants to go home. He wants to warn the Jews that they have danger in front of them. I think that is what Sana wants too. Maybe Berekiah helps her to decide what to do."

"To go home and warn the Palestinians about what?"

Carlotta grimaced. "My English – I do not know if warn is the right word. Maybe she only wants to . . . to motivate her people. To do that, she thinks that maybe dance is not enough."

Mahmoud called us back into the living room shortly after that. We talked about Italian politics for a while. He was convinced that the whole country was corrupt, but especially the tax officials. Carlotta said that wasn't quite true, especially in Bologna, which she called "the most civilized city in Italy."

Mahmoud grunted at that. They argued back and forth in Italian. Sleepiness settled over me. When Carlotta noticed, she proposed meeting me the next day at a café near my hotel. She and Alice would show me a little of the town. Mahmoud agreed to come as well, but he would only be able to stay with us a short time, as he had a great many business calls to make.

We met the next morning at eleven. It was another sunny day, but almost all of Bologna's streets were porticoed, so I kept my sweater on as I walked with Carlotta and Alice. Carlotta took pride in first showing me the frescos of the Oratory of St. Cecilia. She pointed up to the last one, where a haloed St. Cecilia was being carried on a shroud to her burial plot. "Beautiful, no? I come here all the time when I am little. The *freschi*, they are finished in 1506. I remember that date when I read your book, because at the same moment the Christians in Lisbon are killing the Jews, an artist is painting these lovely Christian images here in this room."

On my insistence, we then went to look at Carlotta's childhood home. The façade of the handsome, three-story building was painted bright yellow. On the ground floor was a restaurant with red and pink lanterns hanging by the door. It was called "Da Fantoccini," which Alice translated as "At the house of the puppets."

"There were the most beautiful puppets in the window when I was a girl," Carlotta said. "I was adoring coming here."

The morning was very bright and clean – as though a great wind had swept away all confusion. I was happy to know these people – and grateful to have met Sana, who had brought us all together. It seemed now that I'd been waiting to make peace with her since the moment she fell to the street in Perth.

Carlotta pointed to a second-floor window. "That is my room." She turned and gestured down the street. "You see that . . . that *farmacia*? My father worked there."

"Is he still alive?"

"No. Mamma and Papa are both dead since many years." Her eyes moistened. "Emotions come to me too often now," she said. "I'm sorry."

"No apology is necessary. Do you have any brothers or sisters?"

"No." She wrapped her arms around Alice and kissed the back of her head. "I just have this little one and her brother and their father."

I had my camera with me and took a photo of Alice in her mother's arms. The girl is squirming but grinning. They both look like they are just where they should be.

While having a lunch of soup and salad at an outdoor café, Alice called her father on his cell phone to check where and when he would meet us. Thinking of needing to contact Mahmoud in the future, I asked her to write down the number for me on the back of an automatic teller receipt. She bit her lip and looked at her mother for approval.

"I promise I'll keep it only for emergencies," I assured them.

"It is just that my husband has asked that we do not give it to people," Carlotta explained.

"If you'll let me have your home number, too, I'll always try that one first. I just don't want to lose touch now that I've found you. And I may need to speak with him again."

She nodded with a smile, then told Alice to jot them both down.

I thanked her. The summer sun on our faces was like hot metal, and Alice leaned her head back to exult in all that blessed light. With her eyes closed, I could see the resemblance to her mother in the gentle angles of her profile.

174

On the way to our rendezvous with Mahmoud, Carlotta took me on a small detour. Facing a run-down pink building with a tall horse-chestnut out front, she said, "Please, you guess who lived here."

"Dante or Leonardo." It was the answer I gave in Italy whenever anyone asked that question, since I invariably never came up with the right guess.

She laughed. "Sana and Mahmoud," she said. "They live here when they move from Palestine – when Sana was the same age as Alice."

An upstairs window was fringed at the bottom with red geraniums. I imagined Sana looking down at me. Had she planned all along for me to stand here wondering about her? Was she that good a sorceress?

I moved my hand to the doorframe and pressed, imaging her touching the very same spot forty years earlier. Wanting to leave a little of myself behind, I made a scratch with my nail along the paint.

An hour later, Mahmoud met us at the center of the city, looking tired and haggard. He offered me a cold handshake. It seemed that something must have gone wrong with his calls. Carlotta spoke with him in Italian, and I think she asked him what was wrong, but he gave her a vague and rather curt reply.

We were standing below Bologna's two medieval towers. They looked like a child's dream – the shorter one leaning so far over that its shadow was menacing, the taller one so slender and straight that it seemed to point to the very center of the heavens.

While her parents were talking, I told Alice I had climbed to the top of the 320-foot Torre degli Asinelli almost exactly twenty-four years before. I'd spent the summer on a music program in Assisi, Florence, and Siena, and had taken the train one afternoon from Florence to Bologna to explore.

The girl wanted to lead me up again and tugged on my arm. I joked that I'd only go if she had an oxygen tank waiting at the top. Carlotta had stopped trying to alter her husband's sour mood by now and laughed her agreement with me.

The girl told me in an excited voice that there'd once been two hundred towers in Bologna. "Imagine trying to go to the top of all of them!"

"I sometimes think of those two hundred shadows in the city," Carlotta said, extending her arms way out. "Bologna must be a . . . a *scacchiera* . . ." She frowned at not knowing the word.

"A table for that game . . . chess, I think you call it," Alice said to me.

"A chessboard," I suggested.

"Yes, that's what I mean!" Carlotta exclaimed happily. "It was a chessboard of light and darkness."

"It was the New York of Italy," Alice said definitively. It sounded like a publicity slogan she'd read in a brochure. Carlotta and I smiled at each other.

"Now I know why you want to go to New York," her father said. "To go back in time to medieval Bologna."

I smiled at Mahmoud, but he wouldn't meet my eyes. I wondered if he'd been offended by something I'd asked the day before.

I bought everyone ice cream at a café in the central square. It was already three. I'd have to go back to my hotel soon and leave for the airport. When Carlotta accompanied Alice to the bathroom, I used their absence to apologize to Mahmoud for anything thoughtless I might have said.

"No, no. It is not a problem," he replied, taking out his cigarettes.

His distant tone implied otherwise. Unwilling to lose this opportunity, I said, "I might not be able to get back to Bologna for a while. Do you mind if I ask you a few more questions?"

Looking across the square, he gave me his agreement. I had the feeling he regretted having been so friendly and forthcoming with me the day before.

"Was there any other reason you moved to Italy?" I asked.

"What do you mean?" He turned to me and squinted in puzzlement.

"Besides banking, another motive for coming. A political reason, for instance."

He took the cigarette dangling unlit from his lips and smiled. His black eyes radiated pleasure. "You mean," he said in a gleeful tone, "am I a spy?"

"Something like that."

He laughed. "I'm flattered. But if I am a spy, why did I invite you to my home? I have nothing to hide. Not that I don't have my opinions about Palestine. And I try to help in my own way."

"By . . . ?"

"I told you," he said impatiently. "By arranging loans and grants for Palestinian students to study overseas. When they go back, they are educated. They can help make conditions better and help more students to learn." Mahmoud looked off again into the distance. "I will go to America soon for that very reason. You have many of our students there now."

"When will you go?"

"After the Orient – sometime in late September." He looked as though he was going to say more about that trip, but instead asked, "Do you know of a nice hotel in New York City, by any chance?"

"No, I always stay with my mom. But I can ask my friends – or I'm sure my literary agent will know one."

"Maybe your mother, she knows?"

"No, she lives on Long Island and hasn't lived in the city for fifty years. But I'll ask my agent."

"No, don't bother. I have banking colleagues there. I just thought you might know."

He lit his cigarette and leaned away from me, smoking greedily. His profile was very self-contained.

Hoping to ease Mahmoud's manner with me by showing my interest in the past he and Sana shared, I asked where in London he'd stayed with her. I also wanted to go there – to see where they'd always met. He told me it was the R— Hotel, not far from Marble Arch. It sounded expensive, but he said that they sometimes had a special weekend rate.

When our waiter passed, I requested the bill.

"I'm sure I'm trying your patience, but I have one last

question," I told Mahmoud. "Do you think Sana was thinking of going back to Israel or Palestine?"

"There was nothing in Haifa for her," he said absently. "Everyone was dead or gone. No, she was happy in Brazil."

"Happy?"

He nodded.

"Yet she killed herself?"

He drew in sharply on his cigarette, then let the smoke curl out of his nose, considering his words. "And you are sure she did?" he asked.

"What do you mean?"

"Maybe someone pushed her."

"Who?"

"I don't know. I was not in Perth." His voice was angry now. It seemed as if he was about to accuse me of not looking after her.

"You think someone murdered her?" I asked.

"Maybe yes, maybe no."

I'd thought of that before, of course, but no one had led me to believe that it was a serious possibility. I realized now that this must have been the main reason why Mahmoud had asked me so many detailed questions about Perth.

"Mahmoud, you really have no idea who might have done it?"

"No."

"Do you know who Queen Bee was?" I asked.

"Who?"

"Queen Bee – it was a name for a monster that scared Sana when she was little. You must remember."

"Only vaguely."

"And you don't know if she meant anyone in particular."

He shook his head.

"Sana sometimes referred to Júlio, her boyfriend, as Queen Bee."

"I don't know about that."

"Do you think he might have wanted to kill her?"

"No. She didn't talk about him after they finished their relationship."

178

"Do you think she had enemies anywhere?"

"She was a dancer – who would be her enemy? I don't know anything about enemies."

"I saw her production of *Lysistrata* on video. Some people may have hated the way she characterized Israelis as the enemy."

He glared at me as if I'd said something stupid. "That interpretation you are saying is very simplified."

"Some people are very simple."

"I don't know anything about that."

"But you're saying someone wanted her dead. It would have to be someone in her troupe. They were the only ones who knew she was in Perth. They were probably the only people she knew in all of Australia."

"It's just an idea!" he said in frustration, banging the table between us. "Forget what I said. Forget everything I told you." He tossed his cigarette away. I could see he was about to jump up and rush away. But his wife and daughter were now approaching from behind him. I waved to them to keep him from fleeing. Leaning toward me, he grabbed my hand. His eyes were radiant with righteous anger. He whispered, "I've warned you that it would be much better if you just forgot us all. Remember that!"

I pulled my hand back, but he scared me badly. My heart was drumming, my thoughts scattering. I realized I didn't know him at all – or anything about what he really thought of me. I wasn't sure if I would be able to act as if nothing had happened between us.

By then Alice and Carlotta were sitting down again, and I didn't dare talk of Sana being murdered. Carlotta noticed her husband's coolness right away and gave me an apologetic look. The girl saw it too, but didn't seem concerned. On her insistence, I got out my camera. Mahmoud groaned and said he looked like a cadaver in photos – his cheekbones jutting out and dark eyes too deep in shadow. He pulled his coat over his head, but Alice tugged it back down. I took several photographs of the three of them, and Carlotta took two of me with her husband and daughter. In one, Alice is sitting between me and

179

Mahmoud. He is looking off into the distance, furious, as though biding his time. Alice is waving.

I keep that particular photograph on my desk, next to my favorites of Sana and Helena. What I didn't realize at the time was that Alice was waving goodbye.

Chapter Fifteen

At four in the afternoon, Mahmoud, Carlotta, and Alice walked with me to a taxi stand. The ground felt brittle, as if it might cave in. Carlotta hugged me for a long time. Alice and I kissed cheeks. Mahmoud shook both my hands very hard, as though wanting to press his will into me, then leaned his mouth to my ear and whispered a caustic, tobacco-scented, "Forget Sana and write your novels."

Maybe his hostile advice influenced me. Or maybe I was hesitant about penetrating even further into Sana's story. I know I was even more scared of Mahmoud when I got to Porto. In hindsight, I sensed that he'd never have allowed me into his home if he'd had any other way of learning what I knew about Sana's last day in Perth. Maybe he was as skilled an actor as his daughter.

So I didn't call Helena or Samuel to tell them what I'd learned in Bologna. I kept my notebook closed and neglected my tapes. Alex and I were having our apartment remodelled and were living in our weekend house about an hour north of Porto, near the town of Caminha. I was glad to be able to work twelve hours a day on *Hunting Midnight*. To give myself an occasional break, I'd sit in the garden like a child and pull out weeds. At night I agonized over my characters.

I did call Mário to ask if anyone in the troupe had been so enraged at Sana, or so uncontrollably jealous of her, that they'd have wanted to hurt her. He thought I'd lost my mind.

Helena called a week after my trip to Bologna and I ended up telling her about Mahmoud's new family. Resentment put poison in her voice. "It's absolutely wonderful – I'm just so thrilled!" she snapped. I could hear her thinking, *Sana and Jamal are dead, and that fucking bastard has started his life all over again . . .*

Helena was still staying with her father. Abstaining from alcohol gave her a near-constant headache and both a furious temper and appetite. "It's lucky my mom is dead – she would have shot me by now."

"How's your father's golden feijoa coming along?"

"Nothing yet. But the green ones are just starting to fall from the bushes. I've been making jam – with a gram of powdered Valium in each jar. It's my new peace initiative. Dad says it could make me a fortune in Israel and Palestine."

Samuel took the phone after a while, and he was more forgiving of Mahmoud. "Good for him," he said. "Maybe he did find his honor again in a foreign country."

As for Mahmoud's answer about not being a spy, Samuel thought he'd outwitted me. "By exaggerating what you were asking he could deny everything and still be telling the truth."

"I guess I blew it," I said.

"It doesn't matter. If he didn't tell me, he wouldn't tell you. We'll never know."

I told him about our second day together. "The forceful way he spoke to me – it was a shock."

"I'll bet he was just angry about showing his emotion in front of you the day before," Samuel replied. "He'd see that as weakness, and he probably blamed it on you."

"You really think that's all it is? You don't think he hates Jews, do you?"

"Look, just to be safe, don't get in touch with him again. If you want my advice, you'll leave Mahmoud to his new family. To have peace with the Palestinians, we don't have to be friends, just neighbors."

When I said how nice it would be to see Wadi al-Nisnas, where they all used to live, Samuel said he would meet me in Haifa whenever I wanted and show me around. "I think some blue hydrangeas may even still be growing at our old house!" We made tentative plans to meet during the first week in October. He would ask Helena to join us.

I hadn't mentioned to her what Mahmoud had said about Sana being murdered because I couldn't predict how she'd react. But I told Samuel.

"Frankly, I think it's just wishful thinking," he said.

"Wishful thinking?"

"Take it from me, no father would want to believe that his daughter killed herself. This way there's someone to blame – and maybe to punish."

On September 2nd I received a call from Mark Fleisher, the dance critic living in San Francisco whom I'd tried to contact after speaking to a friend of his at the Joyce Theater. Fleisher told me right away that he remembered Sana's production of *Lysistrata* quite well.

"It was one of those minor disasters that everyone gossips about for forty-five seconds. It only ran for two performances."

"Why?"

"Do you really think an anti-Semitic *Lysistrata* is going to sell tickets in New York?"

"Was it anti-Semitic?" I asked.

"Come on! Your friend altered an ancient Greek play just so she could attack Israel. What would you call that?"

"A reinterpretation for a contemporary audience," I answered.

He laughed and said, "Nice try. Look, what *I* heard at the time was that a critic at the *Times* was going to write something ferocious about it, so the producers pulled the plug before the article had a chance to come out."

"Sana told me she was chased out of New York – nearly lynched."

"Oh, come on, she was just over-dramatizing – dancers do that all the time. They perform in some nightmarish political diatribe and think they're being persecuted when it's forced to close. I can assure you that when that *Lysistrata* went to its grave, we all moved on without giving it – and her – another thought."

Fleisher's waspish tone made it obvious he was cherishing this opportunity to belittle Sana's work. I decided to end the call before I said anything rude.

"Before I let you go," I said, "did you keep a program with the names of the other performers by any chance?"

"Sorry. Nothing. And I'm pretty sure the Soho Dance Theater broke up right afterward. At least I hope they did."

As the summer drew to an end, I felt more and more pressured about the rewrites on *Hunting Midnight* and worked on the book full-time. Even so, I kept in touch with Helena. She had resumed writing her letters to the Israeli newspapers and was getting her death threats forwarded from Paris. One man from Tel Aviv had written, "You should be roasted in hell for inciting attacks on Israel!" With pride in her voice, she told me she'd recently received letters from as far away as Cape Town and Singapore.

"I didn't know there were any Jews in Singapore," I replied.

"Well, there's at least one. Though his vocabulary in Hebrew is very limited. And he makes so many spelling mistakes! He must be an American Jew who learned some Hebrew for his *bar mitzvah*." She said he called her a "bitch" seven times in two brief paragraphs.

I told Helena I didn't understand how people living so far away had found her; they couldn't all know someone working at the newspapers where she published her letters.

"Israel is so small a country," she replied, "that if one person learns my address on Tuesday, by Thursday half the country has it. And by Friday all their relatives in the diaspora have it too."

The letter that bothered her most came from Santiago, Chile. The author – Chaim – had drawn a design of Helena with a swastika on her forehead and her arm upraised in the Nazi salute. Curiously, he drew her with a hooked nose, as well, as if he had absorbed fascist propaganda about Jewish faces. It upset her so much that she didn't want it in the house, and she sent me the original. I thought of burning it, but then decided to keep it to remind myself how cruel people can be. When I said that to her in our next phone call, she went completely silent.

"What's wrong?" I asked.

"Nothing's changed. All those people are dead in the Holocaust and nothing at all is new. You know, there are probably a few old Nazis left who are enjoying all this trouble in Israel. As far as I'm concerned that's more than enough reason to make peace with the Palestinians."

She was thinking of returning to Paris for a while and was feeling stable enough to begin writing her thesis again. "I want to finish it and then work at the pastry shop for a few months. I need my old routine. I need my life back. When I have them, I will decide what I will do next."

After making online reservations for my upcoming trip to Haifa in October, I found a more sensible explanation for how so many people had found Helena's address: initiating a simple search through the Paris White Pages on the internet turned it up in thirty seconds. I meant to call Helena about that, and also to give her the dates I'd chosen for my trip to Israel, but that afternoon I was walking past a café on one of Porto's main shopping streets when I saw a crowd of people leaning expectantly toward the television in the corner. I figured it was a soccer match. But through the window I could see the top floors of the Twin Towers banded by flame and casting billows of dense gray smoke into the sky. I rushed inside. It seemed like science fiction – absolutely impossible. Then one of the towers collapsed. All the people around me seemed to slide away from me and grow dim. From past experience I knew I was about to faint. I sat with my head between my legs. I didn't want to cry. But I did. I also didn't want to be seen, so I kept my head under the table.

I thought of Sana and Helena in their hiding place.

When my dizziness subsided, I sat up and drank a glass of water. I was very cold. A man from the next table recognized me and smiled. I recognized him too – Germano Silva. He was a local journalist and historian who'd interviewed me once. He came over and sat with me. We talked for a few minutes, since he remembered I was from New York, but I cannot recall a single word of our conversation. When I could stand, I rushed off for a taxi and headed for Alex's office. He was in a meeting, but came out to hug me. I remember the scent of him – the scent of all our years together. Then I sat at his secretary's desk. Amazingly, I got through to my mother right away. I expected her to be hysterical, but she was calm with numbed disbelief.

Chapter Sixteen

O ver the next few days, I exchanged e-mails with high school and college friends, my literary agent and editors, my mother's neighbors, and everyone else I could think of in New York. Thankfully, all the people I knew were safe. I spent most of my time in front of the television watching CNN and Sky News.

A week later I remembered about Mahmoud having to go to New York in late September. I wondered if he'd called off his trip – like I'd cancelled mine to Haifa. But his fax was shut off and neither his home phone nor his cell phone was working. There were reports of reprisals against Arabs in Europe and America – I'd even read in the *International Herald Tribune* of an Egyptian student being assaulted in Naples. He'd needed thirty-eight stitches on his face after being slashed with a razor blade. One of the Italian right-wing political parties, the Northern League, was making openly racist threats against immigrants. I guessed Mahmoud had decided it best for his family to disappear for a while.

Helena and Samuel had called right after the attacks, and they were both very kind to me. Helena ended our conversation by telling me that the political situation in Israel and Palestine was going to get much worse now, that there might even be an all-out war with Syria and Iraq. She was back in Paris. I pleaded with her not to publish any more letters and to remove her address from the White Pages; information was coming out now on networks of al-Qaeda terrorists in Europe, particularly in France, and I was convinced that either a Jewish or an Islamic fanatic would take the next logical step and slice a razor across *her* face. She agreed on no more letters.

"At least for now," she added darkly, as though she were making preparations for an all-out assault.

On October 3rd, while scouring the *International Herald Tribune* for articles on suicide that I could put in my collection, I happened upon a curious piece at the top of page four entitled: "Secretive Money-Moving System Scrutinized for bin Laden Funds."

Written by Douglas Frantz, the article discussed how Osama bin Laden and other terrorists moved money around the world using a centuries-old money-transfer system called *hawala*, the Arabic word for trust. Although illegal in most countries, billions of dollars flowed through the system annually.

To send money abroad – whether to buy weapons or schoolbooks, it made no difference – all you had to do was visit a nearby *hawala* trader and hand over the sum in question, along with the name of the city where the person receiving the funds would pick them up. There was no need to identify yourself or the beneficiary receiving the money. The trader would then give you a codeword, which you would phone or fax to your contact on the other end. With that codeword, he or she could pick up the same amount of cash from an associate of the original trader.

I ended up underlining one sentence in red ink: "With nothing more than a telephone and a fax machine, Mr. Khan transfers money almost anywhere in the world – no questions asked, no names used and no trail for law enforcement to follow."

Given what Mahmoud had told me about his business, I began to suspect that this might have been the true nature of his work. Perhaps it always had been, or maybe he'd once worked for a commercial bank and become a *hawala* trader only upon retirement. I guessed that the "birthday present" he'd mentioned on his original fax to me was a codeword for the funds to be transferred.

Although it disturbed me that he was probably involved in illegal money transfers – and might even have had fleeting contact with people funding terrorism – the article made it clear that there were thousands of *hawala* traders who never moved sums around for anything disreputable. Mahmoud's work must have been just as he said – arranging support for Palestinians studying abroad. He rightly considered it valuable work. Yet I was also beginning to believe that he was a far more complex and conflicted man than he had let on. Did he still believe that Jews were keeping Palestine in an eternal winter?

I sent a copy of the article to Helena, and she in turn gave it to her friend at the Sorbonne who had previously translated Mahmoud's fax. He was a Palestinian who had grown up in Cairo and Beirut, and was well informed about the current politics in that part of the world. His name was Michel Khalidi.

"Is that an unusual first name for a Palestinian?" I asked when we first spoke on the phone. We spoke in French because he said his English was hopeless.

"Yes, but my father worked in Marseilles for many years and his favorite soccer player was Michel Platini."

Michel told me that Mahmoud wasn't necessarily involved in *hawala*, explaining that the PLO raised "taxes" from the Palestinian diaspora through representatives abroad. Mahmoud might have been one of these "tax collectors," he suggested. "Or, he could be both a *hawala* trader and a 'tax collector' – the borderline between these professions isn't always very well defined."

"And you don't think there's any chance that he might be involved in terrorist activities, do you?" I asked.

"Who can say? Again, these things don't have strict boundaries."

"What exactly does that mean?"

"Well, let's say Mahmoud raises money for an Islamic school in Paris. Or helps secure funding for it. With that money, the directors bring over teachers from Algeria and Lebanon – for chemistry and math and geography and everything else. But one of them turns out to be a fanatic and starts plotting with some friends to release poison gas in a Paris Metro station. Would you say then that Mahmoud is involved in terrorist activities? Or what if he helped arrange funding for a business – an olive oil importer or clothing manufacturer – and it turned out that the owners were using their profits to recruit men for terrorist training camps in the Sudan? Where is Mahmoud's responsibility in all that?"

"So he wouldn't necessarily know where the money was coming from or going?"

"That's the whole point of the *hawala* system. No one in the middle ever knows."

When I spoke to Helena about what Michel had told me, she didn't seem interested. She was very down and spoke in a hoarse whisper.

"Have you started drinking again?" I asked, dread in my voice.

"No, it's not that. I'm just tired all the time. I have no energy to write my thesis. It's disappointing – I'm very disappointed with myself."

"Maybe you miss all that heat and light in Israel."

"It's not that. But if I tell you, you have to promise not to try to comfort me."

My heart tumbled. "Is it your father? He wasn't attacked again, was he?"

"No, but remember I cut my hair? It wasn't to look better. I was . . . I was told it would fall out."

My mother had had radiation therapy for breast cancer a few years back, so I was pretty sure what Helena was about to divulge to me. Sure enough, her doctor had found a small lump in her right breast. Even though he'd recommended surgery right away, she'd rushed off to stay with her dad instead. "I needed to speak to him and maybe say good-bye."

While with her father, she realized she wanted to have the growth removed in her homeland. "It is odd, I know, but I felt I needed to have an Israeli doctor make the operation," she told me in a confessional voice. "I suppose I still think we're all on the same team."

"And the operation went well?" I asked.

"Yes."

"And now you're having radiation?"

"Yes, here in Paris. The doctors say I will not have to do the chemical therapy, which is very good. So I didn't need to cut my hair, after all."

"But you look much better. Please don't grow it out again."

"You sound like my mother."

"How much more radiation do you have to have?"

"About two more weeks. You know, I'm more scared of dying than I thought possible. I could scream nearly all the time. I'd like to break all my windows."

"You can scream at me if you want."

She laughed. "You and my father are the only two people who I think are amusing any more. That must mean something."

"It means you need to meet more people. Have you been able to go out during the day?"

"Yes. It's very odd, but now that Tia Zeinab's predictions have finally come true for me, I feel freer than I have since I was a little girl – free and old and fragile. That's not so bad a combination, is it?"

I had organized a writers' conference in Porto that was set to begin on October 20th. For three straight weeks we would be hosting four novelists per weekend and each of them would talk about influences on his or her work. Unfortunately, my teaching was starting up at the very same time, so I had a lot of errands to clear out of the way beforehand. One of them was getting the photographs I'd taken in Bologna developed. Alice looked particularly wonderful in them – full of girlish delight. I was so pleased with the results that I had copies made for Mahmoud and Samuel. I figured Mahmoud was in hiding, but I hoped that they would find their way to him sooner or later.

I also hoped my sending them would be interpreted as a friendly gesture. And that he'd forgive me if I'd said anything that had offended him.

Samuel called as soon as he received the pictures. "That man is not Mahmoud," he told me.

"Excuse me?"

"The man in the photographs – he's not Mahmoud."

"What do you mean? I spent a weekend with him talking about Sana."

"I don't care, that's not him."

"But her doctor had him listed as the next of kin. And he replied to the fax I sent."

"I assure you, he is someone else. He doesn't look anything like Sana's father."

I thought of Mahmoud's protests against my taking his picture, even covering himself with his coat. "Samuel, this is insane. I called him Mahmoud all weekend and he never corrected me. His wife and daughter . . . they all knew Sana. They knew her *really well*."

"Maybe Mahmoud is his name too. It's very common. In any case, he's *not* Mahmoud Yasawi. If you want, I can fetch Rosa's old boxes and find a photo. I'll send one to you today."

"No, I believe you, but then who is he?"

Helena had just finished her radiation treatment and was eager to pick up where she'd left off on her thesis. She hoped to be able to hand it in to her supervisor by the end of the year. Her doctors were agreed that she could begin working again at a leisurely pace.

I wrote her a letter, explaining what Mahmoud had told me about Sana, then ran to the post office to express-mail it to her along with two of the photos. On to the top image I stuck a Post-It that read: "Do you recognize this man? Colombowitz isn't sure who he is."

Helena rang the next day. "Should I recognize him?" she asked right away.

192

"He's supposed to be Mahmoud."

"Hah! That's a good one."

"No resemblance?"

"Not unless Mahmoud has bought a new face and taken hormones that make him grow."

"You don't recognize his daughter or wife, I assume?"

"No."

I explained to her about being tricked. My voice was a monotone of stunned disbelief. "I don't understand why they'd do it," I told her.

"Pleasure," she suggested. She ran off to get her cigarettes. When she picked up the phone again I asked, "What's that supposed to mean – pleasure?"

"Fooling someone makes people happy. I feel very pleased with myself every time I tell someone that my mother spent the Second World War making herself tan on the beaches of Smyrna. It gives me a very lovely sense of power."

"But they seemed so . . . so . . ."

"Genuine?"

"Yes."

"And affectionate?"

"That too."

"People are good at pretending – especially Israelis and Palestinians. I think I told you that once, no? Hollywood should recruit us all."

"Okay, but why?"

"Look, you faxed Mahmoud wanting to find out about Sana, and the man who received the fax knew he could tell you all about her. Probably Mahmoud is dead. But he didn't want to say that. And he didn't want you to know his identity. Maybe he's living illegally in Italy. Maybe he has big tax problems, like he told you. Maybe he's a *hawala* trader like you think. Or just maybe he works for Fatah or your old enemy Abu Nidal. Whoever he is, he felt sympathy for you and wanted to help. He liked Sana, and he wanted to be nice to her friends. Or maybe he desperately needed to know from you how she spent her last days in Australia. So he decided to give you what you wanted, but without saying

who he was. He probably thought he was being very gener-
ous. And maybe he was – you found the information you
wanted, after all."

"But maybe what he told me is all lies."

"I don't think so. It's always much simpler to tell the truth.
That way you can't become caught later in any spider webs.
And what he told you about Sana sounds very reasonable to
me."

"But why didn't he just tell me he wasn't her father? He could
have said he was her friend and that I shouldn't say anything to
anyone about him."

"We talked about this already, you and I. Why do you think
you have a right to know someone's personal history? Just
because you ask? Just because you're an American and America
runs the world?"

"Helena," I snarled, "if he didn't want to tell me the truth,
then he shouldn't have spoken to me – or invited me to his
home. That's the least we can expect from other people."

"Look, you said he knew all about Sana. Maybe he thought
of himself as a father of sorts – or as her stepfather. The real
Mahmoud wasn't much good anyway."

"But his wife . . . she played along! And his daughter, too.
It's like they held me in contempt all the time I was with
them."

"They knew it was just two days of pretending. That's not so
much. Some people live their whole lives like that – maybe Sana
did."

The ease in her tone irritated me. "You think this is funny,
don't you?"

"Funny? Not at all. I just think it's . . . it's perfect."

"Perfect? Why?"

"Because this is the way Sana's death should be – all upside
down and tied in knots."

"But when I speak to them again, how are they going to
justify this?"

"Hah! Nobody justifies what they do any more. They just
make up reasons when they need to. You really do live in the
dark, don't you?"

"Thanks for being so supportive."

"Listen, you don't need support right now, you need the truth. So don't become angry with me. I agree with you – what they did was not so very nice. But they probably only did it because they had to – so that this other Mahmoud can protect his identity. Anyway, I simply don't believe it's unusual. If you turn on the lights in that Portuguese cave of yours, you will see we are all living at a masked ball. Nobody knows who the other people are."

Anger made me keep silent. Helena sighed. "Is that a poor metaphor?" She was trying to be amusing. "Look," she continued, "maybe there's an innocent explanation. You could call them and ask."

"I've called a dozen times! But their damn phones aren't working. He's probably taken his family away to escape the violence against Arabs. Or maybe the police are after him because of his *hawala* activities."

"You'll just have to keep trying."

"What do I say when I talk to him?"

"How about, 'What the fuck is your true name and why did you and your family lie to me?'"

After discussing everything with Alex, we came to the conclusion that Sana's real father must have been a business colleague of the man I'd met, sharing the same office and fax number. They must have known each other for many years. Otherwise, he couldn't have known so much about Sana. Assuming Mahmoud had died, this work colleague – the man I'd met – had probably kept in close touch with her for a long time. Maybe he'd even helped fund her studies and professional work. Over the years, she must have grown very close to him and his family. She liked inventing her past and probably told people – including her doctor – that he was her father.

My reasoning sounded logical, but I still couldn't believe it. I suffered a clinging insomnia for several nights. I was too hot, then too cold. My inner thermostat was broken again – as it had been in Perth. Sometimes I'd stare out the window at our garden, bathed in moonlight. It was far too quiet.

In my thoughts, I searched through every conversation Mahmoud and I had had in Bologna, looking for a slip he might have made. I played my tapes over half a dozen times. But my host had been nearly flawless. All I could recall was that he hadn't remembered Queen Bee.

The only other clue I had was that I couldn't remember Carlotta using her husband's name in front of me – except when she said that Mahmoud and Sana had lived in a particular building. Then she might very well have been referring – in her own mind – to the *real* Mahmoud Yasawi. Very possibly, she wanted to be able to tell me at some time in the future that she'd never lied to me.

In point of fact, *he* had never actually said he was the Mahmoud who'd been Sana's father. He'd let me assume it. He'd even told me that his thin turquoise ring had been left to him by Zeinab. That must have been an invention. But he'd convinced me it was the truth by making a point of telling me that he'd lied about it earlier. That was a very clever trick.

I got into several fights with Alex over the next days. I shouted some mean things and so did he. In making up with him, it became clear to me that I was upset that my instincts about other people didn't count for nearly as much as I'd thought. I had no antenna, no radar, no depth of vision. I had no defenses.

But none of us have solid defenses, as it turns out. Over the next weeks, I read a dozen articles in American and British online newspapers about how the terrorists involved in the World Trade Center attack were regarded as nice, quiet people who liked their privacy – immigrants who'd adapted well to the American way of life.

In the *St. Petersburg Times*, for instance, I discovered that neighbors of Abdul Al-Omari, who had helped overpower the crew of American Airlines Flight 11 and steer it into the North Tower, regarded him as a "personable man with a beautiful family and well-behaved, pleasant children." The landlord of their stucco home on 57th Terrace in Vero Beach said, "It's hard to believe that the father knew what was going to happen, and that he knew it for a long time." And yet, every morning, while neighbors watched Abdul leave his home for the school where he was training to be a commercial pilot, murder must have been precisely what he was thinking about and planning for. His wife Halimah, who drove the children to school shortly after her husband took his car to work, must have been thinking a great deal about it too.

If Helena was right, then they must have been very excited to be living a lie – to be secret agents of a very particular sort. Though maybe not – maybe Halimah knew that her young husband was on a suicide mission and hated the idea of having to raise their four children alone.

Abdul Al-Omari and his wife and children disappeared a week before the September 11th attack – just like Mahmoud, Carlotta, and Alice. I was beginning to believe there might have been a connection.

The first weekend of the writers' conference went very well. For the Saturday evening's opening session, with António Lobo Antunes and Luis Sepúlveda, we had over six hundred people in the audience. They spilled over into the aisles and up into the gallery above the auditorium.

The next day, I called Mahmoud and his family again on several occasions. Nothing. On Monday, I took the train from Porto back to our house in the country.

Alex was becoming protective and suggested I'd be better off not trying to reach Mahmoud or his family. I *was* scared of him, and ambivalent about learning more, but I decided to try to find Carlotta through her work. I liked the idea of speaking to her first – I believed I would have an easier time with her. I thought we might even continue as friends if she could just explain herself to me.

I got the phone number for the Orchestra del Teatro Comunale di Bologna from an Italian operator.

"I need to speak to one of the musicians," I told the woman who answered my call. I was attempting to speak Italian.

"Who are you?" she asked.

"An American writer."

"Who is it you want to speak to?"

"Carlotta. She plays violin."

"Carlotta Ciolli?" she questioned.

"Yes, that's her."

"Are you British?" she asked.

"No, American."

"Carlotta no longer plays with the orchestra," she told me in English.

"How come? She's not ill or anything?"

"No, she . . . she went away."

"When . . . when did she leave?"

"Since two . . . two months."

"When exactly? I need to know exactly."

"You are a friend?"

"No. I'm her cousin – her American cousin."

"In early September she has gone."

"There's no answer at her home phone number. I've tried calling every day for a month. All I get is a weird ring, like a quick busy signal."

"She . . . she . . ." The woman spoke Italian to someone, then came back on the line. "She has moved."

"Where?"

"I do not know."

"Can you find out?"

"Hold on."

I waited for a few minutes. A man got on the phone.

"You want to speak with Carlotta Ciolli?"

"Yes. I'm her cousin. I'm visiting Italy. I want to see her."

"She has moved."

"Yes, that's what I've just been told. Where did she move to?"

"We do not know."

"She must have told you something."

"No, she has given us no phone number and no address. She tells us only four days before she leaves. She says she cannot say more because her husband is an Arab. She is worried, she says. She will tell us where she is in some weeks. But she has not contacted us. It is all a great . . . a great rush. Listen, if you find her, you tell us, okay?"

"Of course. And did her kids go with her too?"

"Yes, we have a small party here for them – for Alice and Tomasso."

"Was her husband there – at the party?"

"No, he is not in Bologna when we make it."

"What was Carlotta's husband's name? I haven't seen either of them in a long time and I'm very worried about her."

"Samir."

"Yes, that's right. And his last name?"

"His what?"

"His family name."

"I do not know. Carlotta does not use his family name."

"Would you look it up in your files?"

While holding on, I pictured the dark patch in Mahmoud's wooden floor where the piano had been. They'd had it shipped out, which meant that they'd known they were leaving at least a few weeks before Carlotta gave notice at work. Also, Mahmoud had told me to forget about Sana. What he really meant was that he never intended to let me speak to him about her ever again.

I picked up the photograph of Alice I kept on my desk and now understood she had not been able to resist waving goodbye to me.

Maybe Tomasso had stomped around the house in anger because he'd just been told he would be moving – just like Sana had been told she was going to leave for Italy when she was a girl. Maybe Carlotta had been so emotional at times not because of Sana's death, but because she knew she'd soon be leaving her homeland for ever.

The man from the orchestra got back on the phone. "Samir Nizar al-Hassan," he told me.

"Thank you. Do you know where Carlotta shipped her piano?" I asked.

"No."

"I don't suppose you know the name of the company that might have shipped it for her?"

"No, I'm sorry. We know nothing."

"Look, if you do find out where it was sent, please tell me right away, because that's where Carlotta and Samir went."

I searched on the internet right away for information on Samir Nizar al-Hassan, but I couldn't find a thing. Nor did I discover any references to Mahmoud Yasawi.

On October 29th, I found my first indirect connection to Samir in an article from the *International Herald Tribune* entitled 'Italy Tightens Qaeda Net'. It reported that more than six hundred special police officers had been assigned to the task of cracking down on Osama bin Laden's local financiers. The Italian Treasury Minister, Giulio Tremonti, was quoted as saying, "We are well aware that the terrorist money trail . . . passes through Italy." The article went on to note that the U.S. Treasury Department had named the Islamic Cultural Institute in Milan as the main al-Qaeda station-house in Europe.

I then discovered articles on the institute on dozens of websites. It had first made headlines in 1995, when more than ten of its members were charged by Italian prosecutors with supplying arms to Egyptian terrorists and Bosnian guerrillas. The Egyptian prayer leader at the center fled arrest and was later shot dead by an unknown assailant in Bosnia.

From that point on, the Italian anti-terrorist squad had watched the institute closely, even bugging members' apartments. They soon learned that it was a base for militants from a broad range of Middle Eastern countries, a transfer point for money and arms, and a recruitment hub for terrorist training camps in Afghanistan. Supervising these activities – and apparently appointed directly by bin Laden as his European chief of operations – was a thirty-three-year-old Tunisian named Essid Sami Ben Khemais.

Ben Khemais maintained close links with other al-Qaeda cells operating in Germany, England, and Spain. Phone conversations showed, for example, that he was well aware of the activities of Abu Doha, the Algerian leader of a London terrorist unit also recruiting for bin Laden.

Italian police arrested Ben Khemais and five others in January 2001 for trafficking in arms and explosives, and for using false passports and other documents. In a raid on his apartment, officers found about forty video cassettes showing training scenes in Afghanistan and military battles in Chechnya.

Investigators soon learned that he had been planning to release cyanide gas into the ventilation system of the American embassy in Rome.

"What I need is not an army," Ben Khemais said in a bugged phone call from the spring of 2001, "but two people who have brains, training and nothing to lose or gain. They spread the gas and say goodbye. I only need a barrel of 10 liters and a few documents. God is with us."

After the final weekend of my writers' festival, I flew to London to give a talk at a synagogue in Hampstead on "Being a Secret Jew at the Time of *The Last Kabbalist of Lisbon*." I splurged and got a room at the R— Hotel, where Samir had claimed to have stayed with Sana. It was all very plush and floral, with giant Italian vases everywhere and an antique Turkish rug at the entrance. The ancient doorman wore a red uniform with cordage across his chest. He looked like someone from the "Sgt Pepper's" album cover thirty-five years on. As soon as I showered, I asked at the reception desk if I could have a quick word with the manager.

He came to my table in the lobby a few minutes later. He was an elderly gentleman, tall, with a shaved head, and he showed me a haughty squint on stepping toward me – as if I might be a rather disappointing mirage. He wore a pinstriped double-breasted suit and kept his right hand in the pocket until we shook hands. About six months later, I would see pictures of the Dutch politician Pim Fortuyn after he was assassinated. The manager could have been his elder brother.

I asked him if I could buy him a drink at the bar because I had a strange story to tell him about two of his guests.

"I have a meeting soon. How long do you expect it might take?"

"Fifteen minutes maximum – for the short version. A year and a half for the long one."

He didn't smile. He looked at his watch, which was gold and large. I was wearing a nice blue sweater and my best woolen slacks, but even so, I could see him thinking he ought not to be seen with a rather undistinguished-looking guest like me. To convince him I might have some small cachet – at least as an oddity – I took a copy of *The Last Kabbalist of Lisbon* out of the envelope I was holding. "I want to give you one of my novels. It has something to do with the story I need to tell you."

He leaned his head back as he looked at the cover and squinted again. Maybe he thought I would insist that he read it. "Thank you," he said, without much conviction. Turning it over, he scanned the blurb. His lips moved. "Very nice," he said. "How many novels have you written?"

"Three." I hoped that was enough to win me an audience.

"I can only give you ten minutes," he said.

Three minutes and twenty seconds per novel.

We sat at a table on low-backed blue seats – too stylishly designed to be comfortable. He kept his legs crossed and sipped his tonic water coolly.

Out of nervousness I spoke rather too quickly about Sana liking my book and committing suicide. I explained a bit about her past, too, then about my meeting Samir and his family in Bologna and how they'd recently disappeared. I ended by telling him that I wanted to see if Samir had registered at this hotel under his own name or Mahmoud's.

"So you want to see our records?" the manager asked. His face had become stern – like a school principal's; he'd just

202

realized that all his goodwill in meeting with me had been pointless. I was asking the impossible.

"Maybe it's all on computer now," I replied hopefully. "You could just type in his name and see what comes up."

"I'm afraid we don't give out information on our guests."

"But I don't really want information on him. I just want to know if he was here and what name he used. And if Sana was here."

"If they *registered* here?" he asked, as if I could have meant anything else.

"Yes, that's all – and the dates. Please, I would be very grateful."

He stood up and inserted his hand in his jacket pocket. With a little bow, he said, "No, I'm very sorry, Mr. Zimler, but hotel policy forbids it."

It was becoming clear to me that I would have to call on higher powers to get me the information I needed, and I resolved to make an appeal to my old friend George Miklós, a retired barrister distantly related – through his maternal grandmother – to the British royal family. George and I first met in August 1977, eighteen months before I met Alex, and we'd stayed in touch ever since. When I told him about my difficulties at the hotel, he said he was only too pleased to come to my rescue. In fact, he was overjoyed at the chance to prove his powers of persuasion. He was going to come to my talk in Hampstead anyway, so he decided to have his chauffeur drive him around to the hotel late that afternoon. "We'll have drinks and straighten out your secretive little manager, then head off to the synagogue. I've had a number of important friends stay at the R—, so I'm fairly certain I shall be successful."

I waited for him in the lobby, where he gave me a big hug and kiss as soon as he arrived – he'd been arrested in Brighton for sodomy in 1958 and the resulting notoriety had cured him of all the stiff constraint he'd been raised to demonstrate. "Unlike Oscar Wilde, going to prison was the best thing that ever happened to me," he'd once told me. "I gave up on the rules of English life then and there."

He'd aged since I'd last seen him, and his walk was a hesitant tightrope act, but he still had his bright smile and a full head of silver hair.

He was wearing a paisley waistcoat and a white felt hat with a wide brim. It gave him the air of an Englishman in the colonies. He carried the duck-headed cane he'd always had with him – inherited from his father, a Hungarian diplomat who defected in 1956 when the Russians drove their tanks into Budapest to smother the nascent reform movement. There was something graceful even now about the way he moved and held himself.

England is the place where oddity is most beautiful, I was thinking.

At the reception desk, he told a perky young woman with black hair and bright red lipstick that he needed to see the manager right away. His tone was friendly but also implied, *I am of the aristocracy and you are not, so I'm afraid you'll have to do as I say*. He also turned and began to speak to me immediately after addressing her, so she could hardly raise an objection without appearing rude.

"Now please don't say a word when the manager gets here," he told me *sotto voce*, "even if you think you should. In fact, you know what . . . ?" He caressed my cheek. "Why don't you run off and talk to the barman about Russian literature and I'll join you shortly. Some delicate subjects can only be handled between Englishmen, dear boy."

Ten minutes later he was caning his way toward my table. I stood to help him sit next to me.

"Well?" I asked.

"You will have your list presently. Now what shall we drink? Tell me, do you expect I'll need something strong to survive your talk?"

Fifteen minutes later, the girl we'd seen at the reception desk served me the handwritten list on a silver tray. Sana Yasawi and Samir Nizar al-Hassan had stayed for three days in June 1994, seven days in July 1995, and four days in May 1996. This last stay was just prior to Sana's visit with Helena in Paris. I guessed the database didn't go back any earlier. As for later dates, I was beginning to understand Sana's way of thinking and decided to ask for one more favor.

Twenty minutes later I had another handwritten note in my hands. Helena and Samuel Verga had stayed here three times: for four days in June 1997, nearly two weeks in August 1998, and a week in July 1999.

That night I awoke in a kind of frenzy of lucid madness, sure that Sana had written me a farewell note and placed it in the bag with the soaps she'd given me as a gift. The note would explain why she'd been so distraught and desperate – maybe even warn me about Samir. She had wanted me to read it immediately after her suicide, but I had never been able to take out her gift ever again.

I called Alex at three in the morning. Drowsy and grumbly, he got up and found the soaps. But there was nothing else in the bag from the art gallery giftshop in Perth.

I asked him to cut the bars of soap apart.

"I hope you're kidding," he replied. I could see him standing by the phone in his oversized orange nightshirt.

"Please just do it."

He stumbled down to the kitchen to get a knife. "Nothing," he said when he got back on the phone.

On reaching Porto, I called up Helena. She denied ever having been at the R— Hotel. "You think I lie to you just like that man in Bologna, don't you?! But I have not been in London for years."

"You don't get it, do you?" I asked.

"Get what?"

"Sana stole your passport."

"What?"

"She wanted to register at the hotel under a different name. She stole your passport when she was staying with you and then must have had Samir get someone to substitute her photograph for yours. When you two were kids she was always pretending she was you, right? It's perfect. And Samir must have decided to register as your father to keep things consistent."

"But my father's passport was never stolen – at least he never mentioned it."

"Samir must have had the passport forged. If he's involved in *hawala* then he probably has some very good connections in dark places."

"But someone at the hotel might have noticed the name change. You said they stayed there before."

"Nobody remembers the names of guests who only stay once a year. Besides, the reception people probably don't hang around very long. Maybe Samir and Sana even liked the risk."

"It's impossible. How could Sana know she was going to run into me in Paris? It's a big city. I can't believe it."

"Helena, she didn't run into you. She planned it. She knew where you were living and must have followed you. She might have even had someone else watch you before she visited – to learn your patterns. Maybe that's when you started thinking someone was following you."

"That doesn't seem . . . it doesn't . . . ." Her protest faded to nothing.

"To make sure you'd see her, she started performing on a street where she knew you were in the habit of walking. You were going out during the day then."

"I don't think she'd do that."

"She would. She did! How else could she have registered under your name?"

"Then all that we did together during her stay, our walks around Paris – it's all a lie. She used me. She . . . she only contacted me to use me."

"Helena, she obviously loved you – and was overjoyed to see you. You'd have noticed if she was acting. You knew her too well to be fooled for very long. And it's possible that I'm wrong about her planning everything – maybe she only had the idea of stealing your passport *after* she went to your apartment. I don't know. But she must have realized at some point that she could take your identity. The question is, why did she need to do that? And why did she need your identity beginning in 1996?"

Suleiman Tamari called me a few days later and apologized for taking so long to find out more about the guards who'd brutalized Jamal. He said he'd discovered that both men had quit their jobs several years earlier. N., whom we believed to have held down Jamal's arm, was still living in Israel, in Tel Aviv. Tamari gave me his phone number, but he asked me not to tell N. where I'd gotten it since he needed to protect his sources. As for S., who had probably wielded the ax, he had disappeared without a trace.

"I have a friend at Ashkelon who even managed to check the official records. There's nothing on him anywhere. It's as if he vanished into another universe."

I was very nervous about calling N. A woman answered, but she spoke almost no English. A teenage boy got on the line and, when he understood what I wanted, told me he would call his father. After a few seconds, I could hear an animated conversation in Hebrew.

"Who is it?" he asked when he got on the phone.

I told him my name and that I was an American journalist. "I'm looking for a man named N."

"I'm N.," he confirmed. "What do you want?"

"Did you used to work as a guard at Ashkelon?"

"No."

"You're sure?"

"I program computers," he said. "All I do is that."

"Do you know anyone who worked at Ashkelon?"

He hung up.

I believed that only a fellow Israeli might be able to convince N. to stay on the phone and talk about Jamal. Helena thought she'd be wrong for the job, since she'd only get anxious and flustered. She volunteered her father, who was happy to help. I told him that I wanted to know three things: 1) if N. had ever been contacted by Sana; 2) if he'd ever been threatened by her or anyone else for what had happened with Jamal; and 3) where S. was living and what his phone number was.

I told Samuel that Tamari would have probably managed to track S. down if he was still living in Israel. He must have emigrated. I suggested he'd probably be living in America or Brazil.

"Why there?"

"Because that's where Sana went to live. I think she might have been trying to track him down."

Samuel agreed to call. When he got back to me, he said, "As you guessed, that man is very frightened."

"Of what?"

"He obviously doesn't want to be linked in any way to what happened to Jamal. He lives a quiet life now. He doesn't even want to remember Ashkelon."

"But he worked there?"

"Yes. And someone *did* contact him once before about Jamal. But it wasn't Sana. It was a man. He didn't say so, but I think this man threatened him. And you were right in a way – it happened when he was living in Brazil. He moved there, but he didn't adapt well and returned to Israel. Now he just wants to forget the past."

"What Brazilian city did he live in?"

"He didn't say. I forgot to ask. I'm sorry."

"It's not important. Did he say whether he'd told whoever threatened him where S. was living?"

"He claimed not to know anything about S., at least at first."

"At first?"

"He would not admit to hurting Jamal or confirm the other guard's name to me – which irritated me. So I played dirty."

"What did you do?"

"It's terrible, but I don't care – I owe it to Jamal and Zeinab. I said I'd been contacted by an American human rights group that was going to look into Jamal's case. I said you were a journalist who'd been named to that group – so that your phone call to him would make sense. I said I'd been told that the group would leave him alone if he revealed to me who the other guard was and where he was living. That's all they really wanted."

"And?"

"N. confirmed that S. was the guard who cut off Jamal's hand. He moved to Australia a few years after that. N. didn't know where, however. That's as much as I could get him to tell me. Maybe he's frightened of S. – that he'll come back to hurt him if he says anything more."

I next called Mário and asked if Sana had ever spent any extra days in Australia during either of their tours.

"The last time we went," he replied, "she flew to Perth before the rest of us. She needed to get there to prepare things. And she wanted to see Sydney again. On our first tour, we'd spent three days there and she'd really loved it."

"So when I saw her in Perth, she'd already been to Sydney?"

"Yes."

"For how long?"

"I think maybe a week. I'm not sure – a few days, at least. She paid for her flight and hotel herself – the troupe didn't have any extra money."

"How did she get from Sydney to Perth?"

"She flew. Ana and I went to the airport to pick her up."

"And she was okay?"

"Just fine. She said she'd had a good time."

"She wasn't jittery or upset?"

"No. She looked a little tired, but she said she'd been going out dancing and staying up late."

"And your first tour was two years before that?"

"That's right. We were invited to the Adelaide Festival."

"Did she go to Sydney first that time too?"

"No, afterward – we all went. We did our shows in Adelaide, then went to Sydney for three more performances. She stayed for a few extra days, then flew home alone."

"How did you get the invitation to the Adelaide Festival?"

"Sana said she'd always wanted to go to Australia. So she tried to interest the different festivals there in inviting us by mailing them the video we had of our production of *Waiting for Godot*. I know she sent it to Adelaide and Melbourne. She may have tried Wellington too – in New Zealand. She also included some of the reviews that had come out in Brazil – a very positive one from the *Estado de São Paulo*. They were in Portuguese, so I doubt anyone ever read them, but she figured they looked impressive. The Melbourne and Wellington people never got back to us, at least not that I know of, but she came in one day all excited with a letter from Adelaide. They'd loved the video and wanted us for the next festival. So we went. We got a couple of standing ovations, too. The festival organizers in Perth must have heard about us, so two years later we were invited there. It all worked out great."

"In Perth, did you ever see her talking with anyone from outside the mime troupe?"

Mário laughed. "Sana talked to everyone all the time!"

"Anyone suspicious?"

"Like maybe somebody wearing a black cowboy hat and carrying a gun?"

I admitted it was a stupid question. "Did she have an argument with anyone from the hotel, or from Perth – maybe with someone in the audience?"

"Not that I know of."

"Did she ever talk with anyone who was angry that she had made an anti-Semitic adaptation of *Lysistrata*?"

"It wasn't anti-Semitic!" Mário protested.

"It doesn't matter now. I'm just saying that someone in the audience might have thought so."

"No, no one."

"Did anyone come backstage to see her?"

"Jesus, what's this all about?"

"Imagine that someone was enraged with her and wanted to hurt her. Someone suggested to me that might have happened."

"You mean that she was murdered?"

"Or maybe crashed through the window during a fight – who knows . . ."

"I can't think of anyone."

"Did anyone visit her backstage?"

"Just some journalists."

"Did she speak Hebrew with any of them? Or Arabic?"

"I told you, we never once heard her speak Hebrew or Arabic."

"Did she go out to lunch or dinner with anyone outside the troupe?"

"I don't think so. We went out every night together."

"Did she ever mention visiting London?"

"No, I don't think so."

"Or a man named Samir?"

"No."

"And she never ever spoke about anyone threatening her or bothering her – not while she was in Brazil or Australia?"

"No. She was doing great."

But the point was she wasn't doing great – at least not in Perth, and not if Helena was correct in her interpretation of why Sana was miming her finches and putting a flower behind her ear. She was in desperate trouble and needed some magic to help her. She needed to talk to someone – even a stranger like me.

Chapter Seventeen

I couldn't drop my classes and writing and fly off to Australia, so through some friends I placed an ad in the *Sydney Morning Herald* and *Australian Jewish News* asking for information on a woman named Sana Yasawi or Helena Verga who had visited Sydney in March of 1998 and February of 2000. I included a fairly recent snapshot of Sana that Mário had mailed me and sent it as an e-mail attachment to the newspapers. I wrote in the advertisement: "Yasawi or Verga were probably looking for a friend or acquaintance from Israel."

The ad appeared in the *Sydney Morning Herald* from November 18th to 24th, and in the *Australian Jewish News* for the months of November and December.

I also spent days searching the internet for information on S., but I came up with nothing. If he was still in Sydney, then his phone number and his address were unlisted, and his name had never appeared in any of the local newspapers.

When I called Júlio, he didn't deny having hit Sana. "But it was only once," he rushed to say. "It happened one night, right after we'd been to bed. She suddenly went crazy. She shrieked that I made her feel like nothing – that I did it on purpose. She slapped me. I pushed her away, hard – because I was scared. She fell back against the wall, then came at me like she was possessed. Her eyes – there was something . . . something terrified and furious in them, and it wasn't the Sana I knew. She began punching me, and to defend myself I swung out at her. But I hit her with an open hand. I didn't mean to hurt her. We both stopped and just stared at each other. We were both terrified by what had happened. I never touched her again. She went to the bathroom and locked the door and stayed inside with the lights off for about an hour. She said through the door that she was hiding and couldn't speak to me – she couldn't speak to anyone or even make a sound. When she came out, she was calm. She said it wasn't any big deal. I remained more upset than she did, I assure you. And we still saw each other after that. That should tell you it wasn't all my fault."

"Was that when she started calling you Queen Bee?"

"I have no idea."

"Think – please."

"I don't know. It's been years. I really can't remember."

"Have you ever been to Australia?"

"No."

"And you never hit her again?"

"Never, I swear. I loved Sana. She just didn't love me. Maybe that's what made her strike out at me. I was just never good enough and maybe she was angry at both of us because of the unfairness of it all. I know she didn't want it to be that way – it just was."

Over the next couple of weeks, I let my imagination carry me away and became certain that Queen Bee had to have originally been Mahmoud. As a young girl, Sana must have been frightened he would go further than spank her and really hurt her – even kill her. She couldn't admit her fear, so she invented a name for him. I'd have guessed that Mahmoud was the one who "made her feel like nothing." Júlio probably just reminded her of him.

Why Queen Bee, I didn't know. Maybe because of the sharp sting of being spanked. Maybe she experienced sex with Júlio as being *that* painful.

I also thought it possible – but less likely – that she had once been caught by an Israeli soldier and either raped or made to perform sexually for him. Maybe there was something about this man that reminded her of a bee – or again, Sana could simply have chosen that name because of its association with pain.

213

When I asked Helena and Samuel about the possibility that Sana been sexually abused by a soldier, or even by her father, they both said they'd never once suspected anything like that.

"Though it's not impossible," Helena added. "Sana would have kept it a secret."

I sent some of my notes on her childhood to Cal Arkanian, an old friend from college who was now a child psychologist in Chapel Hill, North Carolina. I asked him what he would say about a girl with her fantasies – particularly her fear of Queen Bee. When we spoke on the phone, he said that it was impossible to come to any conclusions without meeting her. He would have to accompany her for several months even to begin to understand the meaning of her fantasies – what she was trying to tell us without giving herself away. He'd also need time to study how she played by herself and interacted with her parents and any siblings she might have.

"None of that can be arranged," I told him. "And you can't even speak to Sana about what she went through. When she grew up, she committed suicide." After I'd explained about the circumstances of her death, I asked, "Can't you just tell me what you think her specific fantasies might mean?"

He was reticent, but when I pushed him he replied, "I'd say that she was deathly afraid of someone in her immediate surroundings. It could have been the Israeli soldiers. Or even a family member or neighbor. And it could have involved sexual abuse. But whoever it was, and whatever was happening, she was convinced she needed magic to get out of her predicament, which would imply there was no normal escape possible. She was in this person's power and would be as long as she remained a child. As for birds and flying, I'd say she felt so diminished that she saw herself as very tiny. One way a helpless thing can get away is by flying."

"What about her attachment to Helena?"

"Helena was her sorceress, her protectress – but also, conversely, her servant or slave. In a sense, she made Helena feel just the way she felt – diminished, trapped."

"Even used."

"Yes, used."

"Zeinab moved Sana into her bedroom during the girl's childhood. Don't you think that's evidence that she was trying to protect Sana from abuse – maybe from Mahmoud's repeated abuse?"

"Not necessarily. From what you've told me, it was enough that Zeinab saw catastrophe everywhere for her to want to keep Sana with her."

"And why Queen Bee . . . why that particular name?"

Cal gave me much the same explanation that I'd come up with by myself and ended by saying, "In any event, we'll never know for sure." Sensing my deep disappointment, he added, "You want probabilities and certainties, but there are none – not now, so many years after all these things happened and after her death. Maybe Sana wasn't even hurt by anyone in particular. Being hunted all the time by soldiers would be enough to make a kid as sensitive as her start imagining monsters. And kids happen to be afraid of bees, especially big ones that give birth to others that can hurt them. All we can say for sure is that people and events damaged Sana. She was very troubled. And in dire need of help – which she deserved to get no matter who or what was hurting her."

By Christmas of 2001, I'd just about given up on ever making contact with Samir. I still tried his cell phone number once a day, but I always got a message in Italian saying it was unavailable.

By then, I'd gotten forty-seven responses to my ads in the *Sydney Morning Herald* and *Australian Jewish News*. Twenty-eight people wanted to sell me pornography or sex toys. They'd read my words as a coded appeal for everything from phone sex in Hebrew to the telephone numbers of Thai girls living in Australia. Most of the rest believed they'd spotted Sana at one time or other: *I think I saw her waiting at a bus stop on Blues Point Road* or *She looks like a woman I saw on a ferry to Manley a couple of years ago – maybe she's living there.*

Two responses seemed more promising, however, since both correspondents said they'd talked to the woman in the photograph. Neither had learned her name, however, and it became clear after a short exchange of e-mails that the person they'd met could probably not have been Sana.

Helena had a complete check-up just after Christmas, including blood tests. There was no sign of the cancer and her prognosis was excellent. She celebrated by handing in her doctoral thesis.

"It's not very good, but I don't care," she told me. "I learned what I wanted to learn, and it may interest a few people. I'll get my degree. That's enough for me."

To me, her dispirited tone implied just the opposite – that she had expected much more of herself. But she had taught me a little more discipline in my questioning and I said nothing. She planned on spending all of January with her father. Then she would begin managing the tearoom at her pastry shop in Paris once again. Having rediscovered her appetite she was very excited about the opportunity to have constant access to so many sweets. "When next you see me, I will look like an elephant," she warned me.

On January 4th, at 3.20 p.m., Samir answered his cell phone.

"You must stop calling," was the first thing he said. "It is such a nuisance."

"You know who this is?"

"Your number tells me. I know no one else in Portugal. Listen, stop this calling me. I will not answer again if I see your number."

I'd kept my tape machine attached to the downstairs phone and pressed the record button.

"Why did you lie to me?" I asked. On the tape, you can hear the insistent anger in my words, but I remember my fear more than anything else.

Silence.

I repeated my question.

"Listen closely," he said, his voice trembling. "Do not call me again. It is no good for me. And if you want the truth, it is no

216

good for you, too. These are things you will never understand. In Bologna, I told you to forget about us. And to forget about Sana. I am telling you that again. You understand me?"

"I may want to write about her."

"If you do, then do not publish my name! Under no circumstances. Do you hear me?"

He shouted as though he were waving a gun in my face. I've played back the recording many times and I hear panic in his voice as well.

A crab of fear scuttled up my back. I tend to say the most naive things when I'm in danger of drowning in my own emotions. "I don't think you should speak to me like that," I told him. "Not after lying to me for two days."

"Listen, this is bigger than me. You do not know where you are. You do not know how far this goes."

Mistrust stalked the line between us, and I didn't reply for a few seconds. He was confirming my worst suspicions.

"Surely you realize that your name will come out sooner or later," I said finally.

It was curious how we were both circling around any reference to September 11th, as if it was a territory we dared not approach.

"For the sake of Carlotta and Alice, do not give my name. They have no part in what . . . in what has happened. They do not deserve to suffer. Is that too much to ask?"

I gave my word that I wouldn't identify them or him in my writing. (In this book I have changed their names, though I have identified him correctly to the F.B.I. Samir's true name has also been given in at least fourteen Italian press accounts available on the web.)

"I will hang up now," he said.

"Wait! How are Alice and Carlotta?"

"They are well." His voice calmed a bit.

"Where are you living?"

"I cannot tell you that."

"Did Sana's father work with you – is that how you met her?"

"There are some things you do not need to know."

"But I do."

"We were friends – good friends. You can leave it at that in what you write."

"Is he dead?"

"Yes."

"Samir, I have a working theory on why Sana committed suicide."

He made no reply.

"I would guess she knew what kinds of activities you were financing. Tell me if I'm wrong."

Silence.

"The 9/11 attacks must have been planned way in advance. Did she find out about them while she was in Perth? Or just before that? Did you speak to her while she was there and tell her? Maybe she couldn't live knowing someone she loved would help kill so many people."

He hung up and did not answer when I called back. If he had, I wonder if I would have dared to add what I was thinking: "So maybe you were right about her being murdered. You were the one who killed her."

In late January 2002, reports on the website for the Italian news agency ANSA started to include Samir's name.

From January 28th: "Prosecutors believe that funding for the terrorist cell in Milan was channeled for at least the last several years through a private banking firm in Bologna run by Samir Nizar al-Hassan. Al-Hassan, an Egyptian from a well-to-do Cairo family, spent part of his youth in London and is believed to have maintained strong contacts there and across the Middle East. According to neighbors, he and his family disappeared on September 7, 2001, just prior to the attacks in New York and Washington D.C."

From February 11th: "Also allegedly active in the so-called Armed Muslim Resistance Corps (AMRC) was Samir Nizar al-Hassan, an Egyptian national who lived in Bologna before disappearing in September 2001. AMRC has been linked to bombings and hijackings in France and Italy, as well as murders in Algeria and Lebanon."

From February 27th: "In April of 2000, Italian authorities intercepted a series of cell phone calls, placed between Rashid Omar Fu'ad, manager of a Munich safe house for terrorist recruits on their way to training camps in Afghanistan, and Samir Nizar al-Hassan, a Bologna financier, in which Fu'ad makes reference to 'deliveries of "birthday presents" in New Jersey and Florida.' The U.S. Treasury Department now believes that this was a reference to money transfers needed to fund the men who would participate in the September 11th attacks."

Over the next months, Samir would be mentioned in seven other ANSA articles, detailing his contacts with al-Qaeda operations in Germany, Britain, Spain, and Switzerland. He apparently had no Palestinian family connections at all – and no link to any Palestinian terrorist group or even the P.L.O. The last name of Sana's real father, Yasawi, never appeared.

I persuaded Helena to visit us for five days in February, during the holiday period between semesters. Her face was indeed fuller, but she was hardly fat. She looked more relaxed than I'd ever seen her before. We stayed up late on the first night talking about Samir and his family. When I told her I couldn't understand how Carlotta could agree to stay with a man involved in terrorist activities, she said, "Maybe she has no choice. She could be afraid of him, you know."

"No, she seemed confident of herself – and to love him, too. So did Alice."

"Well, that's your answer. Women will do a great many things to hold on to love – and to make certain that their children have a father."

"Still, she's given up everything."

"You said she was tired of the orchestra, so maybe she was ready to move."

"But not under these circumstances. That's too hard to believe."

"Look, she was probably forced to decide what she must do

in a great hurry. She had no time to think. Imagine the pressure she was suffering. She'll only really know what she has done in a few months, when her life becomes calmer. Maybe then she *will* regret it."

The next morning we walked by the ocean for an hour, then sat on a big granite boulder at the beach nearest our apartment and looked out at the sea. "This could be Haifa," she told me. "Sometimes I think I will die as a five-year-old, still wondering about the world and how I came to exist."

She took a yellowing envelope from her pocket. "Here," she said, handing it to me. "I found this while cleaning my apartment. I promised to show it to you."

Inside was a lock of bright pink hair tied with an ancient red ribbon; time was powerless against whatever brand from hell had dyed poor Rosa's hair such a shocking color. I was amused, then moved. Helena and I hugged.

We drove the next morning to our country house. Helena gardened eight hours a day for three straight days, even through the rain – until her fingernails were all chipped and dirty, and she had scars from the blackberries she'd tried to hack down from our old stone walls. During a thunderstorm I wanted to run out to her, since she was getting drenched, but Alex said, "No, just let her be. She'll be fine."

Late that afternoon, when she came in, I wrapped a blanket around her and Alex made her some strong tea. She cried while sitting with us, then ran out of the room. After a while I went to her and dried her hair with a towel. She said that the cancer had badly scared her and she doubted she'd ever feel like herself again. She often imagined her own body betraying her – its cells reproducing endlessly and creating hidden tumors. She wanted to crawl out of her skin every morning upon waking. "Maybe I need to go back to Israel to lose myself in the desert," she said. She looked up at me with puzzled eyes. "Is that what all this drama is about?"

I had no answer. I realized that Helena was not so different from Sana – her country was torn by war and terrorism, and the homeland she truly wished for existed only inside her own head. A good many of her fellow citizens hated her and had even threatened her with death.

Later, over dinner, when I asked if she ever thought of Israel as a foreign country, she made a fist and glared at me. "I'll never let anyone take Haifa from me!" she declared.

I thought she was cured of her fear of daylight and would soon adjust to Paris again, but when she got back home she slipped again into her vampire habits. She worked only in the evenings at her tearoom. She denied that she was drinking again, but a small catch in her voice one night on the phone told me she was lying.

"We might have to drive a stake in your heart to free you," I told her.

"Oh please, if it were that easy," she replied, "I'd do it myself."

By now, a year and a half after the start of the Intifida, Israeli troops had marched into every city in the Occupied Territories and Palestinian suicide bombers were putting the Israelis on a permanent state of alert. On March 31st, a blast at the Matza restaurant in Haifa killed fifteen people. Frantic with worry, Helena spent several days calling all the dozens of people she knew there to make sure they were safe. She discovered she had gone to high school with one of the victims and even managed to reach his parents. "His mother kept losing what she was trying to say," Helena told me. "It was terrible. I think it was all the tranquilizers. His father was so angry, it was like he was on fire. 'Do the Palestinians truly think we'll offer them a peace made out of our children's bodies?' he asked me. What could I say? I tried to tell him that serious peace talks had to begin immediately if the violence was ever to end, but he shouted at me that I was a fool. 'Do you really think the Palestinians are still like they were when you were growing up?' he said. 'When are you going to realize that Yasser Arafat and the others are all just criminals? That's what they've always been, though we didn't know it.' Then he told me that Israel would never negotiate with criminals covered in Jewish blood. 'It would be suicide for us,' he told me. 'And maybe now the rest of the world is beginning to understand that.' "

Undaunted, Helena did her best to contribute to the general atmosphere of malignant lunacy by writing letters to newspapers all over Europe and the Middle East, suggesting that the only people in the world as cowardly as the Palestinian leadership were the ministers of Israel. "Ariel Sharon and the rest of the Israeli government all believe that an automatic rifle in your hand makes you a war hero, and Yasser Arafat and the Palestinian militants think that a bomb around your waist makes you a saint. So God save us from heroes and saints!"

By April 1st, I still hadn't received any promising e-mails from Australia. Some royalty money on my books would be coming in soon, and I decided to run my ad in a larger format for one more week. In response, on April 6th, I got an e-mail from a man named Boaz Cohen, an Israeli who had emigrated to Australia thirty-one years before. For the last twenty-three years, he had worked as a private detective. He wrote: "I'm pretty sure the woman in your ad hired me in 1998. But she used the name Rosa Verga, not Helena. If you're interested, call me. I don't want to discuss this in an e-mail."

When we spoke, the first thing he said was, "I've been waiting for four years to tell this story to someone other than the police."

With his vowels migrating freely between Australian and Hebrew, Boaz told me that on March 16, 1998 (the day after the close of the Adelaide Festival, as it happens), he received a visit from a woman who looked like Sana. "Same eyes, same mouth, but the hair is all different. She was blonde – and her hair fell down to her shoulders."

She must have styled herself to look like Helena's mother

Rosa, who, undeterred by her pink-hair debacle, had been a blonde since the 1950s. Sana probably saw her impersonation as an acting challenge.

"This woman showed me a photograph of a little girl – her daughter. And then she . . ."

"Wait, did she say where she was from?"

"From Haifa."

"She said she was Jewish?"

"She said she was Israeli. With that name, I just assumed she was Jewish."

"You spoke to her in Hebrew?"

"A mixture of English and Hebrew – my Hebrew's all rusty."

"How did she come to find you?"

"Some Israeli friends of hers in Sydney suggested me."

"Did she give you their names?"

"No."

"Go on."

"So she showed me her daughter's photograph and . . ."

"Wait, sorry – did she say her daughter's name was Helena?"

"That's right. You know her?"

"In a way." I told him I'd explain all I knew about Rosa Verga after he finished his story.

"So she says that her daughter is dying with leukemia. Their only hope is a bone marrow transplant. But her bone marrow doesn't match her daughter's. So she wants to get in touch with her ex-husband. The only problem is that after the divorce he wants nothing to do with her or the daughter. He's vanished. She knows he moved to Sydney, but nothing more. He never pays the child support he's supposed to."

I asked if she'd identified him as S., and Boaz confirmed she had. "You sound like you know this story before I even tell it," he observed.

"I'm putting two and two together. I'd guess she described her ex-husband pretty well."

"Yeah. She told me he worked in security back in Israel – as a guard in a bank. She had no photograph, though. I usually get a couple of good photos if I can."

"Didn't that strike you as odd?"

"A bit. But she said that the divorce was a very big mess, and that he came over one day and broke in and stole a lot of her stuff, including her photographs – even ones of her parents that had nothing to do with him. She said he stole all her old records, too – everything by Edith Piaf. And Georges Moustaki, too. You know who he is?"

"A Greek singer who lived in France for a long time."

"That's right. I didn't know who he was when she mentioned him."

I later confirmed with Samuel that Rosa had adored both Piaf and Moustaki.

"Was she convincing?"

"Very. She was crying. Her lips were cracked, and she seemed so thin and tired. It was like she was being eaten away by what was happening with her daughter. I was on her side all the way."

"What else?"

"That's about it. She paid me an advance and we agreed to be in touch. She told me she would call me every month or so, since she moved around a lot because of her work and I might not be able to reach her."

"Did she give you a phone number?"

"Sure did – in Brazil. She said she was based in São Paulo."

"Based there?"

"Yeah, she said she was a stewardess for El Al – the Israeli airline."

"Holy shit."

"I guess she didn't work for them."

"No. Did she say anything else?"

"No, she just paid me and left."

"Did she keep in touch?"

"Absolutely – every month. And she'd send more money every three months or so."

"From Brazil?"

"That's right."

"From a Brazilian account?"

"No, a British account – Barclays Bank on Oxford Street in London."

"How long did it take you to find S.?"

"About a year and a half. He'd changed his name. He wanted to hide and he was good at it."

"And then you gave his name and address to her."

"Yeah, in late August 1999. She was real happy on the phone. She cried again, and she said I was an angel and that she'd contact him right away and that I'd saved her kid's life. A week later I got her last payment and a gift – a CD by Ney something-or-other, a Brazilian singer she must have liked."

"Ney Matogrosso."

"That's him! I felt really good about helping her. I liked her. You know, sometimes you're asked to do not so nice things – to follow wives who meet their lovers at hotels, that sort of thing. But this was different – this was great. I drove around for a month thinking I was Batman."

"Till you heard that S. had been killed." ·

"No, not him. One day I'm reading the *Morning Herald*, and I see an article. It's real small and at the bottom of a page. It says a house was blown up in Glebe. That's a neighborhood in Sydney. And it belonged to S. – though the article didn't use his original name."

"This was in February 2000?"

"That's right – on the 4th. I have the article."

"But S. wasn't killed?"

"No, he and his wife and daughter managed to get out with not much more than broken bones. But it took nearly two hours to free the little boy from the rubble that fell on him. He was burned pretty bad and had internal bleeding. He died the next day at the hospital."

"Oh, Jesus." I felt as though Sana and I were free-falling into an abyss we'd been avoiding since her death. There was no way out now. "Did you make the connection right away to Rosa Verga?" I asked.

"Yeah, I did – more or less. I mean, at first I couldn't believe it. Then I figured I understood what had happened. S. must have refused to help her and her daughter, and she went crazy. Her kid's illness – it was too much for her. So I went to the police and told them what I knew. I was feeling really guilty."

"Did you hear from the police again?"

"Nothing – not a word. And I did my best to forget about it until I saw that ad of yours."

"You never spoke to S. or any of his family?"

"No. The police told me they'd handle all that."

While I was thinking about what else to ask, he said, "So is that the way you see it? She tried to get back at her husband for not helping their daughter, right?"

"It's a bit more complicated than that."

"Has she been caught? Is that why you wanted more information on her activities in Australia?"

"In a way." I told him I'd have to begin with my arrival in Perth, four days after she'd bombed S.'s house.

When I was finished, he said, "That bastard did a terrible thing to her brother, but did his kid deserve to die for it?"

"She probably just intended to scare them."

"No way. I drove by a few days after I read the article. The first floor was gone and the second floor had collapsed. It was a fucking pancake. It's a miracle any of them got out alive."

At the end of *The Last Kabbalist of Lisbon*, the narrator pays an assassin to murder his uncle's killer. Was that why she'd told me in Perth that my book had helped her see her path more clearly? Did she view her brother's death as symbolic of the oppression of all Palestinians? Did she intend her bomb attack as the first act in a long campaign to rectify the injustices in her homeland?

A woman flies across the width of a distant country, worried that she will be found by the police and sent to prison. Maybe that is her greatest fear. She has always had nightmares about a bird being caged – and about what happened to her brother. If she is caught, what will the guards do to her? Cut off her hands? She knows she could not live with that.

She also knows that she has given in to her rage and killed a little boy. It all seems different now than she'd thought – dirtier, and more useless. She never thought she would do anything like this. What might she do in the future?

When she meets a writer whose characters seem to reflect her life, she loses her balance. She tells him she is "particularly sensitive" right now. He hugs her, and she finds herself trembling. Should she say something to him or simply cry in his arms?

Maybe she calls a family friend later that day to hear a fatherly voice. Or he phones her to see how she is doing. She confesses her crime. He comforts her and reassures her that what she has done was justified. In fact, he says, he and his colleagues are planning to strike at the heart of the power that has created so much misery in Palestine and across the Middle East. In just a year or two she will see how the world will change. He begs her not to do anything more – he and his friends will act for her. She only needs to bring beauty to the world with her dance.

"But what are you going to do?" she asks him.

He hesitates, but then tells her – and swears her to secrecy.

When she hangs up, she sits staring out her hotel window at the city of Perth kneeling far below. She has never felt so alone, so lost. She sees her that destiny cannot be undone. Her whole life – the hiding from soldiers, her mother's rape, her father's ruthlessness, Jamal's murder, her break with Helena – everything she has done has led her to this.

She stands up. Feeling strangely powerful, she lifts her chair over her head and shatters her window. Does she close her eyes? Maybe she hears a whisper in her ear that she was never anything at all and that her death will mean nothing. Does she imagine herself about to finally fly for real?

I spent the next several days typing up my notes into some recognizable order and making copies of my tapes and photographs, then added a two-page, single-spaced explanatory letter and sent it all by express mail to F.B.I. Director Robert Mueller. I probably ought to have sent it to an underling, but the F.B.I.'s web pages were astonishingly confusing.

Trying to get even a fraction of Sana's story down on paper

was exhausting; I couldn't say anything the way I wanted. Sometimes, while sitting at my desk, I'd just stare out my window at the early morning fog beyond the red-tile rooftops and let my mind wander off into fantasies of saving her – and the little boy in Sydney as well.

An F.B.I. agent named Stephenson called me about two weeks later. He sounded suspicious of my motives. He told me he'd found my letter interesting, but hard to decipher.

"I'm not surprised – I haven't deciphered it myself," I confessed.

"I guess we might as well go back to the beginning," he replied, drudgery in his voice.

I told him what I knew for more than an hour. It was mostly a monologue. Just prior to hanging up, I asked if he'd already known about Samir and his financial activities, and whether they extended all the way to the United States.

"I can't tell you that," he replied.

"Let me guess – national security reasons."

"That's right."

"Do I sound like I'm likely to compromise America's well-being any time soon?"

He disregarded that question and said roughly, "I really hope you're not taping this call." No doubt he was remembering what I'd said in my letter about taping Helena and Mahmoud. "It's illegal," he added for good measure.

In point of fact, I had been. But the tape had run out about twenty minutes earlier, so I was able to truthfully say no.

When I called Helena to tell her about Sana having killed S.'s son in Australia she refused to believe it. "There's some mistake. The Sana I knew would not have done anything like that."

"No, not the Sana you knew."

I let the ambiguity of that hang in the air. She reached out for the only possibility that would leave her image of her old friend intact. "Someone must have forced her to do it – that son-of-a-bitch you met in Bologna. It was him!"

*

Toward the end of April, Samuel called me, crying. He couldn't reach Helena and said he had to talk to someone outside Israel. The country was making him lose his mind.

"What happened?" I asked.

He explained that Israeli soldiers had destroyed the independent educational television station in Ramallah where he volunteered once a week. What equipment they didn't hack apart they heaved out the window. The station's video archive had been completely destroyed.

"But why'd they do it?" I asked.

He passed over my question. "I've lost all the tapes of my gardening program. It's all gone – three years of work. It's just flowers and fruit. How could that hurt the state of Israel?"

His voice was that of a lost little boy.

"I'm sure you can get everything started again," I said.

"I wish Rosa was here."

"Is there any equipment left to start over?"

"You don't understand. Israeli officers are now occupying the studio. They wanted it as a field office. That's why they did it. They won't go. Do you know what my daughter told me even before this happened?"

"What?"

"She told me to leave Israel while I still can."

"Maybe you should."

"I can't. Israel saved my life. You don't understand what it means to me – to all of us. It's everything. Leaving now would be like abandoning all the good people I've ever known, all the people who built this country from nothing – against all that hostility from the whole world. You don't understand how many courageous people I've known here. The best people I have ever met are *all* Israelis. And these terrible bombs everywhere . . . these Palestinians who are so proud of murdering Jews. You want me to leave while we are being attacked by them? By men who dance with joy when they kill a Jew? You want me to let the madmen on both sides win – the ones who pray to God for constant war between us? If only Rosa was still around," he moaned.

"What would she do?"

229

His voice grew rough. "She'd get the gun she brought with her from Europe and come with me to Ramallah."

"You think she'd shoot the soldiers?"

"I bloody well hope so."

Near the end of our conversation, I remembered to ask Samuel if anyone had ever enquired after his wife sometime during the spring or summer of 1998.

"Enquired after her how?" he asked.

"If she was still alive – or when she died."

"Well, I got a visit from the Israeli police a few years ago – it might have been in 1998 – and they wanted to see some photographs of Rosa."

"Did they say why?"

"They said someone might have been using her name on a stolen driver's license or credit card or something. I can't remember – I didn't understand any of it. Rosa had been dead for years. I didn't keep any credit cards or a driver's license in her name. I thought they'd lost their marbles."

I decided not to tell Samuel about Sana's impersonation of his wife just yet, since he was already upset enough.

By the end of June I was finally finished with my last rewrites on *Hunting Midnight*. I should have been feeling relaxed, but all my notes about Sana were waiting for me. Her life and death clung to my thoughts and dreams.

Starting out on her story, I found myself entangled in her contradictions and my own doubts. After a week, it became clear that the only way to create a sensible narration was by starting with how I'd gotten involved with her – our meeting in Perth. Once I tried that, the writing went swiftly.

Helena passed her oral examination at the beginning of July and was awarded her doctorate. Alex and I flew to Paris for the weekend to celebrate with her. She was playful and kind, and relieved to have completed her work. She confirmed to me that she had been drinking "a tiny amount," as she called it, but she'd stopped again. She would stick to Valium from now on. We agreed she would come again for another visit to Portugal in August.

A few days later, however, tests she'd recently had done by her consultant revealed cancer in the lymph nodes under her right arm. Helena's radiologist also soon discovered a lump close to where the original tumor had been. Devastated, she flew right away to Israel and had an operation in which surgeons removed both her breasts. When I called her at the hospital, she was still groggy. Her voice sounded as though it had fled deep inside her. "I wasn't going to wait to have more cancer in the other one," she whispered to me. "You think I have done the correct thing?"

"Of course. I think you're incredibly brave."

I asked then what the doctors had told her. She said she couldn't talk about it and put her father on. He said they were confident they'd gotten everything, but Helena would have to have chemotherapy this time. She took the phone back to say goodbye and told me she'd be living with friends in Tel Aviv during her treatment period, then return to stay with her father. "After that, who knows? I have to think what I really want to do if I only have a few years left."

"You're scaring me," I told her.

"Sorry. Don't you worry about me. You just complete the book about Sana – that's the best thing you can do for all of us. When I know it has been finished, I'll be more at peace, even if the worst happens."

Unable to stop thinking about Helena, I called her the next morning and said right away, "Sana wouldn't want you to die, you know."

As I spoke, I understood for the first time why what I was saying seemed so true to me.

"How do you know that?" she asked.

"She didn't get in touch with you after seeing you in Paris.

Don't you see? She wanted to be back in your life, but she also wanted to protect you. She needed to know you would be all right. She thought if you came to New York she would only end up dragging you down with her – into whatever she was planning. Helena, you may not want me to say this, but I think you might have been worse off if she'd stayed in touch with you. By not speaking to you, she was saving you."

On August 19th Abu Nidal was found dead in his apartment in Baghdad, having been shot several times. The first reports indicated suicide, but most news stories later said he was probably killed by the Iraqi secret police. I wondered what Clara, the girl whose father I spoke to in Paris in 1982, was thinking now. I wondered if she had any remembrance of the mother killed by Nidal's terrorists, if his death could ever fill in even a small part of that blood-splattered, twenty-year absence.

At the end of that month, Alex and I flew to Porto Santo, a Portuguese island near Madeira, for a week of sun. I printed out the nearly two hundred pages I'd written about Sana and took them with me. Sitting on that golden sand, everything that had happened in Haifa, Perth, Paris, and Bologna seemed far away and unable to disorient me again. Maybe because of that I was able to see where the book needed to go.

Helena's chemotherapy went smoothly, and she stayed with her father throughout the fall. She'd become so used to wearing a knitted red yarmulke over her head that she kept it on even now that her hair was growing back. She wore it in bed, too, since it made her feel protected. "As if I'm a little girl in pajamas," she told me in a happy voice.

What she loved most about where she was living was the sunlight near the Dead Sea, which made the shadows on the desert floor vibrate as if they were seeking to come alive. "But if

232

you want the truth, not even that is enough," she confessed to me one day in November.

"Enough for what?"

"There's not much more they can cut from me if . . . if the cancer returns," she said. Terror filled her voice.

Several weeks earlier a friend in publishing in Tel Aviv had expressed interest in publishing her thesis on Sephardic music as a book, and he had even given her some ideas for a rewrite. I urged her now to accept his offer, but she was reluctant to begin a new project. I was sure she was listening to a clock ticking inside her head, sensing she might not have enough time left to finish it. Instead of admitting that, however, she snapped, "I don't want your advice – you don't know what it's like being sick."

"Helena, I won't apologize for being healthy."

That incensed her. "You just want me to think of something other than my cancer!" she screamed.

"Would that be so damned bad?" I yelled back.

"It's mine. You don't understand. It's all mine." In a broken voice, she added, "What if it's all I have now?"

"Don't you dare go on strike again," I warned her.

"There you are always being clever!" she replied, as if I'd crossed one line too many.

She hung up on me. But when next we spoke, she apologized. "Fear was freezing me in my bones on the day we talked," she told me. She was now working ten hours a day on the revisions to her thesis and the routine was helping. "I stop thinking of the future when I write. Maybe all of Tia Zeinab's catastrophe sickness has finally been cut out of me."

"I hope so."

"There's something else I've been thinking about lately . . ."

"What?"

"When I was in the hospital, after I could stand, I would look at myself in the mirror all the time – to see my terrible scars. In the bed next to me was a young woman. She worked in a bakery, so we talked about that. She must have told her grandfather about me looking in the mirror. He was an Italian Jew, old, very dignified and handsome, with a crest of the most beautiful silver hair – the kind of man who wears a coat and tie all the time. I didn't ask about *back there*, but I could tell he'd been there because he had those liquid black eyes they have. He walked over to me once, and I thought it was because I'd been staring at him. But he pointed to the mirror and said, "So who are you looking at in there?' I was startled. I said, 'I guess I just want to make sure I'm still here.'"

"No, not you, who else?" he insisted. When I told him I didn't know, he said that some people thought the dead could see us through mirrors. That made me shiver – I didn't want any dead people looking at me. But later, I realized I *did* want my mother to see me – I've wanted that for so very long."

"Did you tell the old Italian man what you realized?"

"No, I told his granddaughter. The next time he visited, he came over to me, took my hand, and said, 'It is good you let your mother take a look at you. I know – I am a parent.' Wasn't that a nice thing to say?"

"Yes."

"And now, every time I look in a mirror, I imagine that mom might be there, gazing at me."

"She'd be very happy to see you."

"Yes, but . . . but I'm still not convinced that Sana would be. Though I'd like her to be. I mean, now I know I want to live, even in a world without her. The cancer showed me that."

I finished something close to a final draft of my book about Sana – the book you have in your hands – in November and showed it to Alex, my mother, and Helena. To my great relief, they all liked it. Helena called me all weepy one evening to say it was more than she could have hoped for, which was a monumental relief. She had scribbled down dozens of small corrections for the section about her childhood with Sana and was going to mail them to me.

She was still enjoying the rewrite on her thesis. "I sit in Dad's office, looking out at him caring for the feijoa bushes he loves, feeling all that light soaking into the flowers and him. I know I'm right where I want to be. And all the work I'm doing on my thesis to make it ready to be published is improving it. I'm making it what it should have been. It is like I'm saving a part of my life that I could have lost. It's a blessing."

"So you'll stay in Israel?"

"I don't want to think about my future. My mother once told me to keep walking, and I never really understood her. But after losing my breasts, I think I do." She gave a mocking laugh. "Though maybe it's just one more illusion in my life."

"What do you think your mother meant?"

"That all my indecision – being torn between Paris and Israel, Jews and Palestinians, St. George and the dragon – might never end. The important thing is not to stop while waiting to decide. I'm not a little girl any more. What you said about not going on strike again was right. In spite of my fear, and all I've done wrong, and all my bad faults, I just have to keep walking."

Postscript

I originally intended to end this book with something like this:

When I was at the North Carolina School of the Arts during the summer of 1977, I spoke to a twelve-year-old viola prodigy who had been born blind. I asked him if he saw uniform blackness in front of him. "I see the very same thing that you see out of your hands," he told me.

That reply stunned me, but it has always given me hope, as well. After all, there are so many things way beyond our understanding. Maybe there is even an afterlife and we lack the senses to know what it looks and feels like – or even to imagine it properly. To do that, we'd have to be able to "see" out of our hands.

I wonder what Sana was thinking as she jumped to her death. And what she saw of her past, if anything, on the way down. Was Zeinab with her? Was Helena? I hope they held each of her hands and held them tightly.

Sana's heart must have been banging with fear. I hope death was what she really wanted.

If she did use me, I don't mind. But I wish I'd understood she was in trouble – that I'd been able to understand her fantasy birds and the magic flower behind her ear. How sad it is that we cannot interpret the sign language of others with any accuracy.

I'm fairly certain that the connections between her life and my book that I've mentioned are the ones she saw and felt. I've come to believe, however, that the truest and deepest connections are unlikely to be anywhere in the pages of that novel. What Sana found in my book was intimately tied to her own experiences and journey. To its pages she added what was dearest to her, and now all that is gone.

I have not ended *The Search for Sana* this way because on June 3, 2003, just before the American release of *Hunting Midnight*, I put the first chapter on my website and invited readers to contact me at my hotmail address. I received the following e-mail:

Dear Richard,

I am Samir and Carlotta's daughter, Alice. I hope you remember me. Thank you for the first chapter of *Hunting Midnight*. I would like to read more! I hope you are well. We are fine, although we miss Bologna very much. Excuse me for not to say more, but I should not be writing to you. I would like to see you but that is impossible. Many things seem impossible now. Please forgive me and do not be angry with me. Congratulations for your new novel!

Con i migliori auguri,
Alice

Her e-mail address ended with co.uk, but that didn't necessarily mean she was living in Great Britain. She or Samir could have registered with a provider there and then have had access to mail from anywhere in the world.

I wrote back right away, especially since I read between the lines that she was unhappy. I thanked her for her note and asked her to tell me about her new school and if there was anything I could send her care of a friend or family member in Italy (since she obviously couldn't give me her address). I didn't mention the attacks on the World Trade Center and the Pentagon. I assumed she didn't know much about her father's activities. She'd probably been told they'd had to flee racist reprisals in Italy – or maybe even Samir's tax troubles.

I never got a reply from her.

Helena moved back to Paris early in July and finished the book version of her thesis a couple of months later. It's scheduled to come out in Israel sometime next year. She's free of cancer, at least for now, and she's working at her tearoom in the afternoons. She still writes angry letters to newspapers, and gets a few death threats every month, but they don't prevent her from going out during the day. When I asked her what had changed, she said, "If I were to tell you that I am in Israel even when I am in Paris, would that make any sense to you?"

"Not really."

"Well, when I look in the sky now, I see the same sun that shines on my father's house. And I feel the same earth beneath my feet that my mother walked on in our garden in Haifa. I try to remember that. And I try to remember only the good things about Sana. I don't want the bad things any more – they weigh too much. I'm not like her – I can't toss the stones from my pockets when I want to fly."

By September 2003, my Portuguese publisher had agreed to publish this book, with the ending about the young violist I've mentioned. But I decided to send the manuscript off to Samir. I wanted to give him a chance to disagree with my conclusion that he'd contributed decisively to Sana's desire to kill herself. I sent the entire book as an e-mail attachment to Alice. I asked her not to read it and to simply print it out for her father. I told her that he had no reason to be angry with her for writing to me because I would never give her e-mail address to anyone.

Alice didn't reply. For good measure, I sent the manuscript a second time a few days later.

*

On January 7, 2004, I got a package from Budapest. It was about eight by twelve inches and wrapped in thick brown paper. No return address was written. I assumed it was from my Hungarian publisher – I envisioned a box of chocolates. If I had known it was from Samir, I'd have called the bomb squad.

It contained two videos and a brief note.

The first video showed a training camp in a rocky wasteland. The quality of the images and the sound were poor, as if it was a distant copy of the original. Almost all of the men were wearing camouflage pants and shirts. Many had scruffy beards and some others wore cloth masks over their faces. Holding automatic rifles over their heads, they hustled across a field, then climbed up and over a cement wall – wave after wave of them. To me, they looked like out-of-shape shopkeepers out to prove their toughness.

"Pathetic," Alex said when he first saw it.

The training footage goes on for eight minutes and nine seconds. Then we see seven men seated on the floor, inside a bare room painted light green. One of the men wears white robes and has a long beard. He speaks in Arabic. Some of the others reply from time to time.

This goes on for seven minutes and four seconds.

Helena listened closely to the men when I sent her a copy of the video, but her Arabic wasn't good enough for her to decipher all that they were saying. She thought they were discussing poor driving conditions and the weather – something about snow.

To tell the truth, I didn't really care about getting a proper translation of the footage because in the last scene, back at the training camp, a young man with large dark eyes and several days' growth of beard takes the camera from whoever has been filming and turns the lens around. Sana smiles, then winks, as though she is embarrassed. She carries an automatic rifle in her right hand and wears blue jeans and a large woolen sweater – pink with a black collar. Helena recognized it as a gift she'd given Sana in Paris. So we knew the video was no older than 1996. I also remembered she was wearing it when I saw her sitting in the hotel bar in Perth.

After Sana's friend takes the camera from her, she asks him – using the name Ali – to return it to her. Is he the same Ali she stayed with in Gaza City after Jamal's hand was cut off? When he refuses to accede to her wishes, she swirls her right arm in a great circle, as fast as she can. I thought she was trying to create an imaginary vortex to draw it back to her. But Helena told me that interpretation was wrong; she was making one of the magic gestures that they would use as children to chase Queen Bee away.

"She does not really want the camera back," Helena told me. "She wants it far away."

"But Sana seems happy and relaxed," I protested.

"Don't you see," Helena told me with misery in her voice, "it's all a lie! She's confused. She's scared. That man Samir you met involved Sana in this. And she doesn't know how to escape."

Ali keeps the camera. After a few seconds, Sana's expression grows grave. She points her rifle toward the lens and moves it closer, until all we see is the metallic snout. Then the video ends.

The second video is much shorter – only three minutes and seven seconds. It shows Sana seated with Samir on the red couch of his living room in Bologna, the photographs from Israel and Palestine on the wall above their heads. Long shadows cover the floor like darkened water – it must be late afternoon. They are talking in Arabic about a performance that night by a group called Le Tracce. Samir laughs at one point and says that he will not go no matter what blackmail Sana tries.

I later discovered that the Italian dance company Le Tracce performed in Bologna on February 10, 1999, a year before I met Sana in Perth.

Sana and Samir seem calm and happy. He is smoking. A little more than halfway through the video, he says something inaudible that makes Sana giggle.

"Show us where you got the idea," he then tells her. He turns to the camera and nods as though this will be a treat for the viewer.

Sana gets up and leads the cameraman down a hallway to a bedroom. We see her back, then an open doorway and a blue blanket jumbled up on a slender bed. Above the pillows is a poster of Zucchero, the Italian singer.

It must have been Tomasso's room.

Sana tells the cameraman to point the lens out the window. The image goes hazy until we see the tile rooftops of the city and the medieval towers pointing high into a blue sky. The focus zooms in on them, then shifts back to Sana.

"There used to be two hundred towers in Bologna," she says in Arabic. "And now there are only two."

Lifting her right hand, Sana then imitates a bird flapping its wings. After it perches on her shoulder, she strokes it and gives it a kiss. Cupping it very delicately, she holds it out to the camera, smiling.

She is giving us a gift – her most precious one, I thought.

When I told that to Helena, she said, "Yes, she is giving us herself."

The image goes blank a few seconds later.

I copied both videos at my university right away and express-mailed them to Agent Stephenson at the F.B.I. Despite my begging, he wouldn't tell me whether the conscripts were from al-Qaeda or Hamas, or even hangers-on from my old friend Abu Nidal's group.

"There are a lot of organizations out there," Stephenson told me. "And I think it's better if you don't know which it is."

"I figure it couldn't be al-Qaeda, since Sana isn't wearing any veil."

"I just can't say."

"But it *is* a terrorist group that you know about. Just tell me that."

"No doubt about it."

"One last thing . . ."

"What?"

"I really need you to tell me something. Have you heard

241

anything from the Israelis? I mean, did their secret police know about Sana? Were they following her? Might an agent have murdered her in Perth?"

"I can't speak to you about any of that."

"You have to. I can't rejoin my life if you don't tell me."

After a long silence, he said, "They knew about her. That's all I can say."

"Might they have killed her?"

"I have no indication about that either way. None at all."

"You're telling me the truth. Please . . ."

"I'm telling you what I know – it may not be the truth, but it's all I have."

Helena figured that Samir and his family had probably moved to Iran or Iraq, or maybe even Libya, and that what he wrote in his note to me was just another con. She was convinced, as well, that Sana must have been acting in the videos, from a script prepared by Samir, and that he'd coerced her to participate. Even today, Helena thinks that Sana must not have had any choice, but her absolute belief in her childhood friend may be blinding her. "There are certain things you cannot ask a person to give up," she told me, warning me with her eyes not even to try. "If I lose what I feel about Sana, then I will lose everything else and return to the way I was."

I've tried not to believe what Samir wrote to me in the note that accompanied the videos, but I think he is probably telling the truth – though I'm not sure that blaming Mossad makes much sense; if his claims about Sana are right, then she had one more good reason for feeling guilty enough to take her own life.

The note reads:

Dear Richard,
I think you will have no choice but to alter your conclusions after you watch these tapes. After all, who else but a girl who spent part of her childhood under the towers of Bologna could have thought of such a way to change the world for ever?

Now, too, you can see why I think she was murdered. She shouldn't have gone to Sydney. Mossad must have traced her from there to Perth.

Please remember that I tried to spare you this knowledge and that I had the care to confirm with you that your mother was not living in Manhattan. Do not try to contact me or Alice ever again.

Sincerely,
Samir

A Note from the Author

Some of the people and events described in this book are based on fact, but it is a work of fiction. The issues, however, are real – and important to me.

The form I've chosen has permitted the characters to tell their own version of events without having to censor themselves. In consequence, they say and do things we don't often read about or hear. Furthermore, they're not always sure what's right. They have conflicting ideas about how to fulfil their obligations to themselves, their families, and their communites.

These complex characters are not representatives of any particular viewpoint or illustrations of any theory. As I see it, there are no easy villains or saints. It's left for each reader to draw his or her own conclusions.

For more about the background to the book, go to:
www.constablerobinson.com

Also by Richard Zimler

"Fiction enables a writer to talk about the big issues, and to peel away all the unnecessary elements which confuse people. Fiction lets me deal with the deepest and most intimate truths, to create characters who talk on the most reflective and philosophical level about these huge issues. If I was an historian, I'd be dealing with the facts of history, and wouldn't be able to interpret them through the lens of human emotions. That's why I'm a storyteller." Richard Zimler

Richard Zimler is the author of a bestselling series of novels about different branches and generations of the Portuguese–Jewish Zarco family. The first was *The Last Kabbalist of Lisbon*. The most recent, *Guardian of the Dawn*, is set in the 17th-century Portuguese colony of Goa and exposes the untold brutality of the Catholic Inquisition's drive to convert non-Christians there, including hundreds of Jews. In 19th-century Portugal, Jews were still living in hiding from the Catholic Church, and *Hunting Midnight* tells a different side of this same story. Born into secrecy and persecution, Richard Zimler's characters live with the threat, and reality, of betrayal – both personal and public. Zimler blends vivid historical detail with intriguing plots, real-life characters with universal issues. The results have won him international acclaim as a novelist, and he is also in demand as a commentator on Jewish culture and history, and Middle Eastern politics.

Available now

Guardian of the Dawn

In 17th-century Goa, the Catholic Inquisition was making excellent progress in its mission to keep all "sorcerers" – whether native Hindus or immigrant Jews – from practising their traditional beliefs. Those who refused to betray others or give up their ways were either strangled by executioners or burnt alive in public *autos-da-fé*.

By living just outside colonial territory, the Zarco family manages to stick firm to its Portuguese–Jewish roots. But when both father and son are imprisoned by the Inquisition only one question remains: who can have betrayed them?

£7.99

Hunting Midnight

At the dawn of the 19th century in Portugal, John Zarco Stewart is an inquisitive, hot-headed child and the unwitting inheritor of a faith shrouded in secrecy. As John faces adulthood, the arrival of Midnight – an African healer and freed slave – brings love and friendship, as well as the shattering revelations that will take him from war-ravaged Europe to pre-Civil War America.

This work of visionary scope and beauty takes the reader on a journey – via the colorful marketplaces of Porto, the drowsy plantations of the American south and the mystical Africa of Midnight's memories – as epic as John's own hunt for hope.

£8.99

Constable books are available from all good bookshops or direct from the publisher. Just tick the titles you want to order and fill in the form below.

TBS Direct
Colchester Road, Frating Green, Colchester, Essex CO7 7DW
Tel: +44 (0) 1206 255777
Fax: +44 (0) 1206 255914
Email: sales@tbs-ltd.co.uk

UK/BFPO customers please allow £1.00 for p&p for the first book, plus 50p for the second, plus 30p for each additional book up to a maximum charge of £3.00. Overseas customers (inc. Ireland), please allow £2.00 for the first book, plus £1.00 for the second, plus 50p for each additional book.

Please send me:

Guardian of the Dawn ☐
Hunting Midnight ☐

NAME (Block letters) . . . .
ADDRESS. . . . .
. . . .
POSTCODE. . . . .
I enclose a cheque/PO (payable to TBS Direct) for . . . .
I wish to pay by Switch/Credit card
Number . . . .
Card Expiry Date . . . .
Switch Issue Number . . . .